## SHIPMENT FIVE

*Belonging to Bandera* by Tina Leonard
*Court Me, Cowboy* by Barbara White Daille
*His Best Friend's Bride* by Jodi O'Donnell
*The Cowboy's Return* by Linda Warren
*Baby Be Mine* by Victoria Pade
*The Cattle Baron* by Margaret Way

## SHIPMENT SIX

*Crockett's Seduction* by Tina Leonard
*Coming Home to the Cattleman* by Judy Christenberry
*Almost Perfect* by Judy Duarte
*Cowboy Dad* by Cathy McDavid
*Real Cowboys* by Roz Denny Fox
*The Rancher Wore Suits* by Rita Herron
*Falling for the Texas Tycoon* by Karen Rose Smith

## SHIPMENT SEVEN

*Last's Temptation* by Tina Leonard
*Daddy by Choice* by Marin Thomas
*The Cowboy, the Baby and the Bride-to-Be* by Cara Colter
*Luke's Proposal* by Lois Faye Dyer
*The Truth About Cowboys* by Margot Early
*The Other Side of Paradise* by Laurie Paige

## SHIPMENT EIGHT

*Mason's Marriage* by Tina Leonard
*Bride at Briar's Ridge* by Margaret Way
*Texas Bluff* by Linda Warren
*Cupid and the Cowboy* by Carol Finch
*The Horseman's Son* by Delores Fossen
*Cattleman's Bride-to-Be* by Lois Faye Dyer

**The rugged, masculine and independent men
of America's West know the value of hard work,
honor and family. They may be ranchers, tycoons
or the guy next door, but they're all cowboys at heart.
Don't miss any of the books in this collection!**

Cowboy at Heart

# THE COWBOY AND THE BRIDE

# MARIN THOMAS

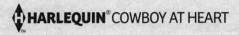

**H HARLEQUIN**®COWBOY AT HEART

Recycling programs
for this product may
not exist in your area.

ISBN-13: 978-0-373-82613-1

THE COWBOY AND THE BRIDE

**Printed in U.S.A.**

## MARIN THOMAS

grew up in Janesville, Wisconsin. She left the Midwest to attend college in Tucson, Arizona, where she earned a B.A. in radio-TV. Following graduation she married her college sweetheart in a five-minute ceremony at the historic Little Chapel of the West in Las Vegas, Nevada. Over the years she and her family have lived in seven different states, but they've now come full circle and returned to Arizona, where the rugged desert and breathtaking sunsets provide plenty of inspiration for Marin's cowboy books.

I wish to thank talented authors Karin Story and Nancy Warren for their feedback on this book, and the Wild Writing Women for their support and enthusiasm. You ladies are the best!

To my family: My husband, Kevin...thanks for Cancún. Each year gets better and better. To my mother, Phyllis Smith, role model extraordinaire. Your courage and faith are always an inspiration. And to my children, Marin and Thomas...nothing else in the world gives me more joy than being your mother. Stick to your goals, don't give up on your dreams, stand your ground when those around you give in, and always believe in yourself. I love you.

And lastly, to my dear friend Karin Dearborn: Thank you for your friendship and encouragement. I could not have made it this far without you.

# Chapter One

"Drat!"

Eyes glued to the gas gauge, Madeline Tate guided the car onto the shoulder of the road. In desperation she pumped the accelerator as the needle slipped over the *E*. The sedan gave one last jerk, then died. She slapped her palm against the steering wheel and glared at the small beaded handbag on the front seat. All she had was an ATM card. She'd left her cell phone in her luggage.

Furious, she gathered all thirty yards of expensive taffeta, grappled for the door handle and almost fell on her head in her haste to get out. Wobbling on two-inch satin pumps, she stumbled toward the front of the car. She stared at the tire, envisioning the missing groom's head, then drew back her leg like a field-goal kicker and let it fly.

"Ouch!"

Jonathon Carter was the biggest ass west of the Mississippi.

And because of him, Madeline was lost.

Not to mention that she didn't know where in the world she was.

She kicked the tire again. Darn it! She should be lying on the beach in the Bahamas, not stuck somewhere in the middle of the Nevada desert.

*Now what?*

Her ears perked. Strange sounds. Short, scuffling, scratchy noises filled the air. Definitely not the sounds she heard when she opened the windows in her Seattle apartment. Images of creepy, crawly varmints scurrying through the brush and weeds made her shudder.

Mr. Ass, her *ex*-fiancé, had removed all their luggage from the hotel room before ditching her at the altar. She'd been so stupid, so blind! She should have known something was up when he'd suggested a quickie wedding in Vegas.

A gust of dry, dusty wind blew the three-foot-long veil in her face, and she swatted at the scratchy lace. At six in the morning, an orangey glow brushed across the horizon, casting shimmering color over the miles and miles of desolate countryside. Surely someone would drive by before too long. After all, it was Friday and people still had to go to work during the week.

*Lights!*

A ranch house, maybe? She studied the fenced-in land alongside the road. Not a single cow, horse or other animal grazed. Aside from a few cactus and scrub brush the only vegetation was one gnarled oak off in the distance, which looked a few hundred years old.

The light appeared to be about a mile away. Under any other circumstance, an easy walk. But hiking across a cow pasture, wearing a wedding gown and two-inch heels, would be a little tricky. She picked at the lace sleeves, careful not to pull any threads. She'd paid a fortune for the designer label, and she was determined to return the cursed thing to Sofia's Wedding Boutique and demand at least part of her three thousand dollars back. She also planned to return the satin pumps, gloves, stockings, beaded purse and even the stupid garter cutting off the circulation in her left thigh. What a fool she'd been to spend so much money on wedding apparel for a Vegas wedding!

Hands full of material, she hiked the dress to her knees and skirted the bushy weeds and prickly thistles as she moved closer to the fence. She studied the barbed wire, resolved to find a way over, under or through it without tearing the gown. Wary of the barbs, she pressed down on the top wire. The rusted metal sagged easily.

Whoever owned the property needed to replace the fence…twenty years ago.

Inching the voluminous folds of satin higher, she raised her right foot and carefully positioned it over the top rung of the fence. The heel on her left foot wobbled precariously as she fought for balance.

Just then a blast filled the air, startling her. She dropped the skirt of the gown, her arms windmilling frantically as she spun toward the road. Her right foot landed on something soft and mushy, causing her to slide backward into the fence.

She heard a tearing sound and froze. Not even daring to breathe, she glared at the two old-timers who stepped out of an ancient pickup that should have found its way to the junkyard a decade ago.

They took off their hats, scratched their balding gray heads and stared at her as if she'd dropped out of the sky.

Grinding her back teeth, she smiled. "Good morning, gentlemen." She wanted to curse the fools for laying on the horn and scaring her to death but under the circumstances thought it prudent to hold her tongue.

"Roy." The taller of the two men spoke. "You ever seen anything like this before?"

The shorter man slapped his hat on his head.

"Nope. Ain't never seen nothin' like this since World War II."

World War II? These guys were that old? She swallowed the scream of frustration clawing its way up her throat.

"Now that I think about it, remember the time we found that widowed gypsy woman out on Henry's property?"

"Oh, yeah—"

"Gentlemen. Would it be too much to ask for a little help, please? You see, I'm stuck to the fence. And this is a very expensive dress. I'd like to get unstuck without tearing it further."

The old cronies stared at her with blank faces.

*Great.* "Maybe one of you could drive into town and get some help." She flung her left arm toward the rental car. "I ran out of—" She gasped. "Shoot!" The lace on the sleeve had caught against a barb. She didn't dare try to tug it off. Carefully, she reached across her body with her right arm and tried to wiggle the material loose. Just when she thought she was making progress, something nasty crawled up her leg and bit her hip.

"Yeow!" She slapped her thigh and jiggled her leg, causing the heel of her shoe to sink into the ground. Reaching back with her hand to gain her balance, she caught the other sleeve on the fence.

"Darnedest female I ever saw."

"Please, misters. I need some help here."

"Holy mother of God."

Startled, Madeline swung her head in the direction of the voice. Her veil slipped over her eyes, and she flung her head from side to side until she could see again. A Hispanic man made the sign of the cross over his chest.

*Where did he come from?* She looked around and spotted a saddled horse grazing across the road.

She stamped her foot. "Will someone please call the sheriff?"

The sound of another truck engine met her ears, and she breathed a sigh of relief. Maybe this idiot would be normal. Loaded down with hay bales, the truck pulled to a stop behind the rental car. Two rangy cowhands got out, spitting tobacco at the ground.

"Well, lookie here," the one with the pock-marked face said. "If it ain't the fairy god-mother." Both men guffawed at the joke. Madeline narrowed her eyes. Just what she needed, a couple of wet-behind-the-ears country bumpkins.

The younger cowboy greeted the older men. "Roy. Roger."

*Roy? Roger?* Oh, great. She was caught in some western version of the *Twilight Zone.* The sun rose higher in the sky, and even though it was early June, the day promised to be a scorcher. "Excuse me if I don't find my predicament amusing. Will someone *please* get me off this fence? It's heating up out here, and I'm not wearing any sunscreen."

"Sunscreen? What's she talking about?" Roy, or maybe it was Roger, asked the others.

The one with the pockmarked face pointed at the front of her gown. "Probably worried about gettin' them melons sunburned."

Madeline glanced at the bodice of her gown and felt her face flame. Good grief! Another inch and her cleavage wouldn't be cleavage anymore.

The roar of another vehicle filled the air. If this jerk didn't have more common sense than the dimwits standing around gaping at her, she'd give up on saving the dress and rip it off the barbed wire.

The approaching truck, towing an empty horse trailer, slowed to a stop right in the middle of the road. *Wonderful.* This guy was as dense as the others. The driver's-side door opened. First came the black Stetson. Then a set of broad, muscular shoulders. Minus the hat, he was a good six inches taller than her own five foot nine. She couldn't tell his age, but assumed it fell somewhere between the wet-behind-the-ears country bumpkins and the two old fuddy-duddies.

When he came around the front end of the silver Ford, her breath left her lungs in a violent whoosh. One look at his muscular thighs and she felt sorry for his horse. He headed straight for her, passing the group of snickering fools, his lean-hipped swagger shouting, *Don't mess with me* from a mile away.

The brim of the Stetson hid most of his face, but the determined line of his mouth and the strong chin looked forbidding. As he approached, she noticed his hair was pitch-black like the hat and his nose had a bump in the middle. She wondered how he'd broken it. He certainly didn't seem like the type to walk into walls.

He stopped two feet away and stared.

She saw her reflection in the mirrored sunglasses and cringed at her tattered appearance. Good Lord. She resembled a fugitive on the run from a state mental hospital. She opened her mouth to speak, but he removed the glasses and she gasped. He had the bluest eyes. A deep, clear, true blue. His captivating eyes, framed by black lashes and eyebrows, sparked with irritation. The cowboy's face was nothing short of compelling. When he cleared his throat, she jumped.

"Name's Jake Montgomery. Mind telling me what you're doing on my property?"

Stunned by the sound of the deep husky voice, she stared into his mesmerizing blue eyes. "Ah." She swallowed hard. "I'm sorry. What did you say?"

His brows dipped dangerously low, and her fingers twitched with the urge to smooth them back in place. His bold gaze left her face, traveled at leisure down her neck, then stopped at the bodice of the gown. Her body temperature shot up several degrees. After a long moment his gaze moved back to her face. "You don't look much like a cattle rustler."

"I'm not a cow stealer. I'm stuck."

He grabbed her right wrist and her pulse accelerated. Not even the scratchy lace could cover the sensuous rub of his calloused fingertips against her flesh.

"No!"

He yanked his hand back.

"I don't want to tear the dress."

The cowboy glanced around him. "Where's the groom?"

"There is no groom. If you could be a bit more careful—"

"He left you alone out here?" The pure outrage in the cowboy's voice sent her heart fluttering like butterfly wings.

"No, he ditched me at the altar in Las Vegas."

Those sexy black eyebrows dipped again. "If he cut out on you in Vegas, what the hell are you doing here?"

"Ah. Exactly where is 'here'?"

"You're just south of the Idaho border. Ten miles outside Ridge City."

"I ran out of gas. I noticed a light coming from there—" she motioned sideways with her head "—I assumed I could make it over the fence and walk to that house for help."

He shook his head. "Of all the blasted, reckless things to do, lady."

"Look, buster. Do you think I'm stupid or what? I know what a fool I've been. Now, are you going to help me off this fence, or just stand there and do nothing like the rest of those useless ignoramuses behind you?"

He glanced over his shoulder, and she thought she saw his lips quirk. The rat. How dare he laugh at her!

"I don't see how I can untangle you and save the dress."

"Please. You have to try. Help me get my arms free and I'll work on the skirt."

He touched her wrist again. This time she thought she was ready. Not. She swallowed a sigh of pleasure at his gentle, almost soothing touch against the red marks on her skin. An image of those hands on a more sensitive part of her body popped into her mind, and she jumped.

"Hold still." He moved closer, accidentally stepping on the gown, causing the bodice to slip farther. She gasped and his head jerked up so suddenly his Stetson caught on the lace veil.

The buffoons guffawed as her rescuer battled the veil. When he got untangled, he gawked at the front of her dress. "Jeez, lady, cover yourself up." He stepped sideways, shielding her from the other men.

She glanced down at the pearl-and-lace bodice of her off-the-shoulder gown and groaned. One deep breath and the dress would be around her waist. Anger, frustration and embarrassment warred inside her. "I need help, you idiot!"

He grimaced. As if he'd been asked to put his fingers in a meat slicer, his hands moved in slow motion toward the front of the dress.

"Just pull it up," she pleaded.

He grabbed the delicate pearl border, the backs of his fingers skimming her flesh, leaving a trail of heat behind. What was happening to her? She didn't even know this man, yet his touch affected her in a way that not even her ex-fiancé's touch had.

"You'll have to pull harder than that." She should have kept her mouth shut.

The blunt edges of his fingertips slid farther

inside the gown, and her lungs stopped functioning. He grabbed a fistful of material and he yanked. Hard enough that her heels came off the ground a good inch.

Lewd remarks filled the air, but her knight in shining armor silenced the two young hayseeds with a dark look and went to work on the sleeves.

His big clumsy fingers were patient and persistent as they freed her arms. She wanted to hug the brute for being so gentle. She couldn't have done a better job herself.

"Thank you so much. If you could show me where the skirt is caught I can—"

"Montgomery?"

"I'm busy."

"But—"

"Roy, I'll be with you in a sec." He sank down on his boot heels and reached up under the second wire, searching for the offending barb.

"You ain't got a sec, Montgomery."

Disgusted, the cowboy stood and faced the group. "What the hell is so important it can't wait until I'm finished?"

The man called Roy opened his mouth, but nothing came out. He raised his arm and pointed beyond the fence.

Madeline glanced over her shoulder and felt the blood drain from her face. She opened her mouth to scream, but just like Roy, nothing came out.

Her rescuer followed her gaze. "Christ!" He reached down and yanked a wicked-looking knife from a leather holder at his waist. "Lady, you're about to be carved up for breakfast."

She wasn't sure if it was the knife coming at her waist or the bull charging the fence from a hundred feet away that jump-started her vocal cords.

Her scream cut off abruptly at the sound of ripping material. "My beautiful gown!" Her eyes darted between the bull and the knife hacking away at the dress as the ground shook beneath her heels.

The cowboy swore when the blade got tangled in the material. The bull was charging at full speed now, and she wasn't sure her legs would hold her up much longer. The animal drew close enough for her to see his angry red eyes and smell his rank odor.

Just as the beast bellowed, the knife broke through the material and the cowboy flung her away from the fence. Inches from the barbed wire, the bull skidded to a stop, kicking up a cloud of dust. Madeline stared in alarm at the animal's flaring nostrils and the drool hanging from his massive mouth. The beast dropped his heavy head and backed up.

She could have died if it hadn't been for the quick thinking of the man next to her. She threw herself at him and wrapped her arms tightly around his neck. "Thank you, thank you, thank you," she mumbled against his skin. Legs shaking, stomach quaking, she breathed in the scents of soap, leather and man. She rubbed her cheek against his neck, enjoying the scratchy feel of beard stubble.

"Daddy, is she a real princess?"

The fingers clutching Madeline's waist bit into her.

She glanced over her shoulder and spotted a little dark-haired girl with a chocolate ring around her mouth. *Oh, my.* Jake Montgomery was a father. Which meant he was married. The sting of disappointment surprised her.

The hands at her waist moved her away from him. Embarrassed, she fingered the lace garter around her thigh. It could be worse. She could have been wearing bikini panties or a thong, instead of the tap pants, which were basically a feminine version of boxer shorts. She scowled at the spectators, who had their gazes glued to her fanny, then faced her rescuer and stamped her heel. "How could you do that?"

His eyes narrowed. "Do what? Save your life?"

"That was a three-thousand-dollar dress you

just cut to pieces!" She took a tentative step toward the fence and reached for the material. The rangy old bull had other ideas. He shuffled forward and skewered the material with a wicked-looking horn, then backed up. A loud rip filled the air as the animal tugged the satin skirt through the barbed-wire fence.

Horrified, Madeline gaped as the beast trotted away, the gown hanging from a horn like a war trophy.

SHE WAS THE DAMNEDEST female Jake Montgomery had ever seen.

Facing the fence, the half-naked redhead planted her fists on her scantily clad hips and shouted obscenities at the bull as he trotted off with half her dress.

If Cyclone knew what was good for him, he'd make himself scarce. At least until the fiery temptress left the area. At the raucous laughter behind him, Jake checked his watch. He'd wasted more time than he could afford. Sliding his sunglasses on, he faced the onlookers.

Billy Boyle spit a stream of tobacco juice at the ground. "She need a lift somewhere, Montgomery?"

When Jake glanced over his shoulder, the bride shuddered. "I'll see to it she gets help."

Boyle whistled through badly yellowed teeth.

"Yeah, I can guess what kind of help you'll be offerin', Montgomery."

Five sets of eyes devoured the bride, and for some crazy reason that ticked Jake off. She wasn't his lady, so why did he care who stared at her silk-covered thighs and sexy torso? He shifted to the side, blocking the rednecks' view. "Show's over. Hit the road."

He kept his back to the beauty until the men climbed into their pickups and drove off. A moment later, Ricky galloped away on his horse. By noon today, the town would be buzzing with gossip about the bride stuck to his barbed-wire fence. He turned to his daughter. "Annie, go get in the truck. Now." With a little huff, she spun away and did as she was told.

"Are you really going to help me?" the woman asked.

Jake bristled. "I said I would."

"Well, you don't seem very happy about it."

He whirled. "Lady, you picked a hell of a time to tangle with my fence." He forgot the rest of what he'd been about to say as a jolt of desire shot through him. He couldn't remember the last time a woman had had this kind of effect on him.

Concealed by the mirrored glasses, he drank in the sight of her. He dragged his eyes from the front of the gown and skimmed over her narrow waist and slim hips on down the length of her long, long legs. Legs encased in white silk stockings and a garter belt with the sexiest little rose-colored buckles he'd ever seen. She looked as if she'd just stepped off the pages of a Victoria's Secret catalog.

Her snooty nose poked in the air. "When you're finished leering, do you think you might get some gas for my car?"

Jake pressed his lips together to keep from chuckling. The fiery hair must be her natural color. Matched her temper. Maybe the missing groom was smarter than he'd assumed after all.

"I don't have time to get gas for your car." He headed for the truck. The sooner he got away from the woman the safer he'd feel.

"You're kidding, right?"

He heard an indignant huff and bit back a grin. "Nope. I've got to be in Pocatello in two hours."

"But…"

Jake glanced over his shoulder and smothered a laugh. Wobbling on her heels, the bride followed, picking her way between clumps of weeds and prickly cactus.

"I'll call the sheriff on my cell phone."

"You can't leave me out here all alone."

"A deputy will arrive shortly."

"I don't have any clothes!"

Damned if he didn't want to ask her why the hell she was out in the middle of nowhere with no clothes but a torn wedding dress. But he wouldn't. The less he knew the better. He halted by the passenger door. Annie was half hanging out the window, her eyes round with curiosity. Gently, he set his palm against her forehead and coaxed her back into the truck. "Sit down, Annie. We're leaving in a minute."

He opened the toolbox in the truck bed and rummaged around for the old set of clothes he kept in case he had to rescue a cow bogged down in mud, or some other emergency. Who'd have thought he'd be loaning the clothes to a runaway bride?

He sensed the moment she stepped behind him. And it wasn't because of the curses she muttered. He could smell her. A soft, sweet odor that made him think of naked bodies entwined on cool cotton sheets in a dark room. He breathed deeply, appreciating the feminine scent. It had been a long time since he'd smelled a woman up close. Until now he hadn't realized how much he missed it.

"I'm not staying behind with those two sleazy rednecks on the loose."

He eyed the proud tilt of her head and her pursed little mouth. He hated to admit it, but she was probably right. Boyle was a sleaze of the worst kind. Before he could say a word, her chin started to quiver, and he felt like a heel. He hadn't pegged her for a bawl-your-eyes-out kind of woman, but obviously the lady had had about as much as she could take for one day. He shoved the pair of jeans and shirt at her. "Here."

Her nose curled. "What are these for?"

Was she dense? "Cover yourself."

She fingered the hem of the shirt. His skin prickled as if those fingers were actually touching him. One thing for sure, he doubted the material would feel the same against his body after today.

"Look, lady. That's all I've got. Take it or leave it." He walked to the driver's side and reached for his cell phone on the seat, then dialed the sheriff's department.

"Hattie. Jake Montgomery. I've got a stranded motorist along my property line north of the turnoff to the ranch. Can you send Karl out with some gas?" The answer wasn't what he'd wanted to hear and he hung up.

"Is he coming?" She clutched the clothes to her chest and glared at him across the hood of the truck.

"No. There's been a bad accident east of here and the patrol cars are tied up." A tight knot formed between his shoulders. "You'll have to ride along with me."

"Can't you drop me off in town on your way to wherever it is you're going?"

"Nope. Don't have time." He opened the driver's-side door. "You coming or not?"

She spun on her heels, went to the car, removed her purse and keys, then stomped back to the truck and slid onto the front seat.

"Are you a real princess?" his daughter asked.

"Annie Jane," Jake warned as he cranked the engine. He almost put the truck in Reverse when a warm smile replaced the redhead's shocked expression. Under any circumstance the woman would be considered gorgeous, but the smile she bestowed upon his daughter revealed two very endearing dimples, softening her features, making her downright irresistible.

The bride stroked Annie's mussed hair. "I'm not a princess, sweetie. I'm a bride. But if I were looking for a princess, I'd think you were one."

Jake stepped on the gas pedal and started down the road. How could he leave the lady after she'd made his daughter smile? He couldn't remember the last time he'd seen Annie Jane's face light up with such pleasure. "Buckle up."

The bride helped Annie secure the belt, then did her own, wiggling her sassy fanny on the seat until she had those blasted satin short things arranged just so.

"What are those for?" Annie asked.

Jake glanced sideways and caught his daughter playing with the little rose snaps on the bride's garter belt. He stared at the expanse of creamy white thigh and shifted uncomfortably against the seat.

"Watch out!" The bride braced her hands against the dashboard.

Jake jerked his attention back to the road and wrenched the wheel to the right seconds before the truck would have drifted into the oncoming lane. The overcorrection caused the horse trailer to swerve violently, and he struggled a good ten seconds to get the trailer and truck under control. A sweat broke out across his forehead that had nothing to do with his reckless driving and everything to do with his reckless thoughts. "Aren't you going to put those damn clothes on?"

The bride ignored him, offering a tender smile to Annie. "Those are called garters. They keep the stockings from falling down. But I'm afraid the stockings are ruined."

The least he could do was offer the woman an apology, since she was being nice to his daughter. "Sorry about Cyclone."

"Cyclone? That nasty bull has a name?" She gazed out the side window as though searching for the recalcitrant animal.

"Yep," Annie answered for him. "He's real

old. Daddy can't sell him 'cause no one wants him."

"Well, I can understand that. How old are you, Annie?"

"Five. How old are you?"

*Good question, Annie.* Jake kept his eyes on the road, determined not to let his gaze wander. For all the good it did. The lower half of the bride's body reflected off the windshield.

"I'm twenty-five."

He glanced across the seat and frowned. Her skin was as smooth as a baby's butt. She didn't appear a day over nineteen.

"What's your name?"

*Keep up the good work, Annie, and we'll find out all kinds of things about the bride before we get to Pocatello.*

"Madeline Tate. You can call me Ms. Madeline if you'd like."

Madeline. Sounded snooty. It fit, though. By the looks of the gown she'd been wearing he'd say she came from money. He cleared his throat. "Exactly where were you headed when you ran out of gas?"

She waved her hand in the air by her head and shrugged. "I don't know. I just wanted to get as far away from Vegas as possible."

The slight tremor in her voice reminded him of how his daughter sounded when he'd gone and stepped on her feelings. "Do you live in Vegas?" Part of him wanted to learn as much about her as he could. He suspected it was the part of him that wouldn't settle down in his pants.

"No. I'm from Seattle. I work for an ad agency there."

Some of the excitement at discovering her attached to his fence died down. "I guess you'll head back to Seattle once you gas up."

She nibbled her lower lip. "Not necessarily. I took a three-week leave of absence from my job to get married."

"What about family?"

A bitter laugh escaped her mouth before she drew in a deep breath, then exhaled in one burst of air. "It's just my father and I. He's in Canada on business."

"You didn't invite your father to your wedding?"

She picked at a run in her stocking. "It was a spur-of-the-moment thing."

*Spur of the moment with a gown like that?* "What about friends?"

"The last thing I want to do right now, Mr. Montgomery, is face my friends." She crossed her legs, and he clenched the wheel to keep the truck steady.

"So you're searching for a place to hole up and lick your wounds for a while."

Her firm little chin jutted in the air. "Exactly."

"Then what?"

Her hands fisted in her lap. "Then I plan to find that...that—" she glanced at Annie "—groom and tell him exactly what I think of him."

Man, he'd like to be there when she laid into the guy. How could any man leave a woman like Madeline Tate standing at the altar? "So what *do* you think of him?" He shrugged at her wide-eyed stare. Hell, she'd be curious, too, if their positions were reversed.

"Was your groom as handsome as a prince?" Jake winced at the rapturous look on his daughter's face when she asked the question.

"Yes, he was handsome. A handsome prince with blond hair."

*She preferred blondes.* What was it with women and men with blonde hair? If you asked him, they were a bunch of prissies. "Annie, don't pry."

Thank God his daughter ignored him. "Is he gonna come rescue you?"

The bride sighed. "I'm afraid not, Annie. I'm on my own now."

"My daddy can be your prince. He can rescue you." Annie yanked on his shirtsleeve. "Won't you, Daddy?"

Before he could form an answer, the red-head's light laughter filled the cab. "Annie, I think your dad has his very own princess already."

"He does?"

Madeline smiled indulgently. "Why, your mother, of course. She's his princess."

Silence filled the truck as Annie stared at the half-eaten cookie in her lap. The bride sent him an anxious glance. "My wife, Sara, died three years ago." Three years that felt like ten, he admitted. Even though he and Sara hadn't had the best marriage, he still missed her presence in the house, the nice things she did for him, like straightening his dresser drawers or cleaning off his mud-caked boots. Things she did for him because she couldn't give him what he'd wished for in the privacy of their bedroom.

The quiet gasp was worse than any apology. The bride's expression softened with sympathy as she took Annie's hands and squeezed gently. "I'm so sorry about your mother, sweetie."

Jake kept his gaze on the road, not willing to risk seeing sympathy or anything close to pity in the siren's green eyes.

"So it's just you and your dad? Or do you have brothers and sisters?"

"I ain't got—"

"Don't have." Both he and the bride spoke in unison, then stared at each other and smiled.

"I don't have no brothers or sisters."

Jake felt her gaze on him but refused to elaborate. He didn't owe the woman any explanations. She'd be out of his hair in another few hours, and by the end of the day she'd be out of his mind. *Yeah, right.*

"Who takes care of you when your father is working?"

"Ms. Catherine. But she quit."

"Quit?"

"Annie, I doubt Ms. Tate wants to hear about our problems."

"She told Daddy her sister broke something, and she gots to go help her."

*Broke something?* His daughter made it sound like a dish. "Her hip."

"Oh, I'm sorry. I hope her sister recovers quickly."

Annie nodded. "Now Daddy gots to take me everywhere."

A knot formed in Jake's gut at the prospect of having to watch Annie every minute of the day while trying to train eight cutting horses for the Bar S Ranch. The Bar S was one of the wealthiest ranches in Idaho. If the owner, Sam William, was impressed with the horses, he'd recommend Jake's training talents to other prominent ranchers in the area. And Jake needed the business. Desperately.

If only Little Bear, his ranch hand and second best horse trainer in the state of Nevada, hadn't decided now was a good time to go on a traditional Blackfoot vision quest with his people, Jake wouldn't be in this mess. As it was, he'd be breaking his back to get those roans trained in three months. And he for sure wouldn't make it if he had to watch over his daughter every second of the day.

He wasn't aware of time passing, or how many miles they'd driven, before he noticed Annie had quit firing questions at the bride. He felt a sting of jealousy at the sight of his daughter, asleep, with her head in the bride's lap. Madeline stared out the window, her pink-painted nails stroking Annie's head.

He swallowed the lump of emotion clogging his throat. If he were better at this father business, his daughter would snuggle against his side, not a stranger's right now. He fought the feeling of guilt that always simmered inside him when he thought about his lack of parenting skills. When Annie had been born, he'd vowed he wouldn't be the same kind of father his old man had been. He'd vowed to spend time with his daughter, to always be there for her. To be someone she could count on.

"What kind of ranch do you have, Mr. Montgomery?"

At the sound of the question, his self-deprecating thoughts scattered. "Jake. Call me Jake."

"Okay. If you call me Madeline."

He nodded. "I train cutting horses."

"Cutting horses?"

"Cattle horses. They're used to move cattle."

"Is that where you're headed right now? To pick up these cutting horses?"

He nodded. "I've got a contract to train eight horses for a ranch in Idaho."

"Did you grow up around here?"

"No. My father worked in the sawmills in Oregon." He clamped his mouth shut. The last thing he wanted to discuss was the way his family roamed from one town to the next because his alcoholic father couldn't hold down a job for more than a few months at a time.

"How did you get interested in horses?"

"My last year in high school I had a part-time job helping out on a ranch. I learned a lot about horses from the owner." He shrugged. "After graduation I followed the rodeo circuit for a few years."

"I'm not familiar with rodeo, but I can't imagine the bull was too happy having someone as big as you on his back."

He chuckled. "No bulls for me. I wasn't that

crazy. I roped calves." He expected her to fire off another question. But when she turned toward the window and stared at the passing scenery in silence, he felt a stab of disappointment. Which was stupid. He didn't even know the woman. Yet something inside him wanted to learn more about her. "So. Did you grow up in the Northwest?"

"I've lived my whole life in Seattle."

He couldn't tell if the wistful note in her voice meant she wanted to stay there all her life or if she wanted to see what the rest of the world was like.

"You said you worked for an ad agency."

"Smith and Bower. I work in sales."

Sales. That figured. With her bossy demeanor he doubted anyone would turn down a sales pitch from her. Unlike him, she probably had a degree from one of the best colleges in the country. He recalled the flimsy certificate shoved in the desk drawer, claiming he'd received an associate degree in business management. He'd wanted to quit a hundred times, but his wife hadn't let him. She'd prodded him into taking one course after another until he'd earned enough credits for the two-year degree.

Annie stirred and sat up, rubbing her eyes. "I'm hungry."

Jake reached behind the seat and grabbed the

soft-sided cooler he'd packed for the trip. He set it in Annie's lap. "Help yourself."

She held up a plastic bag. "Want an Oreo, Ms. Madeline?"

"I'd love a cookie, thank you." She peered over Annie's shoulder. "What else have you got in there?"

"Um. Licorice. A cheese slice. A banana and a root beer."

"That's quite an assortment of snacks."

Jake ignored the heat crawling up his neck and took the exit to the rodeo grounds outside of Pocatello, where the horse auction was already under way. After he paid off the bank, he planned to breed, train and sell his own quarter horses, instead of driving hundreds of miles looking for good ones.

"Annie, when we get there I want you to sit in the truck with Ms. Tate, you hear?" He turned right at the first traffic light. "I shouldn't be more than forty-five minutes." He swung into the gravel lot outside the auction barns and parked near the shade of an oak tree. When it came time to load the horses, he'd pull the truck around to the corrals behind the barns. He stared at the bride. "Take my advice and stay in the truck."

She bristled but held her tongue. He had a

hunch that if Annie hadn't been sitting between them, she would have split his ears.

He lowered the windows, then pocketed the keys. "Give me your purse." He cringed when those gorgeous green eyes spit at him.

"What for?"

He fumbled for the door handle. "So you don't run off with my daughter." He didn't really think she'd take off with Annie. Even if she tried, she wouldn't get far driving his rig in that bridal getup. But letting her know he didn't trust her didn't hurt.

She threw the purse at him. He grinned. "Thanks for keeping an eye on Annie." He stuffed the beaded bag into his back jean pocket, then made it halfway to the first barn, when he noticed a group of cowboys staring at his truck.

He spun around, stomped back and poked his head through the driver's window. "Lady, unless you're planning to replace the missing groom with one of those hayseeds out front, I'd ditch the veil and put on my clothes."

## Chapter Two

*Of all the insufferable, egotistical, hard-headed—*

"Ms. Madeline? Are you gonna come home with Daddy and me?"

Madeline's heart turned over as she gazed down at the brown-eyed brown-haired girl next to her on the seat. The child was too sweet to resist. "No, Annie. I'm afraid I'm only along for the ride. As soon as I get gas for my car, I'll be leaving."

The little girl's mouth formed a cute pout. "Is you going to take off the veil?"

"I can't. It's stuck to my head with lots of tiny hairpins." Not to mention a whole can of hair spray. Even if she was successful in removing the pins, all the tugging and pulling would leave her looking as though a lightning bolt had zapped her in the head. She leaned forward and peered out the windshield. "Right now, I need to find a bathroom. How about you, sweetie? Do you have to go?"

Annie shook her head. "Nope."

Madeline groaned. It was past eight-thirty and the last time she'd visited the ladies' room was when she'd bought chocolate-covered raisins and two bottled waters at an all-night convenience store. She'd been so full of anger and hurt that filling the gas tank hadn't even occurred to her.

She scanned the parking area but saw no signs for a bathroom. Then her gaze landed on the lone Porta Potti across the lot. *Yuck!* She crossed her legs. The temperature inside the truck was steadily climbing. A drop of sweat rolled down between her breasts. "Are you getting hot, Annie?"

"Nope." She stuffed another Oreo in her mouth and offered a cookie-crumb smile.

There had to be something for Madeline to fan herself with. She patted the floor under the seat and discovered a brochure. It had the name of a preschool on the front. Opening the red-and-green colored paper, she saw Annie's name circled and the time and date of last year's Christmas play. Careful not to bend the paper, she fanned her face.

She'd listened to some of her married friends talk about how difficult juggling work and family was. Especially if the woman wanted a career along with motherhood. She could only imagine how much harder it was for a single dad who made his living at a job that wasn't nine-to-five, Monday through Friday. She wondered if Jake Montgomery had even attended his daughter's Christmas play.

Madeline's stomach growled. "Want to split the banana with me?" she asked.

"Okay."

After they'd finished the fruit another twenty minutes passed, and the pressure against Madeline's bladder became painful. "Annie. I've got to use a restroom or I'll wet my...tap pants."

Annie giggled. "Okay."

Madeline scanned the area. The cowboys by the door had lost interest in her and retreated inside the building, but she wasn't taking any chances. She reached into the backseat and grabbed the jeans Jake had given her earlier. After slipping out of her heels, she wiggled her way into the pants. Then she grabbed the shirt and groaned. *Flannel?* "Sit tight, Annie."

Madeline crawled in back and slid down on the seat. "Keep a lookout for me while I change into the shirt."

"Okay." Annie leaned forward and rested her arms on the dashboard.

With both hands twisted behind her, Madeline grabbed the bodice and tore it open. Pearl buttons pinged against the door panels, but she didn't care. It wasn't as if she could salvage the gown. She swallowed a sigh of relief. Too many hours had passed since she'd been able to draw a deep breath. After shimmying into the shirt, she buttoned it, then crawled back into the front seat and stuffed her aching feet into the high heels. "Come on, sweetheart. We'll have to walk fast."

She opened the door and hit the ground staggering. With one hand holding the jeans up and the other tugging Annie, she wobbled toward the Porta Potti like a high-wire circus performer. Halfway there, a raucous group of cowboys spilled from the building.

Madeline froze.

The men gaped at her. She couldn't blame them. It wasn't every day that a cowboy saw a woman wearing men's clothing and a wedding veil on her way to a Porta Potti. But it was too late to turn back. If she didn't reach the bath-room in thirty seconds flat, she'd be putting on a show of another kind in the parking lot. Head held high, she continued across the gravel, the heat of their stares searing her back.

When she made it to the portable toilet, she peeked over her shoulder, and her courage took a nosedive. Jake Montgomery stepped through the crowd. He wasn't wearing his sunglasses, and the stunned disbelief on his face forced her chin up another two inches.

"Annie, stay right here."

"I will."

Madeline opened the door to the stinky compartment and a whiff of putrid odor hit her in the face, gagging her. She stepped inside, shut the door and breathed through her mouth. She couldn't imagine anything smelling worse, except maybe a dead body. The confined space and lack of light made seeing what she was doing difficult and her fingers fumbled with the snaps on the garter. Good grief. Why hadn't she taken her hose off in the truck? *Because that nasty cowboy has you all flustered.*

"Hi, Daddy."

Oh, Lord! The nasty cowboy was standing right outside the door? Her face heated until she thought it might explode. Hurrying as best she could, she fastened and buttoned and snapped everything her fingers came in contact with.

When she stepped out of the portable septic tank, Annie's father was nowhere around. A quick look toward the building confirmed her suspicion. The original group of cowboys had multiplied tenfold.

A horn blast startled her. Across the lot, Jake sat in the truck, waiting—or rather, fuming. From ten yards away, she could see his hands clench and unclench the steering wheel. She stared at the gathering crowd, then back at the fuming cowboy. Neither appealed to her.

"C'mon, Ms. Madeline. Daddy's waiting." Annie took her hand, making the decision for her.

They hurried toward the truck, then she lifted the little girl onto the seat. Big mistake. Jake's jeans dropped to the ground around her ankles. Whoops and hollers filled the lot.

Stone-faced, Jake stared through the windshield. "You through putting on a show now?"

He didn't have to be such a jerk. She couldn't help the fact that she'd had to go to the bathroom. Or that his pants were five sizes too big for her. She tugged up the jeans and got into the truck. "It's not as if I'm naked, you know."

He glanced at her chest. "Might as well be, the way you're bouncing all over under that shirt."

She ignored his rude remark and stared out the side window. Didn't he realize what a fool he'd looked like, sauntering into the auction barn with a pearl-beaded purse sticking out of his butt?

He drove the truck around to the corrals. She refused to watch him load the horses; instead, she read a children's book to Annie that she'd found on the floor. Fifteen minutes later, Jake left the lot and headed back down the interstate. A mile passed in silence. Then two. Then three.

He cleared his throat. "Look, I'm sorry. I was out of line."

Having gone without sleep for over twenty hours, she didn't feel particularly generous, but the sincere tone in his voice did her in. "Apology accepted." She pointed to a gas station sign in the distance. "Would you mind stopping there? I need to purchase a gas can and fill it up for my car."

Jake shook his head. "Can't. One of the stallions isn't trailer broke. If I stop and don't unload him he'll panic and hurt himself trying to get out."

She sighed and stared down at the sleeping little girl nestled in her lap. What did it matter when she got gas for the rental car? She had no place to be at a certain time. She'd never considered herself a weepy kind of woman, but right now she'd give anything for some privacy and a good cry.

Oh, brother. Things like this happened in movies, in books. Not in real life. She should have known something was up when her ex-fiancé's pager went off in the hotel room and he'd told her to go on to the chapel without him. Afraid they'd lose their reservation, she'd hopped into the rental and gone ahead.

God, how she'd wanted to die as she'd stood in the back of the church waiting for her groom to show, while three other happy couples had cast sympathetic glances her way. How humiliating it had been to have the minister escort her out a side door and demand the balance of the chapel fee. Determined to reach the hotel before the weasel made his escape, she'd driven down the Las Vegas Strip as if the train of her gown was on fire, nearly plowing over a group of senior citizens on motorized scooters.

When she'd discovered her fiancé had already checked them out of the hotel and had taken all the pieces of their matching luggage, leaving her with no clothes but the gown on her back, she'd been so furious she hadn't been able to think straight. Instead of doing the logical thing and renting another room for the night, then buying a change of clothes, she'd allowed her anger to overtake her common sense and had driven off in the rental with no destination in mind, except to get as far away as possible.

She stared across the front seat, studying the handsome cowboy's stubborn jaw. *Hmm. What was that old adage? Some things happen for a reason?* She wondered if this was one of them.

After an hour, the truck sped past her midsize rental, sitting abandoned on the shoulder. A few minutes later Jake turned onto a gravel road and drove under a wooden arch with the letters *RF* carved into it.

She took in the vast barren land. "What does *RF* stand for?"

"Royal Flush."

"That's interesting. Did you win the ranch in a card game?" She expected a taciturn response. Instead, he smiled, and her heart quivered. She'd bet her original Andy Warhol painting *Flowers* that those sparkling blue eyes could make an old woman blush.

"No. But the previous owner's great-grandfather did."

"Why did the owner sell to you if the ranch had been in the family so long?"

"He was going on eighty. Suffered a stroke and had no children to take care of him or pass the ranch on to. Sold it to me and moved into one of those assisted-living homes outside of Vegas." He shrugged. "The old guy was pretty attached to the place, so I told him I'd keep the name."

"I like it, too." She didn't know Jake very well, but she suspected that under the rough-and-tough cowboy persona was a man with a true-blue heart.

Annie yawned and sat up. "Daddy, I'm hungry."

"Sit tight. We're almost home." He glanced

across the seat, a trace of sparkle still left in his eyes. "Mind fixing Annie something to eat while I unload the horses?"

"Of course not. It's the least I can do." Thanks to several etiquette courses as a young lady, the response was automatic. But in the back of her mind she thought that the least *he* could do was make *her* lunch for having to wait half a day for a can of gasoline.

A second later the house came into view. It wasn't much. A simple two-story white clapboard. The black shutters added a nice touch, but as the truck drew nearer, she noticed the white exterior paint had yellowed and cracked in several places. There was little landscaping. Scattered bushes here and there. The porch had no rail and ran the length of the house. At the far end hung a swing.

"I'll let you two off here. Key's under the mat."

She unfastened the seat belt and helped Annie out of the truck, catching the waistband of the jeans before they slid down to her knees again. Jake scowled. Sheesh. The man needed to lighten up. He acted as if he'd been the one ditched at the altar. She slammed the door extra hard.

Hand in hand, she and Annie climbed the porch steps. Not sure what pests might be hiding underneath, she cautiously lifted the corner of the doormat, in which the WELCOME had worn off. When nothing slithered out, she grabbed the key. Madeline didn't have much of a chance to take in her surroundings as Annie tugged her through the doorway and down a narrow hall into the kitchen.

Yellow checked curtains and a matching tablecloth brightened the small room. Beautiful green vines had been stenciled around the two windows, one over the sink and the other offering a view of the corrals. On the far side of the room was another doorway, which led to a utility porch. The appliances were outdated and there was no dishwasher.

She washed up at the sink, slipped off her heels by the back door then took the ends of the flannel shirt and threaded them through the belt loops at the front of the jeans and tied them off. At least she wouldn't be caught with her pants around her ankles again. "How about a sandwich, Annie?"

The little girl climbed up on a chair. "Sure."

"Peanut butter and jelly?"

Annie nodded, her eyes drooping. The poor thing was exhausted. Madeline made two sandwiches and poured glasses of milk. After finishing her own meal, she wiped the table and counter. "I'm going to freshen up a bit. Is the bathroom upstairs?"

Annie pushed her half-eaten sandwich away. "Yep. Can I watch TV?"

Although nannies hadn't allowed her to watch much television as a child, she didn't see any harm in children viewing TV as long as they did so in moderation. "Sure." Then she thought of the trashy talk shows on in the afternoons and added, "Be sure it's a children's program."

Annie rolled her eyes. "I won't watch Ms. Catherine's soaps, I promise."

Five minutes later, Madeline had the kitchen back in order. She peeked in on Annie and discovered her fast asleep, curled in a big leather recliner. After turning down the volume on the TV, she padded out of the room and up the stairs.

The second story was small. Three bedrooms and a bathroom. Curiosity got the best of her as she entered Annie's room. The first thing she noticed was Sara Montgomery's feminine signature scrawled beneath the painted tree in the wildlife mural that spread across three of the walls. When Madeline looked up, she gasped. White fluffy clouds and a summer-blue sky floated across the ceiling. A sweet, smiling angel with dark brown hair and eyes sat on one of the clouds. Inside her halo were the words *Sweet Dreams, Annie. Love, Mommy.*

How wonderful that the child could feel her mother's love surround her as she drifted off to sleep each night. A pang of jealousy pricked Madeline. How many nights had she lain awake when she was a little girl, aching for her mother? Yearning to know what a mother's love felt like.

Sighing, she checked out the guest room next to Annie's. It contained a single bed, a plain dresser and an oval rag rug. It didn't feel welcoming at all.

The bathroom was small but quaint. A beautiful pedestal sink and claw-foot tub filled most of the room. On a wooden shelf above the tub sat a stack of towels and a jumbo package of toilet paper. Just like a man to put the toilet paper right out in the open instead of hiding it in a cupboard. On the far wall an oval window faced the ranch yard. For a moment she watched Jake go in and out of the barn, carrying various pieces of equipment.

She shouldn't snoop, but the truth was, Jake Montgomery intrigued her. She told herself it was because he was so different from the polished, sophisticated men she worked side by side with day in and day out. But deep down she admitted that there was something about the cowboy that called to her in a way no other man ever had.

She left the bathroom and stood outside his bedroom several long seconds before she turned the knob and swung the door open. A massive king-size sleigh bed dominated the room. She spotted a small step stool shoved under the bed by the headboard and wondered how tiny Jake's wife had been.

A navy comforter hung half on and half off the mattress, covered by plain beige sheets. Each step closer revealed something more about the man who slept there. She stopped next to the feather pillow that still bore the imprint of his head and felt a twinge near her heart when she noticed the other perfectly plumped pillow. His scent surrounded her—a combination of sleepy male and faded aftershave.

Her eyes widened in shock when she caught sight of the framed picture of Annie and her mother on the nightstand. The woman was plain. Not ugly. Not pretty. Just plain. She thought of what a cute little girl Annie was and realized, that except for their coloring, the mother and daughter barely resembled each other.

Madeline lifted the frame and examined the picture. The camera had captured Sara Montgomery's maternal smile but also a deep, aching sadness in her eyes. She presumed a man as sexy, handsome and earthy as Jake could have had his pick of women. Yet he'd ended up with a plain Jane. So what had Sara had that no other woman could compete with?

Love, maybe? Could it have been as simple as that? Sara had loved Jake. Jake had loved Sara.

A streak of envy took Madeline by surprise. During her all-night flight through the Nevada desert, she'd had a lot of time to think about her relationship with Jonathon. She'd led a fairly sheltered life and he'd been her first serious boy-friend...well, okay, her first boyfriend, period. She admired him. Respected him. But if she was honest with herself, she wasn't sure she loved him. Or he loved her.

But her father had insisted a "smart match" was far better in the long run than a "love match," which he had claimed would inevita-bly lead to disappointment, hurt and pain. Her and Jonathon's marriage would have been one of compatibility. At least to start with.

Even if they hadn't confessed undying love to each other, his leaving her at the altar was a dirty rotten thing to do and she wasn't about to forgive him any time soon. If he had second thoughts, then why had he insisted on changing the wedding plans and running off to Vegas? But the answers to those questions would have to wait. Until she returned home. And right now *home* was the last place she wanted to go.

She set the picture down exactly where it had been, careful not to disturb the dust around it. Turning away, she moved to the bookcase built into the opposite wall. The shelves held several books and magazines on interior design, homemaking and cooking. Annie's mother had been very domestic, probably the perfect wife for a rancher or horse trainer or whatever Jake Montgomery considered himself. She went to the large picture window overlooking the front of the house. She wasn't sure what to make of the view. Depending on the person, the vast miles of land might feel liberating or confining.

She left the room unsure why her heart suddenly felt so heavy. Jake's life was none of her business. He'd made it clear that the sooner she left the better.

She returned to the bathroom and found a washcloth to freshen up with. Then she painstakingly began the process of locating and extracting all the hairpins that held her hair up and that had secured the veil to her head.

Fifteen minutes later, her long hair hung in snarled clumps around her shoulders. Swallowing a groan, she massaged her sore scalp. She opened the medicine cabinet and found a pink-handled hairbrush. Annie's brush. She worked the worst of the knots and the sticky hair spray out.

*Bang.*

Madeline jumped at the sound of a door slamming. She hoped it hadn't woken Annie from her nap. Sucking in a deep breath, she hurried downstairs taking in every detail of the house, knowing she'd never step foot in it again. In comparison to the warm, welcoming feel of Jake's home, her former upscale, trendy apartment had been sterile and cold.

She froze in the hallway outside the kitchen. Jake stood in the back doorway, clutching one of her satin pumps. The size-eight shoe appeared tiny in his large, tanned hand. Her breath hitched when he ran one long finger down the length of the satin-covered heel.

She must have made a noise, because his gaze caught and held hers across the room. His penetrating blue eyes sent a shiver up her legs, across her stomach and straight to her heart.

Madeline prayed that the ornery cowboy couldn't see how his blue-eyed stare made her insides go all gushy. "What?" she croaked.

"Your hair." His husky voice floated across the room.

She patted the messy strands. She knew she resembled a porn queen more than a fairy-tale bride. "The veil was getting itchy."

"Where's Annie?"

"Sleeping in front of the TV." If he would just put her darn shoe down and look away for a moment she might be able to catch her breath.

"I found an extra canister of gas in the shed."

Her throat thickened with emotion. Probably from exhaustion. And if that wasn't enough to make a girl emotional, then being left at the altar, running out of gas on the way to nowhere and having to parade around in half a wedding dress and men's clothing would do the job. She dredged up a smile. "Thank you."

"I'll get Annie." He bent down and picked up her other shoe, then handed her the pair as he slipped past her into the living room.

She sat at the kitchen table and wiggled her swollen feet into the disgustingly filthy pumps.

"Please, Daddy, don't make her go away." The child's sleep-drugged voice floated through the doorway into the kitchen.

"Annie, she has to go."

"She can watch me till Ms. Catherine gets back."

When Jake didn't answer his daughter right away, Madeline's thoughts wandered. Why hadn't it occurred to her earlier that taking care of Annie was the answer to her dilemma? With nowhere to go, no job to report to, nothing to do but feel sorry for herself, the ranch was a perfect spot to catch her breath and pull herself together before returning to Seattle.

She wasn't expected back at work until the end of the month. By then, she'd be ready to face her friends, coworkers and her father. And maybe by then she wouldn't still want to kill her fiancé.

She'd never babysat a day in her life, but watching over a child like Annie couldn't be too difficult. She'd simply do the exact opposite of what her nannies had done when she'd been a little girl. In other words, she and Annie would have fun.

The housekeeping part might be a problem. She didn't know the first thing about picking up after a little girl and a rough-and-tumble cowboy. Her father had always employed a maid, and when she'd moved into her own apartment, the first thing she'd done was hire a cleaning service. As for cooking, well, she wasn't much help there, either. But she did know how to use a microwave. She certainly wouldn't let Annie starve.

Before she allowed herself to consider the reasons she shouldn't stay, she rushed into the living room. Jake sat on the edge of the big leather chair, with Annie in his lap. Madeline took a deep breath and blurted, "I'd be glad to stay and watch Annie."

Jake's eyes bulged.

Annie crawled down from her father's lap and jumped up and down in front of him. "Can she, Daddy? Can she?"

Madeline pressed her hands to her quivering stomach. "I'm at loose ends right now. I'd be happy to stay until you found a permanent replacement."

His blue eyes narrowed. Maybe this was a bad idea. She knew nothing about Jake Montgomery other than his wife was dead, he had a daughter and he trained horses. Considering her groom had just dumped her at the altar, she might not be the best judge of character. But deep in her heart she believed Jake Montgomery was not a fiend or criminal.

Annie tugged her father's pant leg as he stood. "What about the groom? Won't he come looking for you?"

She remembered the crumpled note in the front seat of the rental car, and silently cursed her ex-fiancé. The coward had sent a dozen roses to the chapel with a lame *Sorry* scrawled across the bottom. "I doubt it. If he does, you can send Cyclone after him."

His lips quirked, but he tamped down the smile a second later. "What do you know about kids?"

She considered her own lonely childhood and

winked at Annie "Not a whole lot. Except that they're always hungry and they always want attention."

He didn't crack a smile and her stomach plummeted. He didn't believe she was capable of caring for his daughter. And she could hardly blame him for assuming a childless career woman had little experience raising children.

He shook his head. "I'm sorry, Annie. We need someone with more experience." He grabbed her hand. "C'mon. Let's get Ms. Tate back to her car so she can be on her way." Annie yanked her hand from his hold and stomped out of the room. Well, that was that.

She followed the two out to the truck, biting the inside of her cheek until pinpricks of pain shot through her mouth. Physical pain was easier to handle than the knot forming inside her chest, making it difficult to breathe.

The trip back to the car took forever. When the vehicle came into view, she silently cursed the stupid thing for running out of gas and bringing Annie and the handsome, but grumpy, cowboy into her life. Madeline doubted she'd ever forget this day or these two people.

Jake pulled onto the shoulder in front of the car. He put the truck in Park but kept the engine running, ensuring no long goodbyes. While he filled the car's tank with gas, she hugged Annie, her throat tightening at the sight of the child's quivering chin.

Even though she'd only known the little girl a short while, she wished she could stay and help ease the child's loneliness, which she sensed was caused by her mother's death. Madeline kissed the sweaty little forehead, whispered a heartfelt goodbye, then grappled for the door handle and got out of the truck.

Jake stored the empty gas can in the toolbox. "All set."

She smiled and tugged on the flannel shirt. "Any idea where I can buy a change of clothes?" She cringed, embarrassed by the hitch in her voice.

He removed his shades and pointed down the road. "Turn around and head south. You'll hit Ridge City in ten miles. There's a mercantile on Main Street. They've got shorts, T-shirts." His eyes narrowed on the front of the flannel shirt, then he glanced away and muttered, "Bras."

"I'll leave your clothes with the manager—"

"Whatever." He stared at her with what could only be relief in his eyes.

Stung, Madeline glanced away. "Thank you for all your help. I'm sorry I was such a bother."

"No problem." He spun on his heel and hopped into the truck. She hadn't even opened the driver's-side door of the rental, when the pickup shot forward, spewing gravel. Aching for the stubborn cowboy to change his mind and come back to her, she watched as the vehicle became smaller and smaller, until it was a dot on the horizon.

Who was she fooling? If she couldn't manage a yellow-bellied scumbag like her ex-fiancé, what made her think she could handle a man like Jake Montgomery? She was in no shape emotionally to go head to head with someone that mulish. A woman had to be in top form to handle all that testosterone. She sighed. *Wouldn't it be fun to try, though?*

She opened the door and froze. No longer a dot on the horizon, the pickup was growing larger and larger by the second. She held her breath as the truck barreled toward her in reverse. Her heart doubled its rhythm and her pulse ricocheted off the walls of her veins.

*Don't get your hopes up. He probably wants to insult you one more time.*

The tires squealed as the truck came to a stop next to her. The passenger-side window slid down. Annie wore a huge grin.

Stepping closer, Madeline leaned through the window.

Jake peered over the rim of his glasses. "Two days."

"Two days?"

"I'd be much obliged if you'd watch Annie for two days while I pick up another load of horses."

Excitement surged through her. Madeline wondered why he'd changed his mind, then decided she didn't care. She had two days with an adorable little girl and a sexy, hardheaded cowboy.

What more could a jilted bride ask for?

## Chapter Three

He'd made a mistake.

So what? Jake was man enough to admit when he was wrong and do something about it. He'd asked the bride to stay two days. One day too long. As soon as he returned with the horses tonight he'd send her packing.

He set the coffee mug on the counter and glared at the clock. Nine-thirty in the morning and the woman was still lazing in bed. Annie had woken up at seven, so he'd taken her to the barn with him while he'd looked in on the two horses he'd bought yesterday. Today he had to pick up another two stallions at the Lazy Ace Ranch three hours west of Ridge City and hoped to be back by supper.

That is, if the bride got up any time soon.

He rubbed the dull ache that had been banging against his skull since breakfast yesterday. Madeline Tate twisted his insides worse than the barbed-wire fence she'd gotten herself hung up on. She was a distraction of the worst kind. His washed-out jeans and flannel shirt hadn't disguised the worldliness, education, class and money that surrounded her. She was beautiful and way out of his league. The kind of woman a simple cowboy didn't have the vaguest idea what to do with.

All he had to do was close his eyes and an image of the bride, in her ripped wedding gown, flashed through his mind. Why all of a sudden was conjuring up a likeness of his deceased wife so hard? Sara had been what some might call wholesome looking. She hadn't used much makeup and had worn mostly loose-fitting dresses every day. He sure as hell had never seen his wife in a garter belt. He wondered how Madeline's silky thighs would feel against his rough, weathered hands and how easy those little snaps were to undo.

He shook his head. He had better things to think about than frilly underwear. As he stared out the window at the corrals, his gut tightened. Training eight horses by the end of August would be difficult even if he had extra help. What made him think he could do it on his own?

*Money.*

He chuckled. He needed money a hell of a lot more than he needed that red-haired minx with a broken heart sleeping in the upstairs guest room. When it came right down to it, he didn't know a damn thing about her except that she'd been left in a Vegas wedding chapel. He wasn't such a tough guy that he couldn't feel a little sympathy for her. Strangely enough, she hadn't boo-hooed and carried on as he would have expected a jilted bride to do.

The woman intrigued him, but the idea of her staying at the ranch made him nervous. It wasn't every day a man ran into a female, a gorgeous, stunning female, who seemed oblivious to her beauty and its effect on men.

Earlier he'd notified the sheriff's department that Madeline would be keeping an eye on Annie Jane. Then he'd called the Winstons down the road and told Gladys he'd be gone for the day. She agreed to check up on the two. Not that he didn't trust the bride. He didn't trust himself. The more people who knew she was staying at his place, the harder starting something with her would be.

He dumped his cold coffee into the sink and fixed a second pot. He needed the caffeine. He hadn't slept more than an hour straight last night. He'd dreamed of the bride tossing a lasso over his shoulders and dragging him to the altar. When he'd turned to kiss her, he'd seen his dead wife's face. If that didn't do a job on a man's psyche nothing would.

Sara. She'd been a good mother, a loving mother. These days he felt mostly sad for Annie and regret that he couldn't be everything his daughter deserved.

He thought of what he deserved, and the bride's face popped back into his mind. Even before his marriage to Sara he'd never felt this turned on by a woman. This constant flow of sexual energy buzzing through his body when he looked at Madeline Tate was enough to wear down a man's common sense. He wondered what it would take to coax the princess bride to go to bed with him.

He shook his head in disgust. How could one measly female make a man feel like a thirteen-year-old with his first hard-on? Okay, so the bride wasn't measly. Still, he resented that he couldn't control his body's reaction to her.

The lady was trouble with a capital *T.* As soon as she hauled her pretty butt out of bed, he'd tell her he'd changed his mind and she had to leave.

Sending her packing wasn't just for his sake. Already, after only a day, Annie was getting too attached to her. Maybe his daughter wouldn't be so lonely if he spent more time with her. Guilt knotted his insides. Come the end of August, he'd make sure Annie was his top priority. A shuffling sound from the doorway told him he wasn't alone anymore. He sensed it wasn't Annie, because she didn't shuffle. She sprinted everywhere.

Steeling himself, he turned and got his first look at the bride in over twelve hours. He clenched the coffee mug until his knuckles became as white as the dress shirt he'd loaned her to sleep in. She might as well have been naked. The sun, streaming through the window behind her, made the shirt transparent. He lifted the mug to his mouth as his gaze slid lower, over her breasts, down her stomach… *Good God! What had happened to her underwear!*

He inhaled a gulp of scalding liquid, then spun around and spewed coffee into the kitchen sink.

"Are you okay?" She moved across the room and pounded his back like a construction worker instead of a princess bride.

After a good minute of wheezing, he lifted his head. She stood close enough that he could see the pillow crease along her cheek and neck. If possible, her flame-colored hair was even messier and sexier than yesterday. His fingers itched to grab a handful of the satiny locks and breathe in the scent, test the softness against his face.

Speaking of faces… Devoid of makeup her skin was a creamy ivory, with a smattering of freckles across her narrow nose. This woman gave a whole new meaning to the word *beautiful.* He needed air and space. He stepped around her and put the oak table between them.

He thought she might expect him to wait on her, but she went to the cupboard, got her own mug and filled it with coffee. "I'd like to go into town today to buy a pair of jeans and a couple of T-shirts."

Jake didn't answer. He couldn't. He was too busy staring at the back of her thighs, peeking out from under the hem of the dress shirt.

She drank her first sip, staring out the kitchen window over the sink. Then she moaned. A deep-throated, quivering moan. The sexy noise she made had him thinking she preferred coffee to men.

"I haven't had coffee this good in years."

*Yeah, well, you haven't tried me.* Where the hell had that thought come from? He wasn't— nor had he ever been—a Don Juan with women. "I want to talk to you about staying here."

She blinked. "Okay." She seated herself at the kitchen table and waited for him to continue.

Jake opened his mouth to apologize for having to fire her before she'd even started her two-day job as nanny, when Annie bolted into the room.

"Hi, Ms. Madeline. I didn't think you was ever gonna wake up." Annie sidled next to the bride's chair.

Madeline put her arm around his daughter and hugged her close. "I had to catch up on my beauty sleep. But now that I've done that, what plans do we have for this glorious Saturday, Miss Annie?"

Jake held up a hand in protest, but his daughter kept right on talking. Annie had a hundred different things she hoped to do. He got tired just listening to her.

"Honey, I have to speak to Ms. Tate alone for a few minutes. Why don't you go on outside and swing for a while."

After Annie left the kitchen, Jake sat down across from her. He didn't know where to begin.

She started for him. "You're going to ask me to leave, aren't you?"

"Madeline…"

"Yes, Jake?"

The way his name rolled off her tongue did amazing things to his lower extremities. He rubbed the bridge of his nose, then snatched his hand away and shoved it under the table. "Like I said yesterday, I'll be gone most of the day, won't return until after supper." He was stalling. "Annie's bedtime is eight. Make sure she gets a bath before—"

"Annie and I will be fine."

"There's a list of emergency numbers on the fridge. Annie knows my cell number by heart." He motioned to the kitchen window. "Keep away from the horses and stay out of the barn. Annie might try to talk you into looking at the horses, but she's not allowed to unless she's with me."

"Okay."

He shoved a hand through his hair. "Any questions?"

"Is it all right if we go into town today?" She smiled and plucked at the collar of his dress shirt. "I really need to expand my wardrobe."

His mouth went dry. He didn't plan to wash that shirt for a month of Sundays.

"Jake?"

"What?"

The corners of her mouth curved. "You never answered my question. Is it all right if we go into town later today?"

"Ah, sure. But you'd better not wear that shirt."

She crossed her arms over her breasts. "There's nothing wrong with this shirt. Besides, it's much cooler than the flannel one you loaned me yesterday."

"You're asking for trouble if you do."

She stood and went to the sink. "What kind

of trouble?" she asked, keeping her back to him as she rinsed the mug.

Had she no idea what the sight of her legs was doing to him? The redhead deserved a lesson on the repercussions of teasing a man unknowingly or otherwise. And he was just the man to give it.

He moved around the table and came up behind her. She froze when he set his hands on her waist and leaned close. Her hair smelled like Annie's baby shampoo, and against his nose it felt as soft as it looked. Blood pumping through his veins like an oil gusher, he slid one hand under the hem of the shirt and smoothed it up the side of her thigh, stopping at her hip. "This kind of trouble."

Her head fell back against his shoulder and her eyes drifted shut. Her lips parted.

Oh, yeah, she wanted his mouth on hers. He removed his hand from under her shirt and spun her around. Her green eyes darkened and her tongue darted out to lick her lower lip. With one finger he traced the line of freckles across her nose, stroked her satiny cheek.

Tiny puffs of mint toothpaste and coffee-scented breath hit his face as he lowered his head. He wondered whose toothbrush she'd used. The air around their mouths crackled, like desert heat lightning. He'd never forced himself on a woman before. Like a fool, he stood at her mercy, waiting for an invitation. He was just about to move away, when she lifted her face and brought her mouth in contact with his.

Sparks jolted his body. He held her face between his hands and widened his mouth. His first taste of her sent his head spinning. Rich and sweet. Addicting. With his tongue he explored the cool cavern, tracing her teeth, then retreating to lick and nibble her lower lip.

Her hands curled around his neck, and he lost control when she feathered her fingers into his hair. She thrust her hips against him and all hell broke loose inside his jeans. He showed her with his tongue what he yearned to do with his body. Slowly. In and out. In and out.

Over and over. And over.

She collapsed against his chest, and his hands automatically clutched the shirt collar and tugged her close. He couldn't ever remember kissing a woman like this…like there was no tomorrow…just today. Just this moment—

"Daddy, I can't find Wilma!"

Jake jerked back so violently Madeline dug her nails into his shoulders to keep her balance. He dropped his hands from her and stepped back as if she were a lit stick of dynamite.

Annie barreled into the kitchen, then skidded to a stop. "I can't find—" She glanced between the two adults. "Why's Ms. Madeline's shirt all crooked?"

Both he and Madeline glanced down. The dress shirt had ridden up her thigh on one side, nearly to her waist. Jake snatched the tails and yanked so hard Madeline's feet almost went out from under her.

"I don't know where Wilma is, Daddy."

Jake shoved a hand through his hair and faced his daughter. "Did you check under the porch?"

"Oops. I forgot."

The door slammed, and he clenched his jaw to keep from calling Annie back to chaperon him and the princess bride.

"I think I understand about the shirt now." Her voice shook and he ached to pull her into his arms again.

*This isn't going to work. She has to leave. Now.*

Jake inhaled deeply and forced himself to look her in the eye. "How would you like to stay and watch Annie for two weeks instead of two days?"

TWO WEEKS? WHAT in the world had gotten into her?

Madeline pressed her hands to her hot face and groaned as she listened to the truck engine rev outside. She should have said no. After that kiss, she definitely should have said no.

She stood at the kitchen window, watching Jake maneuver the truck and horse trailer. As he drove past the house, he slowed, casting a glance toward the window. For a brief moment their eyes met. Her heart stuttered to a stop, as his expression changed from anxiety to wariness to…oh, my. *Desire.*

The heat of his stare scorched her and she raised her fingertips to her lips, to make sure they hadn't melted. She had very little experience with so much testosterone. But whatever message the cowboy had sent out, her body still clamored to accommodate. With or without her consent.

Feeling shaken, excited and very unsure, she turned from the window. There had to be a million places in the country to hide out and feel sorry for herself. Why here? Why with this man?

Because Jake Montgomery was real. Not polished and phony like the professional men she worked with.

Due to her natural beauty, everyone assumed she'd had her fair share of boyfriends. When it came to men, though, Madeline was anything but experienced. She'd led a sheltered life. Mainly because her father hadn't known what to do with her after her mother's death. She'd attended private girls' schools, and by the time she'd enrolled in college she'd had such little contact with the opposite sex that she'd tended to avoid boys whenever possible.

When she'd entered the work world, she'd found out quickly that most men thought of intelligent, confident women as their competition. If not for her father introducing her to Jonathon, she wasn't sure how long it would have taken her to become involved with a man.

Jonathon was smart, sophisticated and successful. But next to Jake, her ex-fiancé seemed fake. Cold, smooth steel compared with rough, warm rawhide. And all Jonathon's kisses combined couldn't compare with just one of Jake's.

Not that she was going to jump into bed with the man. She wasn't that bold. But if she played her cards right, she might get lucky and finagle another kiss out of Jake before the end of her two-week stay. She licked her lips and sighed at the taste of his unique flavor, which still clung to her mouth.

A nagging voice in her head insisted the cowboy was a temptation she should avoid at all costs. They had nothing in common. His life was filled with horses, barbecue and wide-open spaces. Her life consisted of high-rise buildings, conference calls and five-star restaurants. Anything long-term with Jake Montgomery was out of the question.

But she couldn't deny they had one thing in common. *Need.*

She sensed a loneliness inside Jake that needed comforting. It was the way his hand had tightened for a fraction against her skin, as if he couldn't bear to let her go. The moan that had vibrated deep in his throat before his lips'd caressed hers. The glazed look in his eyes after he'd pulled away. Jake might not admit it, but he needed someone.

And she couldn't forget about Annie. Annie needed her, too. Madeline knew firsthand the loneliness of growing up without a mother. She looked forward to giving Annie a little extra care and love for a couple of weeks.

And she couldn't forget about herself. Madeline needed to be needed. She jumped at the loud bang of the front door. "Daddy says I get to go to town with you today. He gave me five whole dollars to buy a hair bow."

She laughed at Annie's enthusiasm. "Give me thirty minutes and I'll be ready to go."

Changing into one of Jake's well-worn T-shirts and the same jeans he'd loaned her yesterday didn't take long. She found a belt on the back of the bathroom door and used that to keep the jeans from falling down.

Ten minutes later, behind the wheel of the rental car, she stared at mile after mile of ranch land spreading out in all directions. "Annie, is everything always this dry and lifeless?" The lush green grass and foliage in the Seattle area would look fake next to the brown and yellow vegetation along the highway. She knew one thing for sure. If she had to live in this environment, she'd paint her house grass green.

"Daddy says we live in the Great Bowl."

Madeline smiled. "You mean the Great Basin?"

"Yep."

She turned the air conditioner up a notch. "Does it ever cool down?"

"It's cold at Christmas."

She glanced in the rearview mirror, and her heart wrenched at the sad expression that came over Annie's face. "What is it, honey?"

"That's how Mama got sick."

Sympathy surged inside her. Even now, after so many years, Madeline felt a sense of deep loss when she thought of her own mother. As a little girl, she'd always imagined what her mother's hugs and kisses would have felt like. But every time she'd questioned her father about her mother, he'd remained tight-lipped and had changed the subject. To this very day, she had no idea if her father had even loved her mother.

At least Annie had had the chance to know her mother. But the sadness in the young girl's eyes reminded her that Annie had memories to deal with. Madeline had only photographs. She wasn't sure whether she or Annie was more blessed.

"How long was your mommy sick?"

Annie shrugged. "She coughed a lot. Then Daddy came home and took her to the hospital, and she never came back."

"I'm sorry, sweetie, that your mommy died. You must miss her very much."

"Yeah. Daddy misses Mommy, too." She dragged her fingers down her cheeks, stretching the skin. "His face gets all funny when I talk about Mommy."

For a quick second Madeline envied Sara Montgomery. If her husband still grieved after three years, she was a lucky woman to have known that kind of love.

Madeline wondered if she'd even crossed her ex-fiancé's mind after he'd ditched her. Maybe when he'd opened their luggage and discovered all her honeymoon lingerie. "I don't have a mother, either, Annie."

"What happened to your mommy?"

"She got sick and died after I was born." Her father had never discussed the details of her mother's death. The only thing he would say was she'd hemorrhaged and there was nothing the doctors could do to stop the bleeding.

"Oh. What store are we gonna go to?"

So much for her counseling skills. "First, I need to fill the gas tank and get cash from an ATM. Then we'll go look at hair bows."

Five minutes later they arrived in Ridge City. She wondered what fool had named the one-horse town a city. Good grief, there wasn't a stop sign in sight.

She spotted the Gas-'n'-Go as she turned right on Main, and pulled up to a gas pump and lowered the windows. Annie vaulted over the front seat and hung her head out the window to watch.

Madeline filled the tank, then paid with her debit card. When they entered the convenience store, she pointed to the candy aisle. "Pick out a treat for yourself, honey."

While Annie was occupied, Madeline withdrew five hundred dollars from the ATM machine at the back of the store. She doubted she'd use up all the money during her minivacation in the Great Basin, but she didn't want Jake Montgomery paying her way these next two weeks.

Thank goodness she hadn't opened a joint bank account after she and Jonathon had gotten engaged. At least the schmuck wouldn't get his traitorous paws on her money. "Let's go,

Annie." She watched Annie hop from one foot to the other, agonizing over the three rows of candy bars, gum and other snacks. Madeline laughed. "Okay, pick two."

When they approached the cash register, she offered a friendly smile to the pimply-faced teenager behind the counter. The adolescent's mouth dropped open. "Sure is warm today," she offered, stepping to the side in order to feel the blast of frigid air coming from the air conditioner behind the counter.

His eyes dropped to her chest and his mouth sagged another inch. Oh, good grief. So she was wearing a T-shirt without a bra. This was the Gas-'n'-Go. Surely women came in here dressed in less than that. She dug two dollars out of her purse and set it on the counter, then froze.

A fly landed on the teen's lower lip. Madeline watched it scurry from one corner to the other, dipping its green bug-eyed head inside the dark cavern for a look around. "You have a fly on your lip."

Still in a trance, the kid snapped his mouth shut, trapping the insect inside. She gasped, and Annie clamped a hand over her lips and giggled.

"Uh, keep the change." She took Annie's hand and left the store. Once inside the car they burst into laughter. By the time they parked across the street from Coot's Mercantile they were both gasping for breath.

When they stepped into the store, ceiling fans, with a decade of dust clinging to the blades, whirred above their heads, circulating warm air. The walls were peppered with stuffed animal carcasses ranging from deer, elk, rabbit, raccoon, to some animal-like thing that had two heads. The wood floor creaked and groaned as they walked down the center aisle. Madeline sniffed and her nose curled at the musty smell.

The sound of a throat being cleared halted her progress through the store. She turned and spotted an old man—make that ancient man— standing by an office door several feet away. He leered. Well, okay, it was probably just a smile, but it resembled a leer, because he had no teeth. He ran a knobby arthritic hand over the single strand of gray hair crossing the top of his bald head. The sun's rays streaking through the window bounced off his shiny noggin as he gimped toward Annie and her, dragging his left foot sideways across the dusty floor.

When he stopped near them, she caught a whiff of strong hair tonic. No wonder his skull shone like a lightbulb if he oiled it every day.

Annie tugged her hand free of Madeline's grasp and scurried over to a display of hair accessories, leaving her alone with the store owner. "Hello."

"Howdy, ma'am. Ain't you the barbed-wire bride?"

*Barbed-wire bride?* She stifled a groan and held her hand out. "Madeline Tate. Nice to meet you."

His fingers wrapped around her hand as if it were a fragile piece of china. "Name's Coot. Welcome to Coot's Mercantile."

"Well, Coot. I need a pair of jeans."

"Got me the best Wrangler's in town." His eyes twinkled as he hitched up his sagging pants.

"Wrangler's it is, then. Show me the way."

In less than twenty minutes, she'd selected three pairs of jeans, and several T-shirts from the buy-one-get-one-free rack. She shuddered when she picked out a couple of bras and a week's worth of panties. The white starchy cotton reminded her of the material used to make flour sacks back in…oh, 1876. After a ten-minute goodbye and a promise to return soon, she and Annie left the store and started across the street to the car. They were in the middle of the intersection, when the whining sound of a siren cut through the air.

Madeline drew Annie close as a patrol car whipped around the corner and screeched to a halt in front of them. Great. She'd gotten caught jaywalking. The car window lowered and she opened her mouth to beg her way out of a ticket, but the officer held up a hand, then reached for his radio and contacted the dispatcher.

"Hattie, this is Deputy Karl. I'm at Main and Harwood. I've located the barbed-wire bride."

Madeline's eyes rounded. News of her unfortunate predicament yesterday sure had traveled fast.

"Is backup necessary?" a squeaky voice cackled.

Madeline bit her lip to keep from laughing out loud.

"Everything's under control. Ten-four."

She edged closer to the car window. "Problem, Deputy Karl?"

The man's face turned red. "Depends."

"On what?"

The officer nodded at Annie, who was blessedly preoccupied with her new hair bow. "On where you're going next with Jake's little girl."

"We're heading back to the ranch right now."

"Fine. I'll just follow and make sure you don't lose your way."

"My. Is everyone this friendly in town?"

"Yes, ma'am. We like everyone to feel welcome here."

She grabbed Annie's hand. "Good day, Deputy."

Madeline should have laughed off the whole incident, but the fact that Deputy Karl tailed her all the way back to the ranch made it difficult. She didn't blame Jake for not trusting her with his daughter. If the situation were reversed, she'd feel the same way.

For Jake to be concerned when his daughter's welfare was in the hands of a woman he knew next to nothing about was only logical. Heck, she might be the head of a baby-stealing ring, masquerading as a runaway bride.

But he'd kissed her!

That kiss had changed things. At least for her. A man and woman didn't kiss like that if they didn't at least trust each other a little. She shook her head, doubting she'd ever figure out the opposite sex.

She turned under the arches of the Royal Flush Ranch and honked her horn as Deputy Karl sped by. At least he hadn't planned to follow her up to the house.

If she hoped to find peace and quiet at the ranch, she was sadly mistaken. The phone rang on and off all afternoon. Thankfully, Jake had a cordless phone, which she could take outside while she and Annie played. She thought about inviting Mrs. Winston, Jake's neighbor, over for coffee just so the woman wouldn't have to tax her brain to think up different reasons for calling every half hour.

Annie stepped into the kitchen, her cheeks covered in dirty streaks. "What's for supper, Ms. Madeline?"

She smiled at the child's messy face. She'd actually enjoyed swinging, playing tag and everything else Annie's young imagination had come up with. Even though Madeline was worn out, she felt better than she had in a long time.

Not once during the day had she had the urge to log on to her computer and check email. Not once had she wished she were having lunch with her peers or working on closing a sale for a new ad campaign. And the most amazing thing of all, not once had she thought of her ex-fiancé.

If she'd had to describe herself a few days ago, she'd have said she thrived on the challenges of a stressful career. She'd have said she liked living in a metropolitan area, making lots of money, dining out and enjoying cultural events.

That she'd had more fun digging in the dirt with a five-year-old made her wonder if she had a clue about who she really was and what she wanted out of life. "How about grilled cheese?"

"Okay."

While she fixed dinner, Annie found some

scrap paper and colored at the kitchen table. "Honey, are there any cookie cutters in the house?"

Annie shrugged.

Madeline checked the pantry. After searching every shelf, she found a bag of Christmas cut-outs stuffed inside an old soda-cracker tin. She picked the star and the tree shapes, then used those to cut the sandwiches.

When she set the platter on the table, Annie squealed in delight. "Wow!"

Pleasure filled Madeline. Even her Sales Manager of the Year award hadn't made her feel this good inside.

But pleasure gave way to an overwhelming urge to weep. Shocked at the stinging sensation burning the back of her eyes, she returned to the stove and stared at her own sandwich. She missed her mother and all that a mother repre-sented.

But how could she miss something she'd never had?

An image of herself as a little girl flashed through her mind. Eating alone at the kitchen table, night after night, because her father worked late hours. Her only company, the housekeeper washing dishes or mopping the floor. Always the same food. A piece of meat, potato or rice and a veggie.

The stupid sandwich wavering in front of her represented everything lacking in her childhood. Everything magical, everything warm, safe and loving. A lone tear escaped an eye, and she brushed it away. After selecting the Christmas-tree cutout, she used it on her own sandwich, then joined Annie at the table.

"How about a bath after supper before we watch TV."

"I gots a Disney movie about a tooth fairy."

"That sounds good."

An hour later, after Annie had played in a tub of bubbles with her Barbies, they sat on the couch in the living room and watched the movie. Madeline made popcorn and strawberry Kool-Aid, and by the end of the show, Annie's eyes were drooping. Madeline helped the little girl to bed, read from a book of nursery rhymes for fifteen minutes, then snuggled the animal-print sheet around her shoulders and kissed her sweet-smelling cheek.

Madeline spent the following half hour cleaning up the popcorn mess before retreating to the front porch. She slunk down on the swing, flipping her ponytail over the back, allowing the cool breeze to tickle the patch of moist skin at the back of her neck.

Off to the west, the sky looked as if someone had taken a paintbrush and smeared a dark pink color with a hint of orange across the horizon. A deep sense of contentment filled her as she breathed in the earthy smells of warm wood, dusty gravel, animal and grass.

The only thing missing was the fragrant scent of blooming flowers. If she lived in this house, she'd have hanging plants and potted flowers on the porch. She'd plant some rosebushes by the steps and wild daisies out by the barn.

A soft nicker floated through the air and she shifted sideways on the seat to observe the two horses in the corral. They were beautiful animals, strong and proud. She looked forward to watching Jake's progress with them during her stay.

At the end of two weeks she'd leave. Go back to Seattle and face friends and family. And return to her job. But right now the idea of selling anything, let alone advertising, gave her heartburn. Closing her eyes, she rubbed her temples, easing the pounding that seemed to erupt every time she thought about the future.

The future would always be there. But Jake Montgomery, his daughter and their ranch wouldn't. And right now she needed them as much as they needed her.

Speaking of the cowboy, she glanced at her watch. It was almost nine. She worried that he might have run into trouble on the road. Towing a loaded horse trailer was bound to be hazardous. If he didn't return by ten she'd call his cell phone number.

Her stomach clenched with anxiety. Anxiety that had nothing to do with how Jake might view her job performance today and everything to do with the wonderfully devastating kiss he'd given her that morning.

She yearned for another taste of the dangerous, moody cowboy. Playing with this kind of fire was sheer madness. After a failed attempt at the altar, letting a man like Jake get close to her so soon was a heartache in the making.

She was a smart woman. That she hadn't shed too many tears over Jonathon's abandonment was a sure sign she'd never really been in love with him. She wondered if a woman like her, one lacking experience with the opposite sex, would even be able to recognize true love if it stared her straight in the face.

If an I-can't-live-without-you kind of love really existed in the world, then Madeline was positive Jake was a man who could inspire it in a woman. Her heart might not have suffered a mortal wound from being jilted, but it was still vulnerable. Yet eager. Wanting.

Which made it fair game for the cowboy.

A few minutes later, the deep purr of a diesel

engine competed with the chirping night sounds in the air. She held her breath, waiting, her eyes searching the distant rise in the road.

# Chapter Four

Exhausted, hungry and damn grumpy, Jake pulled the truck and horse trailer to a stop outside the corral. He flipped off the headlights and took a deep breath, then exhaled forcefully. It had been a hell of a day.

A day that had started out bad and had gone downhill from there. And he had no one to blame but himself. First off, he should never have kissed the temporary nanny earlier that morning.

The memory of her mouth under his had stuck with him all day like a burr in a horse blanket. Twelve hours later he could still taste that kiss. Not even the double cheeseburger and fries for lunch could erase the warm, sensuous flavor of Madeline's mouth.

The second mistake he'd made was asking the temptress to stay on two weeks to watch Annie. Having her underfoot would create more problems than it solved. Like, how the hell was he supposed to keep his hands off her, let alone his mind?

Third, somewhere during the long stretches of driving, he'd decided he wanted to be Madeline's hero. To chase away the pain and hurt caused by her jerk of a fiancé. The thought had shocked him. How could he be Madeline's hero when he'd been guilty of the same thing as her fiancé—abandonment.

Oh, hell! He hadn't asked for a jilted bride to drop into his life out of nowhere. If the attraction he felt for Madeline was purely sexual, he knew without a doubt those hero thoughts wouldn't have entered his mind. But emotions were involved. Exactly what emotions he couldn't say for sure. Only that something inside him wanted to make everything right in Madeline's world again.

He slipped the key from the ignition. He had two horses to unload, then he'd grab a bite to eat and check on Annie. He'd missed his daughter today. Maybe tomorrow he'd find a way to carve out some time with her.

A tap on the passenger-side window startled him. He looked sideways and chuckled at the Cowgirls Rule slogan in glittering gold across the front of Madeline's T-shirt. The bride was the furthest thing from a cowgirl he'd ever seen.

T-shirts and jeans couldn't quite hide her sassy confidence and take-charge executive attitude.

He slid from the truck and stared across the roof at her. Her red ponytail gleamed like a brand-new copper penny, and her green eyes glowed with the warmth of welcome he knew he didn't deserve after the way he'd practically mauled her in the kitchen that morning.

Whatever makeup she'd started the day with was long gone. Her skin looked creamy and soft in the shadows cast by the outdoor corral lights. She was drop-dead gorgeous. It didn't seem possible, but Madeline truly acted as if she was unaware of the effect her beauty had on the opposite sex.

He wanted her. Wanted her so badly that he'd do anything, risk everything, to have her right now. The shock of the realization almost knocked his legs out from under him.

She offered a smile.

His gaze fell to her lips. Lips that begged for a man's mouth. *His* mouth. "How's Annie? Everything go okay today?"

"She's in bed, and yes, we had a good day." Her left eyebrow lifted. "Amazing how friendly everyone is around here."

"Friendly?" The reckless desire, the painful need just seeing her created in him, was unlike anything he'd ever experienced. One look at her and it was as though the ground shook beneath him.

She sighed. The sexy, velvet sound rolled across the truck roof and landed against his chest with a gentle thud. He gripped the door until sharp pains shot up his arm.

"Deputy Karl stopped me in town to say hello." She frowned. "Mrs. Winston had a hard day."

He should unload the horses, but that would mean taking his eyes off her. And he wasn't ready to do that yet. "Hard day?"

"She kept calling and forgetting what it was she needed to ask me."

Jake bit back a smile. "She means well." Gladys Winston drove him nuts, but she'd been there for him and Annie when Sara had taken a turn for the worst. He owed the woman his patience at the very least.

"Are you hungry?"

*Oh, babe, you have no idea.*

"I don't suppose I could talk you into Christmas-tree grilled-cheese sandwiches."

"Huh?"

Her laughter floated on the night breeze. "Didn't think so. How does an omelette sound?"

*An omelette for supper?* "Ah, yeah, sure."

She turned away and hadn't taken five steps before his lungs seized up on him. Madeline in a pair of jeans was something to see. Before he could stop the words they were out of his mouth. "Nice jeans."

She kept walking but smiled over her shoulder. "Wrangler's, cowboy. There's a difference, you know. Or so Coot tells me." After that there was a definite twitch to her hips, which he suspected was purely for his benefit.

"I'll be in shortly," he called out.

"No rush. I'm not going anywhere."

He was afraid of that. Jake took his time, giving the horses a chance to settle in and his hormone levels a chance to return to normal. When he entered the kitchen a half hour later, the smell of burned egg assaulted his nose.

She waved an oven mitt in front of her face. "I'm not used to cooking with cast iron."

"Don't worry about it. There's a can of beef stew in the pantry. I'll have that."

"Oh, no. The omelette's fine."

He frowned at the discolored yellow blob in the skillet.

"Really. I'll cut off the edges." She slid the rubbery mass onto a plate, hacked off four corners, then put it on the table next to a paper napkin, a knife, fork and spoon. What was he supposed to do with all those utensils?

When she returned with a glass of water, he

thought about switching it for a beer, but knew it would be suicide.

"I need to wash up." He moved from the doorway, taking the long way around the oak table to avoid passing by her. Less than five minutes later he was back in the kitchen, washed up and wearing a clean shirt.

He sank onto the seat and poked at the omelette with the fork. "Thanks for making supper." A long time had gone by since anyone had cooked for him.

Madeline stood at the sink, suds up to her elbows, washing the skillet. "You're welcome. So, how was your day?"

He didn't answer right away. Couldn't. His jaws were too busy trying to grind down the elastic wad in his mouth. He had to admit, though, that if he could eat a meal while staring at Madeline's backside, he could swallow just about anything. "Fine," he managed to say, after switching the half-chewed lump into the pocket of his other cheek.

Her laughter filled the room. "I guess you're one of those strong silent types." She grabbed a handful of utensils and set them in the soapy water. "I wish I worked with more men like you. The ones I deal with day in and day out could talk a deaf person's ear off."

Jake tucked that tidbit of information away

to ponder later. "Besides going into town, what did you and Annie do all day?"

She turned from the sink. He was glad he hadn't swallowed the food in his mouth yet, or he'd have likely choked. A large wet spot covered the front of her T-shirt. He stared. Couldn't help it.

"We played outside most of the day. I don't know how you keep up with her. She wore me out." Her smile lit up her whole face, making her green eyes glow and her cheeks flush. Rag in hand, she approached the table. He held his breath, hoping, praying, she just wanted to wipe the surface off.

Nope. The air left his lungs in one long rush when she pulled out a chair and sat. Her fingers played with the cotton rag. "Let's see. We played tag, sat on the swing, collected rocks, swept the porch, had a tea party. You know, girl stuff. She had a bath after dinner, then we watched a movie before bedtime."

Madeline Tate's fiancé was an idiot. That was all there was to it. Any man who would walk away from a woman like her was dumber than a worm.

"Jake?"

He blinked. "What?"

"I made a pot of coffee. Would you like a cup?"

"Sure. Thanks." He shoved the last bite of egg into his mouth and choked it down while Madeline poured two cups of coffee.

"What kind of horses are in the barn?" she asked, setting the mugs on the table.

"Three quarter horses. One paint."

"That's nice."

Nothing like a *That's nice* to remind him of the different worlds they came from. His male ego reared its ugly head and he had to clamp his mouth shut to keep from bragging that he had a couple of trophies collecting dust in his bedroom closet for training two world-champion quarter horses.

He patted his empty shirt pocket. He hadn't smoked since Annie had been born. He didn't want to light up now, but it was tempting. At least the cigarette smoke would mask the sweet, womanly scent drifting across the table. After chasing around with his daughter all day, Madeline should have smelled dusty and dirty, like one of the horses. Instead, traces of faded perfume, a little bit of outdoor and a whole lot of warm woman rolled off her.

"Tell me to mind my own business if you want." Her gaze fell to the tabletop, and she scratched at an imaginary speck with her nail. "What was Annie's mother like?"

He opened his mouth, then shut it. Sara was

a good, decent woman. He wouldn't place any blame on her for their less-than-perfect marriage. Living each day with the guilt that he'd caused her death was bad enough. He sure as hell didn't want to share *that* with Madeline.

"I'm sorry. I shouldn't have asked."

He cupped his hands around the coffee mug and stared across the room. Things between him and Sara had been fine until he'd lost his head. Thinking back on it now, he should have stayed and dealt with it, instead of running off to lick his wounds, leaving Sara and Annie to fend for themselves. He looked at Madeline. "What do you want to know?"

A cautious light filled her eyes. "Was Sara as outgoing and vivacious as Annie is?"

*Sara, vivacious?* "No. She was quiet. Reserved."

Jake remembered exactly two times he'd heard his wife laugh during their marriage. The first, when Annie had tried to walk in Jake's boots. The second, when their daughter had made mud pies, then had tried to eat one.

"Her parents were very religious. Strict. She'd never socialized much growing up." Neither had he, for that matter. He'd been too busy working odd jobs to pay for his own clothes and, more often than not, his own food.

"So Annie takes after you?" She smiled. "I

guess it must be hard for your vivaciousness to break through all that macho-cowboy swagger."

He fought the grin tugging at the corner of his mouth.

Madeline shrugged, the delicate slope of her shoulders sagging a few inches. "I wasn't very social, either."

Not social? How could someone with her looks, education and background not be social? "You're telling me you weren't a party girl?"

"Hardly. I was a bookworm." She laughed, but it sounded off-key. "The private girls' school I attended sponsored a dance each year with a nearby boys' academy. It wasn't until I stood three hours in the corner waiting to be asked to dance that I figured out boys were allergic to smart girls." Her smile was a little too bright. "It was no big deal."

But Jake sensed it *was* a big deal. Sure, some of the boys may have been intimidated by Madeline's academic accomplishments. But there was more to it than that. Simply put, her budding beauty and sensuality had scared off the young men caught in the throes of their first hormonal surges.

He glanced at the clock. He should go out and work the horses. Instead, he slouched in the chair. "Your turn. Tell me about your fiancé."

She crinkled her nose. "*Ex*-fiancé."

Jake purposefully ignored the sense of relief he felt when she muttered *ex*.

"Jonathon's a lawyer."

He had sensed she was attracted to high achievers. That definitely put him out of the running...not that he'd ever considered entering the race.

"After I turned twenty-five, I offhandedly mentioned to my father that I'd been contemplating marriage and starting a family."

Children? He had a hard time picturing Ms. Corporation with a baby on her hip and a phone in her hand. Then the image of her stroking Annie's head popped into his mind. Maybe there was some maternal instinct buried under that businesslike veneer.

"Two months later, Father introduced me to Jonathon, the newest member of his legal team." She waved her hand in the air by her face. "Jonathon was the first man I'd met who didn't seem threatened by my success. He was actually impressed that I'd become a vice president at twenty-four."

*Vice president?* Just how driven was this woman?

"He never came right out and said as much, but I sensed Jonathon had aspirations of making partner in my father's firm."

"What did your father say about your engagement to him?"

"He thought we made a good team."

"Team?"

"Father views marriage as a business arrangement, not a love match."

Well, Jake was no authority on marriage. His and Sara's hadn't been a love match, yet it hadn't been a business arrangement, either. He wondered what it *had* been. "After you were engaged, did your father offer him a partnership?"

"Yes. The very next day in fact. I guess it was his reward for popping the question."

*Ouch.* Jake hurt for Madeline. He wished he had the right to take her in his arms and chase the sadness from her eyes. "Any idea why he suddenly got cold feet?"

She shook her head. "Not a clue. We'd planned a church wedding this November, then a week ago he begged me to go to Vegas. Like a ninny, I assumed it was because he was so eager to be my husband. And I'd already had my dress, so I thought, why not?"

Jake grimaced when a picture of Madeline frolicking in a honeymoon suite with a faceless man popped into his mind. "You want to call him?"

"No. I don't want to kiss and make up."

Speaking of kisses… He dragged his gaze

from her face and focused on the coffeepot across the room. "About this morning." He squirmed against the seat, feeling like a little kid caught stealing candy from a drugstore. "You have my word, it won't happen again."

He expected a sigh of relief. A look of gratitude. Instead, she gave him her back when she rose from the chair and crossed the room. He waited, the muscles in his body burning with tension. Not knowing what was going through her mind drove him crazy.

"What if I don't want your word?"

If he hadn't already been seated he'd have fallen on his rump. Had he heard right? Did she say she wanted him to kiss her again? *Oh, man.*

He clutched at his shirt collar, which suddenly felt like a noose around his neck. She liked his kisses. So what? That didn't mean she wanted to take a tumble in the hayloft with him.

He couldn't risk kissing her again. Because if he did, he wasn't so sure he'd be able to stop at just a kiss. He'd want more. A heck of a lot more. And he knew from experience that could only lead to trouble. "Like I said. It won't happen again."

Nodding, she wiped her hands on a towel, then faced him. She braved a smile, but the shadows in her eyes socked him in the gut. She could tell herself she was over her miserable fiancé. But Jake knew Madeline needed reassurance that she was still a great catch, a desirable woman. No matter how badly he wanted to be the man to show her, he didn't dare.

Because he *liked* Madeline. Genuinely liked her. A surge of protectiveness toward her filled him. He didn't want to see her hurt again. He wasn't the right man for her...not even on a temporary basis. If he allowed himself to explore this...*whatever* between them, she'd end up hurt again.

"I think I'll get a shower and go to bed." She paused in the doorway. "Will you be here tomorrow, or are you off to gather more horses?"

*I wish.* "I'll be here."

"Good night."

Her scent stayed long after she left the room. He sat at the table, calling himself every kind of fool. When the sound of running water rattled the pipes in the walls, he took his plate to the sink, slammed his Stetson on and headed for the corrals. He'd be damned if he'd sit there and conjure up images of a naked, wet Madeline standing under the showerhead.

MADELINE STEPPED AWAY from the bedroom window and slid under the cool sheet on the bed. For the past hour she'd watched Jake hold the end of a rope while a horse trotted circles around him. Both man and beast were moving shadows under the glow of a full moon.

She closed her eyes, allowing her imagination to run wild with images of Jake kissing her. She wasn't sure how much time had passed, when the faint sound of a creaking door brought her musings to an abrupt end. A moment later the soft hiss of running water filtered into the hall-way. Jake was in the shower.

When she envisioned his naked body under the cool spray, a deep, tugging sensation settled low in her belly. She plopped the pillow on top of her face to muffle a scream of frustration. Honestly, she was acting like a virgin.

Jonathon might have been her first, but they'd had sex several times. At least three times she could remember. So why hadn't her body re-acted to Jonathon the way it reacted to Jake?

*Because Jake is a real man.*

Madeline sighed. She had to admit, sex with Jonathon had been, well…okay. Not that she'd had enough experience to know the difference between good sex and bad sex. It was just that he'd made love as if he'd been following a ten-step guide to fulfillment. His moves had been too smooth, too choreographed.

If Jake's kiss was any indication, Madeline had a feeling making love with the cowboy would be spontaneous, hot and, best of all, wild.

She yearned to experience another of his kisses, to feel her whole body tingle and quiver.

She wished her need for Jake were just about sex. Good, satisfying sex. But she admitted it was more complicated than that. Jake made her *feel*. One touch of his mouth and she was lost in him. There was something inside him that called out to her. Not bodily, but spiritually. She may have been the one dumped, but she sensed that Jake carried his own scars when it came to matters of the heart.

All of a sudden, the room became stifling. She kicked off the sheet and flopped over on her stomach. The bathroom door creaked, and she held her breath. She listened to Jake's feet padding against the wood floor in the hall. Instead of growing fainter, the sound grew louder.

He stopped outside her door and whispered, "Madeline? You awake?"

"I'm awake."

He gripped the edge of the door and eased it open a crack farther. "Can I come in?"

"Sure." She rolled over and sat up against the headboard.

He wore a fresh pair of jeans, zipped but unsnapped. No shirt.

His hair was wet, the strands reminding her of black liquid ink. He leaned against the wall by the door, crossed one leg over the other and stuffed his hands in the front pockets. He looked tired, and...glum.

She wanted to bolt from the bed and hug him until the sadness left his eyes. Instead, she plumped the pillow and hugged *it* to her chest. Something weighed heavy on his mind, but she worried she'd scare him away by asking too many questions.

He rubbed the bridge of his nose—an endearing habit that Madeline had noticed he resorted to when he seemed unsure of himself. Then he lifted his head and studied her openly. She suddenly wished she were wearing something nicer than the extra-large nightshirt that stopped an inch above her knee.

"I wanted to talk to you about Annie."

Annie? He stood in her doorway in the middle of the night, sexy as all get-out and he wanted to talk about his daughter? Madeline hid her disappointment and smiled. "Of course." She patted the mattress next to her.

Indecision warred in Jake's eyes as he stared at the spot where her hand lay. He moved closer, settling at the bottom of the mattress.

She bit back a smile. She'd never thought of herself as threatening. The idea that she made Jake nervous intrigued her.

He rested his forearms on his thighs and studied the floor. "I was wondering if Annie said anything today."

"Said anything? She talked my ear off."

Her comment brought a weak smile to his face. "Yeah, she's a chatter bug. What I meant is, did she say anything about me?"

The hopeful expression on his face tugged at her heartstrings. "Well, let me think. Yes, she did. She said you were the best horse trainer ever. You don't know how to iron. And your face gets sad when you talk about her mother."

He stared at the floor again and cleared his voice. "She's right. I suck at ironing. And I am a damn good horse trainer." He expelled a long breath, then looked up. "And I guess I don't smile when I talk about Sara."

Madeline couldn't stand not trying to comfort him. She leaned forward and laid her hand across his forearm, enjoying the way his muscle jumped under her fingers. "You must have loved your wife very much."

He pulled his arm away. "I don't want to talk about Sara." He got up and paced in front of the window. "I know deep down Annie isn't happy. I'll be the first to admit she deserves a better father than me." He drew a hand down his face. "I was hoping that you could give me some advice."

"Advice?"

"On being a good father."

She thought of her own father and cringed. Based on their relationship, the only advice she had for Jake was what *not* to do as a father. Before she could say anything, he stopped pacing and gazed out the window.

"I don't know what she needs from me."

"Attention and love," Madeline whispered.

He glanced over his shoulder, his eyebrows dipping. "I do love her."

"Do you tell her?"

He turned back to the window. "No." The word came out sounding so strangled that it was all Madeline could do not to vault off the bed and go to him.

"The words are wonderful, but they aren't always necessary. A hug will do. Pulling her pigtails when you walk past her. A special nickname. A bedtime story each night. Those are little things that say *I love you*."

Jake turned away from the window. "I don't spend enough time with her."

"I think you're being too hard on yourself. Training horses isn't a nine-to-five job. There are going to be days when you don't have as much time to spend with Annie as you'd like. Quantity isn't as important as quality." At his puzzled look she continued. "What you do with your time with Annie is more important than how much time you spend with her."

"Where do I start?"

"How about reading Annie a bedtime story each night?"

He nodded, then his face brightened. "Maybe Annie could help me with the horses."

"I'm sure she'd be thrilled to fill the water troughs or dish out their food."

The shadows that had been in his eyes when he'd entered the room fled and his lips curved into a half smile. "Thank you for listening."

Lord, how the man made her heart stumble. "I'm always here if you need to talk." Her throat tightened at the lie.

Eventually, she would have to leave.

## Chapter Five

"C'mon, Quicksilver. You're not going to win this one, buddy." Jake gathered up the lunge line used to force the stallion to trot in circles, walked the animal several feet outside the corral, then stopped.

Of all the eight horses to train, this one was his favorite. And the most stubborn. Horses by nature were emotional animals, but Quicksilver won the prize. Especially in the willful category. Jake admired the animal's independent streak and took extra time with the stallion, making sure he didn't break the horse's spirit.

He stepped back and looped the lunge line around one foreleg. The animal didn't like anything or anyone near his legs. Jake's job was to change the stallion's mind. Cattle horses had to get used to cows bumping into them and calves running under their bellies. If the reins got caught or snagged around the animal's legs, it was vital the horse keep his composure and not throw the rider headlong into a fray of milling cows. Not to mention that a horse had to get shoed by a farrier every now and then.

When he tugged the line, Quicksilver balked and reared, pawing the air.

"Fine. We'll do this your way." Jake led the horse back into the round pen and forced him to trot in circles for another two minutes. He repeated the procedure outside the pen, looping the rope around the horse's leg and tugging. This time the stallion cooperated. Jake rewarded the animal with softly spoken words of praise and a good long scratch behind the ears. "I knew you'd eventually figure out who the boss is around here. You've earned a recess, big guy."

"What about you, Jake? Do you get recess today?"

At the sound of Madeline's voice, his hands tensed around the halter. It was almost the middle of June. She'd been at the ranch ten days. You'd think he'd have gotten used to her sneaking up on him at the damnedest times, but her husky voice always caught him off guard.

He glanced over his shoulder. She stood a safe distance away, gently swinging a picnic basket in her right hand. Her hair was pulled back in its usual ponytail high on her head, the reddish strands dangling down her back. She looked young, pretty and carefree.

For the past week and a half he'd witnessed the newly hired nanny and his daughter get themselves into more trouble than a litter of puppies on the loose. Sometimes he wondered who was the nanny and who was the charge. He knew one thing for sure. His daughter was happy. Annie didn't care one way or the other if Madeline bumbled her way through this nannying thing. Annie just liked being with her.

And he had to admit, he wished he could be with both of them, instead of watching from a distance. Yet he'd learned a lot from watching. Most days, Madeline appeared on the path to recovery after her failed engagement. But occasionally, he'd catch her staring down the ranch road with a wistful expression on her face. He figured she was hoping her ex-fiancé would come for her.

He eyed the basket in her hand. "What do you have in there?"

"If I said fried chicken, would you believe me?"

He laughed. "No. But as long as it isn't burned stew, I'll eat it."

Last week she'd left a bowl of stew in the oven, warming for his supper. Everything would have been fine if she hadn't set the temperature on broil. Thank God he'd had an extinguisher in the pantry to put the fire out.

"No, it isn't stew. Annie and I have a place all picked out."

"I hope you're not thinking of spreading a blanket in the backyard." He could picture it now. The bride, his daughter and him picnicking in front of ol' Wiley's grave marker. He wondered how much trouble Madeline was going to stir up before she left.

"I suppose you girls want to eat by that rock." Three days ago, Madeline had tried to make Play-Doh from scratch. Turned out hard as a rock. So Annie had painted it and scrawled the name Wiley across the glob. Then she'd placed it under the tree out back where the barn cat had been buried last year. Now the first thing he saw every time he walked out the back door was a pink tombstone.

"Annie wanted to include Wiley." Her smile was brighter than the noon sun.

He wasn't eating next to a tombstone. "I know a better place. One where there's no skunk stench." He loved watching her cheeks turn pink. For a woman who strutted around with a sassy, bold attitude she sure did blush a lot.

She wrinkled her nose. "It doesn't smell *that* bad anymore."

He laughed and patted the horse's neck. Yesterday, she'd taken Annie into town and bought her a plastic play pool. They'd had a grand time sitting in that thing, drinking Kool-Aid and eating snacks all afternoon. But they'd forgotten to empty the water out and clean up the food. This morning the backyard looked like a local watering hole. The house stank, the yard stank—Jeez, even the horses had protested when he'd brought them out of the barn this morning.

Quicksilver bumped his shoulder with his nose and Jake turned his attention to the animal. "Okay, big fella, time to play." He walked the horse into the corral and led him to the gate on the opposite side, which opened to a pasture. He flipped the latch, and the intelligent animal nudged the gate open with his nose.

He stood for a moment watching the powerful horse race the wind, relishing his freedom. The stallion crested a small hill, then reared, pawing the air with his forelegs. Jake laughed. "Yeah, I know. Screw me, right?"

He latched the gate, gathered the ropes and other equipment he'd used throughout the morning and returned them to the tack room inside the barn. As much as lazing on a blanket with Madeline and his daughter appealed to him, he didn't have time for a picnic. He came out of the barn and made his way to where Madeline waited. He'd just opened his mouth to decline the lunch invitation but caught sight of Annie slumped on the bottom porch step, drawing lines in the dirt with a stick. A stab of guilt pricked him. Since his talk with Madeline, he hadn't spent as much time with his daughter as he'd intended.

He'd make time for her now. "Meet me at the truck in ten minutes," he said over his shoulder as he headed back inside the barn to wash the smell of horse from his hands.

Twenty minutes later, Jake pulled the truck to a stop near a small spring-fed pond off one of the three roads dissecting the ranch. As soon as he opened the door, Annie piled out and sprinted toward the water.

Madeline scooped up a blanket and headed for the piñon tree several yards from the pond. She spread the quilt under the shade of the tree, tugged her boots off, cuffed her jeans and went after Annie. "Is it cold?"

Amused, he stood by the blanket, watching the two females kick up enough water to rival a broken fire hydrant. He set the basket on one corner of the blanket, then eased down, using the tree trunk as a backrest. He took a deep breath and exhaled slowly, feeling the tension slip from his body. Jake tugged his Stetson over his eyes, but not too low that he couldn't watch the girls gallivanting through the pond. After fifteen minutes, Madeline returned to the blanket and plopped down near him.

"Look, Daddy, I caught a frog!" Standing in the water, Annie lifted her cupped hands in the air.

"I see that. Now, don't squish him." Jake chuckled.

"I won't, Daddy!"

He felt Madeline's gaze on him, but kept his eyes on his daughter. "It's so damn good to hear her laugh."

Madeline reached for the picnic basket. "Hasn't she always been this bubbly?"

"No." His daughter had gone through a lot when her mother had died, and he hadn't been much help. He'd handled Sara's death by throwing himself into the ranch, working until exhaustion took over and he wasn't capable of thinking, much less dealing with his emotions. But Annie hadn't been so lucky.

"Talk to me, Jake." Madeline's softly spoken request ate away at his defenses. He guessed it wouldn't hurt to confide some things in her.

"After Sara died, Annie suffered nightmares, calling out her mother's name in the middle of the night."

"I would think that's pretty normal under the circumstances."

He plucked a blade of grass and twirled it

between his fingers. "Then Annie quit talking. The doc said the silence would only last a couple of months. Thank God he was right. One morning out of the blue, she woke up and chatted my ear off at the breakfast table."

"Oh, Jake, that must have been so hard on you both." Madeline scooted forward and shared the tree with him. He should have inched over and given her more room, but he liked her shoulder pressing into his arm, so he stayed where he was.

They sat in silence and he wondered at the contentment filling him. This is what it would feel like if the three of them were a real family. *Whoa, where did that thought come from?* He wasn't fit husband material. Madeline had already been hurt by one jerk; he didn't want to be the second.

Annie squealed and came dashing out of the water straight for the blanket.

He shifted sideways. "Hey, you're dripping all over me."

"Here, Daddy. It's for you."

Jake held out his hand and Annie dumped a small frog in his palm.

"Eeeuu!" Madeline leaned away, wrinkling her nose.

Jake grinned. "Go catch some more, Annie. We'll have frog legs for supper."

"You can't eat frog legs, Daddy." Annie scurried back to the pond.

"She certainly likes frogs."

"Sara bought her a frog book when she turned two. Ever since, she's been in love with the amphibians."

Madeline smiled, then clasped her hands in front of her and stared off into space. He couldn't stand that she might be thinking about her ex-fiancé. Suddenly feeling ornery, he warned in a hushed voice, "Don't move, Madeline."

Her head snapped toward him. "What's wrong?"

"Shh. Don't move a single muscle."

"Jake, you're scaring me."

"There's a black widow spider clinging to your ponytail."

"Jaaake. Get it off me!"

"Stay calm."

The blood drained from her face, leaving her skin a pasty white. For all of one second he considered coming clean. Then he remembered she was the cause of the constant state of arousal plaguing his body since he'd unhooked her from his fence. He shifted, bringing his face inches from hers. "Sit tight, honey. It'll crawl away in a minute."

"Can't you flick it off or something?"

"No, black widows are fast little devils. It

would sink its fangs into my hand before I even felt the bite."

"I don't think I can sit still any longer." Her worried green eyes beseeched him.

"I'll distract you." Leaning closer, he whispered, "Remember that morning in the kitchen when I kissed you?"

Two bright pink patches dotted her cheeks. *Good.* At least he knew she wasn't thinking of the lawyer. He lowered his voice. "I swear I can still feel the softness of your lips, the satisfied sigh you exhaled into my mouth."

Her eyelashes fluttered and her breath shuddered against his face.

"Am I doing a good job of distracting you?"

"Real good." Her whispered response made him smile.

"Then I slid my hand under the shirt and touched your bare hip." He nuzzled his lips against her ear. Catching a whiff of tantalizing perfume and Madeline's own body heat, he needed all his concentration to keep from tossing her down on the blanket and falling on top of her.

"Is Annie okay?"

He glanced at the pond. "She's busy hunting frogs. Now, where was I?"

"Your hand was on my hip."

Jake chuckled. "That's right. I touched your

hip, ran my fingers up the length of your smooth, silky thigh."

The quiet moan that rumbled through her chest indicated she was just as aroused as he was. The gentlemanly thing to do would be to come clean and confess there was no spider stuck in her hair. But he was way past gentleman, bordering on rogue.

He cupped her chin and turned her face toward him. Her breath mingled with his. "Have you any idea what you do to me?" He settled his mouth on hers. Gentle. Chaste. The kiss could be nothing more. Not with Annie nearby and his body wound like a toy top.

She pulled back first. "There is no spider, is there, Jake?"

He rubbed an imaginary speck from her cheek. "Nope. I lied."

"If you wanted a kiss, all you had to do was ask." Her eyes twinkled, and suddenly the joke was on him.

"Are you kissing Ms. Madeline, Daddy?"

Jake bolted off the blanket, nearly knocking Annie to the ground. "No. We're not kissing."

Madeline sputtered and coughed. Jake glared at her. "You're not helping."

She burst out laughing, clutching her stomach and doubling over.

Annie smiled. "What's so funny, Ms. Madeline?"

Madeline pointed to Jake. "Your father."

Jake tried. Tried like hell to keep from busting up. But Madeline's laughter was contagious. Then Annie joined her on the blanket and started to giggle. Madeline kept wiping her eyes, and damn it, he couldn't hold back any longer. He gave in to the hopelessness of the situation, fell down on the blanket and let loose a bellyful of raucous laughter.

After several minutes the three of them quieted, with only an occasional hiccup between gasps of air. "How about some lunch? I'm so hungry I could eat a—" he grabbed Annie and tickled her ribs "—little girl."

Annie squealed, and another five minutes passed before they settled down for the second time. Jake lay back on the blanket and grinned up at the cloudless sky. A moment later, Annie curled up at his side. "I love you, Daddy."

Holding her was a little awkward, but he managed to get his arm around his daughter's shoulder and hug her close. "I love you, too, Annie."

"Okay, no more lazing around. Time to eat."

Jake sat up and watched Madeline set out the food. With hands that weren't quite steady, he accepted a plate. He wanted to thank her for this picnic, for giving him this moment with his daughter. But the words stuck in his throat. Her gentle smile and the light touch of her fingertips against his cheek told him she understood.

They ate in silence. As soon as Annie finished her half sandwich she scurried away to collect rocks. He helped Madeline put the food back in the basket, barely able to keep his eyes off her.

"I hope you're not mad at me for pulling your leg about the spider."

"I should be, but I'm not."

He removed his hat and set it aside, then stretched out on the blanket and crossed his arms beneath his head. "I don't usually behave this way. But you're different."

She playfully punched his shoulder. "Different? I don't know whether to be insulted or amused."

He grabbed her arm and tugged until she lay next to him. Talking without having to look into her beautiful green eyes would be easier. He cleared his throat. "I like being with you. You're fun."

"Not the most romantic thing I've heard, but I'm in no position to be picky."

He grinned. "That's what I mean. You don't take things too seriously."

"Was Sara pretty serious?"

"Yeah. But it wasn't her fault. She couldn't help it."

"Tell me more about her."

"I don't know where to start."

"Start at the beginning."

"Sara and I met our senior year of high school. I was new in town and we got to know each other in study hall. We became friends. Nothing more."

"Why didn't you ask her out?"

"It wasn't like that between us. Sara was soft-spoken. Quiet. Smart. She'd earned a scholarship to college and had planned to be a teacher. After graduation I drove off down a different road."

"What did you do?"

"Rodeoed. Worked some as a ranch hand here or there. Sara and I lost touch. Then four years after high school my parents were killed in a car accident."

"Oh, Jake, I'm sorry."

"Don't be." He expelled a frustrated breath. "I suppose they tried, but mostly they stunk at being parents." From as far back as he could remember, his dad had gone on drinking binges, then lost whatever job he'd had. The pattern hadn't ended until his death. His mother had steered clear of his dad by working two jobs, so

Jake had seen little of her at home. In the end, he had fended for himself.

"I came back to make the burial arrangements. That's when I found out Sara was pregnant and had dropped out of college a month earlier."

He'd never told a soul about Sara's past. The sudden need to share it with someone, with Madeline, was unsettling. "Turns out she'd been raped in her dorm room."

Madeline's gasp went straight to his heart. "Sara's parents were religious zealots. When they found out she was pregnant, they disowned her and kicked her out of the house. I found her living in a dumpy one-room hovel above the convenience store where she worked. I told her I'd marry her." He shrugged. "The guy who'd hit my parents had been drunk. I'd threatened to sue. We settled out of court, and I used the money as a down payment on the ranch for Sara and me."

"What a heroic thing to do, Jake. Sara must have loved you very much."

His laugh sounded bitter and cold. "I'm no hero, Madeline." He rubbed the small scar that was hidden in the hairline above his forehead... a reminder of just how unheroic he'd acted in the bedroom with his wife.

Thinking about it still made him sick to his stomach.

"How did Sara die?"

*The truth?* No. He couldn't bear to see the look on Madeline's face if he told her the truth. Told her he'd run out on his wife when she'd needed him most. He'd stick with the prettied-up version. "Pneumonia." He'd sat by her hospital bed for three days, holding her hand, urging her to fight, to stay alive for Annie. But deep in his gut, he knew she'd given up. And it was because of him. "Jake, I'm so sorry."

He sat up and watched his daughter wade through the water. "Annie might not be mine, but I've never regretted being her father." Loving Annie, taking care of her, was his chance to make it up to Sara. Madeline moved closer and hugged his arm. "She's a wonderful child. Any parent would be thrilled to have her for a daughter."

The silence between them grew uncomfortable. He shifted on the blanket and cleared his throat. Finally, he forced his thoughts of the past aside and screwed up the courage to finish. "Maddy—I hope you don't mind me calling you Maddy—you scare me spitless."

He stared into her soft green eyes. "It's a hell of a thing for a man to admit a woman rocks his world." He resisted the urge to stroke the pink blush across the bridge of her nose.

Shyly, she looked away. "Thank you for telling me that."

"Thank you?" His chest shook with silent laughter. "I expect most women would head for the mountains after a confession like that from a man like me."

"What do you mean, 'a man like you'?"

He shrugged. He couldn't find the words or the courage to tell her he was a sorry excuse for a man. Even sorrier than her ex-fiancé, Jonathon whatever-his-name was.

She got up on her knees and brushed at the cookie crumbs clinging to her jeans. He had to move away, or he'd take her in his arms and show her the kind of man he wanted to be if given a second chance.

He checked his watch. Another half hour wasn't going to throw him that far off schedule. "Hey, Annie!"

She sprinted back to the blanket.

"I've got a football in the toolbox. Want to toss it around?"

She frowned. "Football?"

"Football."

Annie shrugged. "Okay."

He headed toward the truck. "Two against one. Madeline can be your quarterback."

Madeline's laughter caught up with him as he reached the truck. "Right, Montgomery. Like I know anything about football."

He thought of his attraction to her. "Just catch it and run the opposite way!"

"WHEN DO YOU gotta go, Ms. Madeline?" Annie snuggled deeper under the covers, clutching a stuffed pink-and-green frog.

"Soon." She smoothed a strand of soft brown hair from the child's face, battling the ache squeezing her heart. "Today is Friday, June 20. I leave on Sunday."

Annie's eyes widened like an owl's. "I don't want you to go." The little girl deserved an Oscar for the heart-wrenching pout her mouth formed.

How could this child have wormed her way into Madeline's heart in such a short time? "We've had a lot of fun together. I'll miss you very much."

The prospect of not being with Annie left a hole in her chest. Instinctively, she knew the child was destined for great things, and she would have liked to be around to cheer her accomplishments and hug away her disappointments. She kissed the tip of her freckled nose. "Sweet dreams, Annie."

"Ms. Maddy?"

Madeline's heart ached at hearing Annie use the nickname Jake had given her. She hesitated at the door, her hand on the wall switch. "What, sweetie?"

"I love you just like a mommy."

A stinging sensation burned her eyes. Before she said something she couldn't take back, like *I wish you were my little girl,* Madeline flipped off the lights and hurried to her own room. The last thing she wanted was to fall apart in front of Jake's daughter.

After tossing and turning most of the night, Madeline awoke Saturday morning to booming thunder, rain battering the bedroom window and jagged lightning splitting the sky. She thought of Annie and worried that the storm might have frightened her. She remembered too well what it felt like to be a little girl all alone in a bedroom with no one to hold her during a thunderstorm. She scrambled out of bed, hurried across the hall and peeked around the half-open door. Then froze.

Jake sat in a chair, with Annie snuggled in his lap. They were both sound asleep. He must have gone to check on her when the storm started. As she watched the two from the doorway, a surge of loneliness assailed her. Turning her back on the homey scene, she shut the door, then returned to her room to dress for the day.

An hour later, Jake stepped into the kitchen. "You're up early."

He hadn't taken the time to shave, and Madeline thought his beard stubble made him look like an outlaw.

"The storm woke me."

He ran a hand through his mussed hair and headed for the coffeepot on the counter. She didn't want to pry, but she was curious. "Is Annie all right?"

"She's fine. Did she wake you when she cried out?" He finished pouring his coffee, then gestured toward Madeline's half-empty mug.

She slid the cup across the counter. "No, I didn't even hear her."

"She's always been frightened of storms. She used to crawl into bed with Sara, but..." He cleared his throat. "I sat with her until she fell back asleep." The warmth in Jake's voice gladdened Madeline, yet at the same time made her sad. He was finding his way with Annie...without her help.

"As soon as this storm blows over, I'm taking a couple of horses to the Winstons' place. I want to get the horses used to being around cattle, and the Winstons are castrating calves today." He grinned over the rim of his cup. "I'd invite you along, but I don't think you'd like listening to a bunch of bawling babies."

"No, thank you. Annie and I will be just fine at home." She shuddered at the picture that came to mind of what ranchers did to the poor calves. "Sit down and eat." She shoveled a stack of pancakes onto a plate and set the plate in front of Jake.

As she stirred another batch for herself and Annie, she realized that she'd never shared breakfast with Jonathon. She could count on one hand the number of nights they'd spent together and awoken the next morning in the same bed. But why hadn't it ever occurred to her to offer him breakfast?

What was it about Jake that made Madeline want to please him?

"Thanks for breakfast. I'll call if I'm going to be late for supper."

She stared at him over her shoulder, thinking how like a married couple they acted sometimes. "Have a good day." All that was missing was a kiss on the cheek goodbye.

The door slammed. She stared at his half-eaten breakfast and tried not to smile. He still didn't like her cooking.

"Where's Daddy going?" Annie stood in the kitchen doorway, rubbing her knuckles across her sleep-swollen eyes.

"Good morning, sweetie. He's taking the

horses to your neighbors to introduce them to the cows."

Annie smiled as she hopped up onto a chair. "I like pancakes. Daddy doesn't never cook 'em."

"Most daddies don't know how. Here you go." She set the bottle of syrup next to the plate and poured a glass of milk. "What should we do today when it stops raining?"

Annie shrugged. "We could look for frogs."

Frogs? Good grief. "You sure do like frogs."

"Yep. We gots big bullfrogs down the hill."

"What hill?" Madeline admitted she hadn't seen much of the ranch except the backyard, barn and the pond where they'd picnicked yesterday.

"Behind the barn. Daddy says I can't go there alone 'cause it's a steep hill and the stream's too deep."

Madeline took her coffee to the table and sat down. "You mean there's a stream back behind the barn?"

"Yep. Has lots of frogs." Annie stuffed another bite into her mouth. At least *she* liked Madeline's pancakes.

"When the rain lets up I'll take you down there and we'll try to catch frogs. But I'll warn you right now, I'm not a good frog catcher." She glanced around the kitchen, wondering what on earth they could use to scoop up frogs with.

By midmorning, the storm had passed on, giving way to sunny skies and a spike in humidity. Annie stood in the kitchen doorway, a green fishing net in one hand and rubber boots on her feet. "You can wear Daddy's boots."

"I guess you're eager to go?" Drat, she'd been hoping Annie would forget all about frog hunting. No such luck. She followed Annie onto the utility porch and slipped into Jake's rubber boots. "Do I need a net?"

"No. You gets to hold the bucket." Annie stood on tiptoe and grabbed a pail from a hook on the wall.

What would her coworkers think if they could see her now? Grinning, Madeline grabbed Annie's hand and off they went. Twenty minutes later, they stood on the banks of a fast-rushing, narrow stream a hundred yards beyond the barn.

Madeline warned Annie not to walk too far ahead, then they spent the next half hour poking the muddy bank with sticks, hoping to find a frog. Just as Madeline was beginning to think they'd go home without one, a huge bullfrog croaked when Annie pushed her stick in the mud. Annie got down on her knees and scooped away handfuls of mud from around the frog until she exposed most of its fat body. Then she wiggled the net under the frog and scooped it up.

Madeline laughed. "Good going, Annie. Looks like you found your Prince Charming." They put the frog in the bucket, added some mud and water, then left the bucket in the grass and walked farther downstream.

She didn't know how long they'd been poking around when Annie's scream rent the air. Shocked that they'd become so separated, Madeline turned around and sprinted back to where Annie stood as if her feet were set in cement. At the look of fright on the little girl's face, Madeline's chest clenched with icy fear.

She reached Annie's side only to suffer a second jolt. Slithering around Annie's rubber boots was a snake. A menacing one.

"Good girl, Annie. You did the right thing by standing real still."

When Annie didn't answer, she glanced at her face. Her skin was pasty white, as if she'd dusted herself with talcum powder. Panic pounded inside Madeline's chest. Had the snake already bit Annie? *Please, God, no.* She edged closer, watching the reptile's movement, slowing as it wound itself around Annie's ankles.

*Don't panic. Whatever you do, don't panic.* Nothing in her college education or career in corporate America had prepared her for something like this. She looked around frantically for something to attack the reptile with. Then she thought of the frog. "Annie, I know you want to show the bullfrog to your dad, but honey, I need that frog to coax the snake to move away from you."

Annie's eyes glazed over. She was so scared her little lips had turned blue. Madeline had to entice the snake away before Annie fainted on top of it. "If I set the frog down near the snake, the snake will go after it."

Tears welled in Annie's eyes, but she nodded her agreement.

"Promise me you won't move. Please, Annie, it's *important*." As she ran back to get the bucket, she prayed the little girl would obey.

In what seemed like hours but was only seconds, she returned to Annie. "That's a good girl. You're being very courageous. Your daddy will be so proud of you."

Gritting her teeth, Madeline reached into the bucket and folded her hands around the frog. The amphibian squirmed in her grasp and she jumped, but she didn't drop it as she lifted it out of the pail. Then she inched around Annie's backside, pausing when she heard the tell-tale rattle.

Annie whimpered.

"Be brave, honey. This'll be over in a minute."

Madeline took a few more steps, then stopped when she was within three feet of the snake. Striking distance for the reptile. The proximity couldn't be helped, though. She wanted the frog close enough to tempt the snake. Slowly, she crouched until her hands rested on the ground. Gently, she let go, praying the snake wouldn't lunge before she got out of the way.

The frog didn't move and neither did the snake. She held her breath, backing up one slow step at a time, her eyes never leaving the snake. After a long minute, she wondered if she'd have to offer her own ankle to entice the reptile away from Annie.

A few moments later the snake relaxed its hold on Annie's boots. It slithered a few inches toward the frog but made no move to strike. "Keep still, Annie. Just a bit longer."

Another minute, and Madeline was beginning to think the stupid snake wasn't hungry. Then the frog croaked and the snake pounced, striking its prey. Annie screamed and Madeline rushed forward, scooped the child up and bolted. Running in Jake's large rubber boots was no easy task, but Madeline kept her footing over the slippery grass and mud. Until she reached the hill.

By the time she saw the rock poking up out of the ground, it was too late. Her wet boot crashed down on the uneven surface, sending her fly-ing through the air. Annie hit the soft wet grass, but Madeline wasn't so lucky. She half fell, half slid against a patch of gravel. The stones tore at her knees and the palms of her hands, but she managed to turn her face at the last minute to avoid scraping it.

Her body throbbed as she struggled to catch her breath. "Annie? Are you all right? Did you hit your head?"

"I'm okay. You're bleeding, Ms. Maddy."

She glanced down. Her jeans were ripped, exposing her bloodied knees. She looked at her hands and groaned. Bits of dirt and gravel were embedded in the torn flesh. "I'll be okay, sweetie. Let's get out of here before that snake decides to bother us again."

Annie held her wrist as they made their way back to the house. Madeline tried not to limp, but her knees were stiffening up on her. They made it to the porch steps just as Jake was driv-ing into the ranch yard, towing an empty horse trailer. *Drat.* Why was he back so early?

"What happened!" he yelled, hurrying around the hood of the truck. His worried gaze swung from Madeline to Annie, then back to Made-line, where it stayed.

Even though she yearned for Jake to hold and comfort her, Madeline bit down on her lip to keep from crying. She didn't want to upset Annie further. The little girl had already suffered enough fright for one day.

"Maddy fell down saving me, Daddy."

Jake took hold of Madeline's wrists and studied her palms. "You're a mess." His gaze dropped to her torn jeans. "Annie, run and get the first-aid kit out from under the kitchen sink." As soon as Annie sprinted away, Jake cupped her cheek with his warm, calloused palm. "Do you think you broke anything? Twisted your ankle?"

She lost her battle with tears. First one, then two, then a whole stream, rolled down her cheeks. Jake wiped them away with his fingers, then pulled her close and rocked her. "Aw, babe, I'm sorry you got hurt. What's this about saving Annie? What were you two girls up to?"

"A snake," she muttered, using his shirtfront to wipe her runny nose.

He held her at arm's length. "Snake? What snake?"

"Behind the barn, down by the stream."

"You went down to the stream? Annie knows she's not supposed to go down there."

"Sorry, Daddy." They both looked up to see the little girl standing several feet away, rubbing the toe of her rubber boot in the wet dirt.

"I'll deal with you later, young lady. Let's get Maddy patched up first."

Jake's big cowboy hands were gentle and tender as he cleaned and bandaged her cuts and scrapes after he'd walked her inside. He gave her some pain medication, then helped her to the couch, insisting she keep ice packs on her knees. "I'll make some sandwiches for lunch," he offered. He was halfway across the room, when he stopped and came back to the couch. Leaning down, he gently kissed her lips. "Thank you for keeping Annie safe."

# Chapter Six

Madeline pointed the remote at the TV and pressed the off button. She was restless. Lonely. Annie had been sent to bed early as punishment for disobeying Jake's orders to stay away from the stream. Annie hadn't protested. The day had been traumatic for her and she'd promptly fallen to sleep at seven when Madeline and Jake had tucked her in. Madeline had hoped Jake would spend the evening with her, maybe watch a movie, but he'd excused himself and hurried to the barn to check on the horses.

She knew Jake was hiding from her. Hiding from his strong reaction to seeing her hurt this afternoon. She went into the kitchen and stared out the window toward the barn. A yellow glow spilled from the open doors.

She pressed a fist to her stomach. Myriad emotions twisted her insides into a tight little ball, making her queasy and light-headed.

Tomorrow she had to leave.

It didn't matter that Jake hadn't found some-one to watch Annie. Or that he hadn't really tried. Her two weeks were up.

She admitted, much to her shame, that the main reason she'd volunteered to take care of Annie the past two weeks had been for her sake more than the child's. Jake intrigued her. And what woman in her right mind could resist a cowboy?

She hadn't considered that Annie might start thinking of the three of them as a family. Or that she might start thinking of Annie as her little girl. Tomorrow's goodbye would not be easy.

Stupidly, she'd allowed emotions to get in the way of common sense. She waited for the knot in her stomach to unravel, but when it didn't, she let out a long, keening moan of frustration.

It was too soon for her battered and bruised heart to admit anything more than falling in lust with the cowboy. But the picnic had changed things. Changed her feelings for Jake. He was raising a child who wasn't his and had married a woman who'd been raped. She'd never known a man more honorable, more committed, with such a deep sense of goodness and uncondi-tional love.

She sensed that Jake had held something back from her when he'd talked about his marriage to Sara, but she didn't care. His tender looks and touches made her wonder if she was already halfway in love with the man. Jake deserved a little happiness in his life. Was she crazy to believe *she* might be the one who could make him happy?

She'd never considered having an affair before, but didn't think one night of lovemaking qualified as one. A few short hours of intimacy. Nothing more. No strings. No regrets. Besides, one evening wasn't enough time to fall the rest of the way in love with the man. Her heart would be safe.

Before she lost her courage, she left the house and marched stiff-kneed to the barn. The smell of fresh hay filled her nostrils as the soft whinnies of the horses met her ears.

His back to her, Jake stood several feet away, scooping feed into pails. "Annie still asleep?" The sound of his husky voice floated back to her.

She wasn't in the mood for mundane conversation. "I wasn't sure if you remembered or not. My two weeks are up tomorrow."

For a second he froze. Then slowly, his arm came up and out of the grain barrel. When he turned around, the shocked expression on his face startled her. Had he truly forgotten the two-week agreement?

He opened his mouth, then snapped it shut.

He was speechless. A tiny sliver of hope worked its way into her heart.

He walked toward her, one rolling hip at a time, then stopped a foot away. She could smell him now. A trace of woodsy aftershave and hardworking male. She breathed deeply, amazed that it took as little as his scent to arouse her. She yearned to bury her nose in his chest and let herself drown in his essence.

He stroked a strand of hair that had come loose from her ponytail. "Ah, Madeline."

She pressed a finger to his lips. "I like 'Maddy' better." She leaned forward, and felt hope spring loose in her chest when he didn't move away. She noticed a small scar at the base of his neck and touched it with the tip of her index finger. His skin was moist and warm.

She raised her head, and the heat simmering in his gaze was enough to melt her. "Being with you can't be wrong, Jake. You make me feel things I've never felt before. I can't walk away tomorrow wondering what it would have felt like to be in your arms, to feel you love me."

He shoved a hand through his coal-black hair, mussing it, making her want to smooth it back in place. "It'll only lead to heartache."

She sensed him wavering and gripped his arm, ignoring the sting from her scraped palms. "We won't let it."

The muscle along his jaw clenched and un-clenched until a great shudder wracked his body. He closed his eyes as if praying for strength. When he opened them, she saw aching arousal mixed with anguish and pain.

He cupped her face, his hand flexing against her skin. She turned her head, nuzzling the center of his palm. Oh, how she wanted to comfort this man. To receive comfort in return.

The first touch was tentative. The second bold. The third buckled her sore knees. He hauled her up against him, his hand pressing her bottom closer, letting her feel how she affected him. She smoothed her hands up his chest and wrapped her arms around his neck. Clinging to his strength, she opened her mouth to his thrusting tongue, answering the rumble in his chest with her own breathless whimpers.

He chanted her name over and over, the adoration in his voice filling her with joy. She relished his rich, dark flavor, his mouth hot, gentle, yet firm.

Never had she wanted a man more or thought she might perish if she didn't have all of him around her...on her...in her. He clutched her leg, lifting it over his thigh, arranging her more snugly against the hardness at the front of his jeans. Both hands on her bottom, he rocked against her, and she gasped, sure she would burst into flames.

Then he stopped.

He pressed his face to her neck, his breath blasting against her skin, his chest falling and rising like great ocean swells. Aroused, stunned and shaky, she clung to his shirt.

His hands clutched her hips, and she feared he'd push her away. Instead, his fingers moved upward, caressing her rib cage. She wiggled sideways, wanting him to touch her, to knead the aching mounds near his fingertips.

He did.

Flinging her head back, she emitted an unladylike sound and dug her nails into his upper arms. She was terrified of the sensations flooding her body, yet at the same time she reveled in her first taste of true ecstasy.

Without warning, he thrust her from him roughly, reaching out at the last second to steady her when her foot slid on the uneven floor. His smoldering blue eyes pleaded for mercy. "Go back to the house."

"But—"

"This isn't going to happen." He shook his head, his mouth tugging down at the corners. "I won't let it."

The turmoil in his eyes eased some of the pain gripping Madeline's insides. She took a cautious step back, afraid if she didn't she'd embarrass herself and try to change his mind. Good Lord, what had gotten into her? She'd never begged a man for anything in her life and she refused to start now.

Ashamed at her behavior, she blinked back tears. "Don't worry, cowboy. I won't throw myself at you again." She made it to the door.

"Maddy."

The choked sound of her name was enough to jerk her to a standstill.

"Lock your bedroom door tonight."

She did.

Madeline lay awake long into the wee morning hours, her body and heart aching from the sting of Jake's rejection. If not for Annie, she'd have packed her bag and driven off tonight.

"HEY, BUDDY. YOU'VE got to work with me here." Jake patted Quicksilver's silky nose. The horse continued to be the toughest to train, and his favorite. The stallion, chock-full of spunk and pride, resisted him at every turn. He unlatched the gate and slapped the horse's rump. The animal bolted for freedom.

He glanced at his watch. Almost suppertime. And Maddy still hadn't come out of the house. Like a chicken he'd snuck out this morning before the girls had gotten out of bed. He knew it was cowardly, but he couldn't face Maddy with Annie around. He couldn't pretend her leaving didn't bother him…didn't tie his insides up in knots. So he'd worked with the horses, and hadn't even bothered to eat lunch.

Midmorning, Annie had come out to the barn to tell him that their neighbor Gladys was picking her up after church to take her strawberry picking. He'd waited just inside the doors and watched, hoping to catch a glimpse of Maddy saying a final goodbye to his daughter. But she'd stayed in the house.

Then he'd hung out in the barn the rest of the afternoon, thinking Maddy would come say goodbye to him, but she hadn't. He wondered if she was staying until Annie returned. Regardless, all this waiting was eating him up inside.

*I should have never gone on that damn picnic with the girls.*

It was no use trying to kid himself into thinking what he felt for Maddy was simple lust. Purely physical. His heart had jumped into the game. How much of his heart, he wasn't sure. He just hoped like hell Maddy's leaving today wouldn't tear the sensitive organ from his chest. He took a deep breath, then exhaled forcibly. Maybe she expected an apology from him before she left.

He hadn't used much finesse when he'd

turned down her invitation in the barn last night. She'd caught him off guard when she'd mentioned her two weeks were up, and he'd panicked.

His body had wanted to jump at her offer. But his mind put up a fuss at the last second. He'd never been around a woman like Maddy before. A well-educated-money-making-knows-what-she-wants-and-goes-and-gets-it kind of woman. He was a simple, nothing-to-fuss-over cowboy… with enough baggage to fill a plane. Most of the time he felt as if he had two left feet around her.

Maddy might believe she only wanted a quick roll in the hay, but no matter how bold and brassy she acted, she wasn't the kind of woman to sleep with a man unless she felt something for him. After being dumped by her fiancé, Jake hated that his rejection might have made her doubt herself even more. He had to explain it was nothing personal.

*Yeah, right. Like she'll really believe you?*

He'd make her believe him. He'd tell her he'd messed up so badly with Sara that she was better off not getting involved with him. Besides, she was too special to waste herself on a guy like him.

He removed his Stetson and wiped his dusty shirtsleeve across his sweaty forehead. Aw, hell. It would be so much easier if she hadn't already gotten to him…deep inside. Making him want things he didn't deserve.

Before he could change his mind again, he marched up to the house, only to find the kitchen empty and Maddy's packed duffel bag by the door. He removed his boots in the mud-room, then padded through the house, pausing in each doorway as if he expected to find her. What he found was a spanking-clean house. Not a speck of dust on the furniture. The carpets had been vacuumed. And stacks of his and Annie's laundered clothes sat neatly on the stairs, ready to be put away. Feeling like scum, he took the stairs two at a time. When he reached the top landing, country music filtered into the hall-way from under the closed guest-bedroom door.

If he was dead set on apologizing, the least he could do was take a shower first. She might forgive him if he smelled better than a ripe cow pie. Ten minutes later, dressed in a pair of jeans and nothing else, he stepped out of the bath-room, then froze.

Maddy stood in the hallway, her green eyes wary, her expression reserved. Her pretty, red hair hung loose around her shoulders, slightly tousled, as if she were going out on a date. She looked younger than her twenty-five years, sexy and so out of his league it hurt to look at her.

He stared at her body, ignoring the little zing

that shot through him at the sight of her in jeans and a tight T-shirt. Then he spotted ten glossy pink toenails peeping out from under the blue denim. Jeez, even her toes were sexy.

"Annie should be home soon," he mumbled, not knowing where to begin, feeling like a clumsy fool.

Her gaze settled on something down at the end of the hall. "Gladys asked if Annie wanted a sleepover with some of her friends."

*Oh, hell.*

"She's bringing her back tomorrow before supper."

*Oh, double hell.* A sweat broke out across his forehead and a slow throb started in his groin.

"I should be going now." She turned toward the stairs.

"Wait." She stopped, her hand resting lightly on the railing, her back to him. He supposed he deserved her back.

"I owe you an apology. For last night. I had no right to—"

"Don't." She spun around, her hair lifting off her shoulders before settling in waves around her face. "It doesn't matter."

She might want him to believe it didn't matter, but the hurt in her voice and the defensive tilt of her chin were dead giveaways. He shoved a hand through his wet hair, hating that he was the cause of her pain.

He hadn't realized he'd moved, but there he stood, gazing into a pair of the most incredible green eyes he'd ever seen. How had he missed the tiny flecks of gold ringing the pupils, making her eyes glow with warmth? She amazed him. Awed him. So much fire, such emotion. Her scented heat pulled at him, tempting him even closer.

He'd tried to ignore this attraction between them for two weeks. He'd tried to ignore the sultry scent of her womanly body, permeating every room in the house—even finding its way under the crack of his bedroom door, keeping him awake until the early-morning hours. He'd tried to ignore her smile, her laugh, her touch. Her everything.

Well, damn it, he was tired of trying.

He cupped her face, and when she didn't bat his hand away, he smoothed a calloused thumb over the dark shadow under one eye.

He wanted to haul her into his arms, lose himself in her heat. But he held back, knowing that this woman was capable of reducing him to a pile of smoldering ash.

He slid his hand down the warm skin of her slender neck, then pressed a fingertip to the pounding pulse at the base of her throat. Maddy was so real, so vibrant, so alive.

He stared at her face, terrified of the damage he knew she'd inflict upon his soul, his heart.

She set her palm against his chest, her touch searing his skin. Desire and need swam in the two green pools that gazed up at his face.

Would a man like him be enough for a woman like her?

*Yes!* His pure male pride roared.

He moved closer, his chest brushing the white lettering across the front of her T-shirt. Her nipples pebbled and he stared, awed by how her body reacted to his. With one cautious step after another he guided her away from the stairs and backed her up against the wall.

Bracing his hands beside her head, he leaned in, then paused, their ragged breaths mingling and dancing between them. "I want you, Maddy. Bad. Since the first moment I saw you stuck to my fence. But I can't give you more than once, more than right now. Right here."

Her gaze dropped, and his body clenched as if he'd been gut-kicked. Then her hand settled against his hip. Inch by inch, she lifted her mouth to his. Relief that she wasn't turning him away made his legs shake, and he had to lock his knees to keep from falling at her feet.

The first tentative brush of her lips across his

turned his heart upside down. Her mouth clung to his, her lashes fluttering against his cheeks like butterfly wings.

When her nails dug into his pectorals, he sank his mouth deeper into hers, his tongue delving inside, stroking the wet sweetness until he was convinced he'd never tasted anything so right, so perfect.

He pressed against her, chest, hips, thighs, letting her feel all of him, how every inch of his body burned for her. He told himself to go slow. To be gentle. But her passion, her enthusiastic response, made it impossible. The thrill of having an eager, willing woman in his arms drove him dangerously close to insanity.

She took everything he gave and asked for more. She wasn't afraid of him, his strength, his desire, his need. And God help him, he needed her. He was afraid to admit how much this woman had come to mean to him in such a short time.

One kiss. Only one kiss and already she made him *feel* like a man. Her touch, the mewling sounds that vibrated in her throat, the way her fingers tensed against his flesh, brought to the surface desires and emotions he'd buried deep inside after marrying Sara. For Sara's sake he'd denied himself. How could he have ever thought he could live the rest of his life without this kind of intimacy?

Without Maddy.

*Whoa, slow down, buddy. This is a onetime deal. Don't complicate things by trying to make it more than it is.*

He held her face between his hands and feasted on her mouth. God, he loved her mouth. He gently bit the fleshy center of her lower lip, then soothed the redness with his tongue. He nuzzled her dimples, then had to kiss her mouth again. He couldn't remember ever spending this much time just kissing.

A deep shudder racked his body, when she rubbed her bare foot along the back of his calf. He let go of her head and grappled with the hem of her T-shirt. His fingers slid under, gliding over her trim waist. He soothed his hands upward, exploring the slight indent of each rib, stopping only when he bumped the edge of her coarse cotton bra. While his fingers traced the outer swell of each breast, his mouth trailed kisses down her neck. "You're so beautiful."

He pulled his hands out from under her shirt and tugged her fumbling fingers from the front of his jeans. He leaned forward, resting his head against the wall, trying like hell to slow his raging hormones. His harsh breathing mocked the country ballad about love and commitment filtering into the hallway.

"Please, Jake. Please don't stop."

Her raw plea brought his head up. Fear of rejection shimmered in her eyes. To hell with him and his hang-ups. Lifting her into his arms, he crossed the hall in two strides and entered his bedroom, shouldering the door shut. He set her down next to the bed. Before he could remind her that this was nothing more than simple, uncomplicated sex between two consenting adults, her lips against his mouth promised to prove him a liar.

Her eagerness urged him to do his damnedest to make it good for her. For them. To erase the pain and hurt from both their pasts.

Her hands scorched his skin, fanning out over his chest and down his stomach. When one finger dipped inside the waistband of his B.V.D.s, he clamped a hand around her wrist and held his breath.

"What's wrong, Jake?" Her quiet voice squeezed him like a loving hug.

He didn't know where to begin. "I want this to be good for you."

She nuzzled her head under his chin and wrapped her arms around his waist. "It will be."

He held her to him, fearing the look on her

face when he admitted his lack of prowess in bed. "Maddy, it's been a long time for me."

"That's okay."

He hugged her harder. "No, it's not okay. I don't have a clue what a woman like you expects in bed."

She struggled against his hold and he finally relented and dropped his arms. She touched his cheek, forcing him to look her in the eye. He should have figured she wouldn't let him off the hook easily.

"What do you mean, 'a woman like me'?"

He expelled a long breath. "Maddy, the only women I've slept with over the years have been buckle bunnies. Immature, flighty, self-centered girls. I don't know the first thing about what a classy, sophisticated woman like you needs from a man in bed."

"Oh, Jake," she sighed against his mouth. "Everything you do pleases me."

He was lost—something, he was beginning to understand, her kisses would always make him feel. Being with Maddy almost made him believe he could forgive himself and let go of the past. Now, how insane was that? He smoothed a hand over her wild red mane. Maddy was real, vibrant, alive.

And she scared him spitless.

It was hell to admit he was afraid of this woman.

Afraid of what she made him feel. Really feel, deep down inside, beyond physical gratification.

"Slow down, honey." He coaxed her arms around his neck. "I can't promise that—"

"I don't need promises. I need you."

He shut up. No use talking if she wouldn't listen. With unsteady hands he tugged the T-shirt up and over her head, then let it drop to the floor behind her. Then he just stared. How could her breasts look so damn sexy in a contraption that resembled a horse harness more than a woman's bra? He felt a twinge of regret that Coot didn't stock lace and satin underthings for women. He'd love to see Maddy in black lace.

Her nipples beaded against the white cotton, begging for his mouth. His hands. He aimed to please.

Cupping both mounds, he feasted on the hard peaks, laving and sucking the sweet little tips through the rough cotton. Her back arched, and she offered herself up like a pagan goddess. Her moans and sighs urged him on, reassuring him that she liked his mouth on her.

Wanting only her softness against his lips, he tugged and pulled until her breasts popped free. There was so much of her. He nuzzled the plush mounds, never dreaming he'd ever hold such an incredibly beautiful woman in his arms.

She was more than he deserved, and he feared more than he could handle.

With a flick of his finger, he unhooked the bra and let it slide down between their bodies, where it landed on his bare foot. Then he wrapped his arms around her and hauled her up against his chest, savoring the sensation of their beating hearts melding. Savoring her scent, her warmth. Her closeness.

He could have held her forever, but her hips moved impatiently against his arousal and his tenuous control slipped a heck of a lot more than a notch. Her lips seemed to be everywhere at once. His face, his shoulders, his neck. When she sucked on the end of his ear, he thought his head would pop clean off and hit the ceiling.

She touched him as though she couldn't get enough of his body. Heady stuff for a man whose former wife had once looked at him with revulsion in her eyes.

His fingers dug into Maddy's narrow waist. He was afraid of where her mouth would go next, yet even more afraid to stop her. When she nuzzled his belly, he set her from him and made quick work of stripping off her Wrangler's and white granny briefs.

He tumbled her to the bed. Followed her

down, sliding his body along hers. For a long moment, lips, mouths, hands, arms and legs tangled and moved with urgency.

She sighed in his ear as her fingers fumbled with the zipper on his jeans. He trapped her hand against the front of his fly. "Not yet, darlin'. I plan on taking my time with you first."

The little hitch in her breath went a long way in easing his raw nerves.

He sprawled across the bottom of the bed and started at her feet. Tracing the curve of her arch, kissing the delicate bones in her ankles, caressing her smooth calf. Then he leaned over and gently kissed her sore knees before sliding his hands up the firm length of her thighs.

He never would have believed touching a woman slowly, carefully, gently could be so satisfying, so intimate. He knew that what he was about to share with Maddy was something he'd never find again with another woman. Something that was theirs only to cherish. Something he'd tuck away in the corner of his heart to treasure the rest of his life.

He caressed her belly, watching as her eyes glazed over. When he slid a hand between her thighs and touched her warmth, her back arched off the bed and her fingers threaded through his hair, tugging at the strands. Her uninhibited response threatened his composure, and his chest tightened at her unvoiced trust.

He pressed tender kisses against her belly and gently curved hips. Then he raised his head and stared into her eyes, waiting, wondering if she'd allow him the kind of intimacy with her body he craved. A feminine smile flirted at the corners of her mouth, then she pressed her fingers against the back of his head.

He shuddered with joy at his first taste of ambrosia. Her body twisted under him. He gave her everything she asked for and more, desperately wanting to make her come apart in his arms.

It didn't take long until she surrendered to him. He stayed with her through each tremor, each sob.

A fierce sense of pride tightened his chest at the pleasure he'd been able to give her. That his body hadn't found fulfillment didn't matter. He gathered her in his arms and held her close, rubbing his hands along her curves. "Maddy, you amaze me."

She leaned over him, her hair falling around his face, over his chest. He lifted his mouth to hers. Tried to tell her without words what her trust meant to him. How bringing her pleasure made him feel bigger than life. He could only imagine what it would be like when he was finally inside her. Surrounded by her warmth, her fire.

MADELINE RUBBED HER cheek against the expanse of smooth, tanned muscle her head rested on.

*Jake.*

She purred in contentment and slipped a leg between his scratchy denim-clad limbs. The feel of the rough material reminded her that things had been a little one-sided a few minutes ago. She lifted her knee higher, nudging the hardness straining at the zipper. His body tensed and his smooth chest hardened into granite beneath her cheek.

His fingers tightened against her back a second before sliding sensuously over her bottom, down her thigh, then up again, curving around her right breast, where it stayed, gently thumbing the nipple.

"Mmm." She wiggled closer. "Your turn now."

He grinned. "Maddy, you're more than I bargained for. I don't know if I can handle any more."

Lord, this man was good for her heart. Afraid her voice would betray her shaky emotions, she opted for showing instead of telling. She levered herself up and slid her mouth over his. She loved Jake's mouth.

His loving touch had reached deep inside her. She'd never lost herself so completely the way she had in Jake's arms moments ago. "Mmm." She pressed her hips provocatively against him.

A deep groan rumbled through his chest a moment before he flipped her under him. "Once I'm inside you, Maddy, I won't... I don't think I can—"

"Shh."

He hesitated only a second before fumbling with his jeans and B.V.D.s. Madeline smiled at his obvious excitement and enthusiasm. He flung his clothing to the bottom of the bed, then grappled for protection in the nightstand drawer.

She watched him roll on the condom. His size startled her, and he must have caught her reaction, because his hand paused midway through the process. "It's okay if you've changed your mind, Maddy."

She trailed one finger down the length of him. "No. I want you."

He finished rolling on the condom. But instead of gathering her in his arms, he stared at the pillow beneath her head. For a moment she feared he was thinking of his dead wife.

Madeline wanted no ghosts in bed with them. She wished she knew what Jake needed from her now. How to help him through this. Lifting her head, she softly kissed his heart.

The faraway look in his eyes vanished, replaced with gleaming heat as he pulled her to him. With one hard thrust he was inside her.

Sliding her hands over his muscled buttocks, she clung for dear life. He rode her hard. Wild, tender. Fast, slow. What he lacked in finesse he made up for in enthusiasm. Madeline let Jake do with her what he would, mesmerized by his astonishing delight in her body.

It didn't last long, but then, he'd warned her it wouldn't. With one more wild thrust he shouted his release into the pillow beneath her ear. He hugged her tightly, his sweat-slicked chest heaving and sliding against her breasts.

Something near Madeline's heart shifted and moved.

After a minute or two, his breathing quieted and he rolled away, bringing her with him, snuggling her to his side. She kissed his jaw, then his chin and finally his mouth.

"Maddy." His lips brushed hers. "That was more than incredible."

Her heart smiled. She, too, believed that what they had just shared could have only happened between them and not anyone else. She believed. Her heart believed.

Which changed everything. Yet nothing.

## Chapter Seven

A cloud of dust billowed up on the horizon, and Jake stepped outside the barn to watch Gladys Winston's old Dodge bump along the ranch road. She was bringing Annie back from the sleepover.

Maddy was up at the house right now, waiting to say goodbye to Annie. After a night of mind-blowing sex with the redheaded spitfire, the prospect of Maddy walking away from him and his daughter was burning a hole in Jake's gut.

Breakfast had been stressful. Sitting at the table, watching her nibble on toast as if they hadn't just devoured each other in the shower minutes earlier, had been awkward as hell. He'd tried to eat, but his upset stomach had revolted at the food. He'd settled for guzzling coffee.

Neither of them had mentioned her leaving. To Jake's way of thinking, there was nothing to discuss. They both knew that today was the day. Which had made it so damn difficult not to drag her back upstairs and have his way with her again. But, miserable coward that he was, he hadn't had the guts.

Then the phone had rung and his upset stomach developed an ulcer. Little Bear had called to tell him he wasn't returning until late September. So he was on his own with the horses.

As Gladys's car drew nearer, Jake left the shadows of the barn to meet Annie and Gladys by the front porch. Jake cringed as he considered his daughter's reaction to her nanny hitting the road. Annie hopped out of the backseat and headed straight for him with the biggest, happiest smile he'd seen in a long time. Now that he thought about it, Annie had been smiling a lot lately. And he knew the reason.

*Maddy.*

He opened his arms, and Annie vaulted into them. Caught up in her good mood, he twirled her around in the air and chuckled. "Maybe I ought to go pick strawberries if it'll make me this happy."

"Daddy, Mrs. Winston let Becky, Julia, Emily and me sleep on the floor and we ate popcorn and watched movies until ten o'clock."

"Ten o'clock?" Jake tried to look outraged, but his daughter saw through his bluster and giggled.

"Yep. And Mrs. Winston braided our hair, and we had matching ribbons. See?" She held her braids up like Pippi Longstocking's.

Gladys smiled as she got out the driver's side of the vehicle and shut the door. "Annie was a delightful guest."

Jake propped his daughter on his hip. "It was generous of you to allow the girls a sleepover."

"She said she'd never had one, and well, with Sara gone now, sometimes fathers don't think of those things."

The comment sliced through Jake and felt like a criticism.

He set Annie on the ground. "Did you bring your overnight bag back?"

Annie nodded.

"Why don't you get your stuff and go say hello to Maddy. She missed you last night."

"I can't wait to show her my toenails. Mrs. Winston painted ladybugs on them." She ran back to the car, removed a canvas bag, then stopped in front of Gladys. "You're the best, Mrs. Winston." She flung her arms around the older woman's legs and squeezed hard.

Gladys laughed in delight and returned the hug. "We'll do it again sometime before the summer's over."

"Did you hear that, Daddy? We get to have another sleepover."

"Yeah, I heard. Now, get inside." When Jake glanced at the house, he spotted Maddy in the doorway. How long had she been there? Why hadn't she come out to greet Gladys? After spending long hours making love to Maddy, he'd thought he'd be able to understand her better, but the opposite was true. The closer he got to her the less he could read her mind.

"Jake."

He looked at Gladys.

"I'm old enough to be your mother, so I have no qualms about sticking my nose into your business." She softened the remark with a smile. "Everyone in town is asking about that bride you found out on your property."

"Ms. Tate?" He felt like a phony, using Maddy's proper name.

"I'm not one to pay much attention to gossip. Lord knows my four boys caused enough ruckus in this town to keep the rumor mills churning while they grew up."

"What's your point, Gladys?" He felt like a teenager being lectured for some unknown wrongdoing.

"I assume the woman's just passing through?"

"That's right. She's leaving today." Jake winced at the sudden stitch in his side.

"Good. I'm worried that Annie's getting too attached to her. All she talked about was her nanny. She told the other girls she had her very own fairy-tale princess living with her and someday her father would marry the princess and they'd live happily ever after."

Princess? After last night he'd be more inclined to describe Maddy as a siren. He stared the older woman straight in the eye and ignored the heat rising up his neck. "There's nothing serious going on between Ms. Tate and me. And if there was, it certainly wouldn't be anybody's business."

She touched his arm. "No one's saying you don't deserve some happiness, Jake. But you should be careful for Annie's sake. She's very vulnerable. It took her a long time to come around after losing Sara. I've never seen her this happy since before her mother got sick." Gladys dropped her hand from his arm.

He'd had all the advice he could stomach. "I've got work to do. Thanks again for showing Annie a good time."

"My pleasure." She hesitated at the car door. "If you get in a bind with Annie, call me."

"Thanks, I will." Jake watched his neighbor drive away, wondering what the hell to do. Damn. He should have known his daughter would look to Maddy as a replacement mother. Why hadn't he seen it happening?

*Because you were so wrapped up in your own*

*feelings for Maddy that you were blind to anyone else's.* Shame filled him.

He removed his hat and smacked it against his thigh. His neighbor was right about one thing. Annie had suffered greatly after Sara died. He'd hate to see his daughter go through something like that again. He glanced at the house. He'd better go inside and see if Maddy needed help getting her things together.

At the thought of her leaving he flinched. Everything in him wanted her to stay. In all his twenty-seven years he hadn't fallen for a woman the way he'd fallen for Maddy. His Maddy.

He closed his eyes and pictured the serene expression on her face after they'd made love for the third time last night. He could almost feel her fingers sift through his hair, her hands stroke his back and shoulders, her sigh ripple across his neck.

Ah, hell. Sometimes life just plain sucked.

He didn't bother removing his dusty boots when he entered the house. Just stood in the kitchen doorway, soaking up the sight of Maddy at the sink, peeling potatoes.

Her sassy little fanny twitched and swayed to the rock 'n' roll tune playing on the kitchen radio. Like every other day, she wore her hair up in a ponytail, showing off her beautiful neck. He cleared his throat. "Where's Annie?"

She tossed an inviting smile over her shoulder. "She's upstairs unpacking her bag."

He wanted to move across the room and press his mouth to hers. Lose himself in her one more time. But he didn't dare. Instead, he leaned against the doorjamb and rubbed the bridge of his nose. "I was wondering if you'd said goodbye to Annie yet."

She went so still he couldn't tell if she was even breathing.

His gut clenched. "Gladys said Annie's getting real attached to you." He shifted from one boot to the other and took a deep breath. "Anyway, I wanted to make sure you still planned on leaving today. I think it's best…for Annie."

The potato in Maddy's hand slipped, hitting the bottom of the sink with a loud thud. Her chest rose and fell in one long deep breath, then she faced him. "But I thought after…"

The wounded look in her eyes reminded him of an abused animal.

It was clear that she'd thought things had changed between them. And they had. But he couldn't let her know that. Not when there wasn't a chance in hell of happy ever after for them.

He wanted to shout at the unfairness of life. Instead, he stared into her beautiful, hurting green eyes. "If I didn't have Annie." Remorse slammed into him. He loved Annie. He didn't regret having to raise her. But he was only human, and sometimes he wondered how different his life would be if he hadn't married Sara.

A mask of indifference slid over Maddy's face. He might have been stung by it if he hadn't seen the flash of hurt in her eyes moments before. Her chin lifted. "I don't suppose I can change your mind?"

He opened his mouth, but nothing came out. Embarrassed, he glanced away and coughed. "No."

She set the potato peeler down and wiped her hands on a towel, each movement jerky and unsure. "Fine. There're a couple of things I need to get in town before I drive back to Seattle."

He gave up the fight to keep his distance and moved across the room. Standing before her, he willed her to look at him. She refused. He wished he knew what to say. Wished he had the courage to tell her what she meant to him. Wished...ah, hell. He wished for things he couldn't have. Didn't deserve.

When she attempted to move past him, he touched her arm and swallowed the feeling of hopelessness clogging his throat. "Maddy." Finally, she lifted her face, and the naked agony in her eyes made his own burn.

She pressed her fingertip to his lips, and the

simple touch almost brought him to his knees. She sniffed once, grabbed her purse and keys from the counter, then left the house without a backward glance.

He barely had time to regroup before Annie clomped down the stairs and skidded to a halt inside the kitchen doorway. "Where's Maddy going?"

He almost chickened out, but the innocent expression on his daughter's face shamed him. She deserved a better father than him. "Sit down, Annie. We have to talk."

Her lower lip jutted out. "I'm hungry."

Jake glanced at the clock, wondering where the afternoon had gone. He had no idea what Madeline had planned for supper besides the potatoes sitting in the sink. "How about a snack?"

She pulled out a chair and crawled onto it. "Okay, but I don't want cookies."

He swallowed a sigh of relief. Maybe this would be easier than he thought. "How about a bowl of cereal?"

She wrinkled her nose.

"Okay. Scrambled eggs?"

The wrinkle got deeper.

He shoved a hand through his hair and scowled. "Ice cream?"

"No."

The quiet whisper twisted his gut. He forced

his face muscles to relax. He felt like a heel for letting his frustration show. It wasn't Annie's fault Maddy had him tied in knots. "Nah. I'm kind of tired of ice cream."

Some of the wariness left her eyes. "You are?"

He forced a smile and patted his stomach. "Yeah, it's making me fat. How about a club sandwich?"

"What's that?"

"Ham, turkey, lettuce, tomato—"

"Yuck!" She pinched her nose as she slid off the chair. "I can make us a snack."

Jake stood in the middle of the kitchen while Annie whirled around him like a minitornado. In less than a minute, she had the ingredients for peanut-butter-and-jelly sandwiches set out on the counter.

"Beep, beep." Annie grabbed the back of one of the table chairs and dragged it to the counter. "Maddy showed me how to make Christmas-tree samiches."

The last thing he wanted was a gummy peanut-butter-and-jelly sandwich, but he was powerless against the eager light in his daughter's eyes and the enthusiasm in her voice. "Sure."

Feeling useless, he seated himself at the table. Annie reached for a paper towel and almost teetered off the chair. He opened his mouth to caution her but stopped. It seemed all he ever did was tell Annie what she should and shouldn't do.

He realized, as he watched her deftly wield a butter knife, that the five-year-old was more capable than he'd given her credit for. If she had to, he realized, she could probably take care of herself all day while he worked with the horses. For a moment, pride filled him at her show of independence. But the feeling was short-lived.

When had Annie learned not to depend on him?

Despair ate at him. Maybe his daughter no longer needed him. Annie had paid a higher price than he'd been aware of when her mother died.

He cleared his throat. "So you had a good time at Mrs. Winston's?"

"Yeah. She said I could call her 'Grandma Winston.'" Annie glanced over her shoulder, and her tiny white teeth sank into her lower lip. "Is that okay?"

Mrs. Winston was the closet thing to a grandma his daughter would ever know. His own parents were dead and Sara's parents wanted nothing to do with the offspring of a rapist. "Sure, you can call her grandma. I bet she likes that."

Annie's smile loosened some of the knots inside him. "Grandma Winston said girls are prettier and smell better than boys." She giggled. "Emily wet her pants when we was playing tag outside, but we didn't laugh at her. Then I accidentally dropped a plate of chocolate-chip cookies, and Barney the dog ate them all, then threw up on Grandma Winston's foot. I thought she was gonna get real mad, but she laughed."

As Jake listened halfheartedly to Annie describe the previous night's activities, he wondered how to approach the subject of Madeline's impending departure. When Annie paused to take a deep breath, he blurted out, "Maddy's leaving today, Annie."

She stared at him, eyes round, face pale.

He winced at the less-than-tactful approach.

"Make her stay, Daddy. Please."

Her whispered plea cut through him. When her lower lip wobbled, he pushed back the chair, crossed the kitchen and gathered her into his arms. Annie snuggled against his chest and sniffled. It wasn't often he and his daughter hugged like this. Her small body trembled against him, and he admitted he could use the hug as much as she could. Stroking her silky brown hair, he forced the words out of his mouth, recognizing they weren't what she wanted to hear. "Maddy has to go home, honey. She has family and a job waiting for her."

Annie lifted her head. "Uh-uh. She said her daddy's on a trip right now, and just like me, her mommy died when she was little."

*Died?* God, when it came to Maddy there was still so much he wasn't aware of. No wonder she'd become attached so quickly to his daughter. They had more in common than he realized. He rubbed a hand down his face. "She has her own home to get back to, honey."

Annie grabbed the front of his shirt, shaking her head. "She doesn't got a home no more."

"What?"

"She said she gave her 'partment away 'cause she was 'pposed to live somewhere else."

How come his daughter was more familiar with Maddy's life than he was? *Because you didn't ask. You didn't want to know.* Feeling put out, he grumbled, "That's even more reason for her to leave today. She'll have to find a new home."

Annie went up on tiptoe, clasping his cheeks between her sticky hands. "We can share our house with her, Daddy."

Jake swallowed hard. The conversation was getting out of control. "No, honey, we can't. Maddy has a job and a life somewhere else."

The urgency in his daughter's eyes dimmed to sadness as her hands dropped from his face. She turned her back to him, and shoulders slumped, she finished making the sandwiches. With no enthusiasm she mumbled, "You wanna star or a Christmas tree?"

Like a little boy, Jake wanted to stomp his boots in frustration. "I'll have whatever you're having."

She pressed the cookie cutter into the bread, then pushed the tree-shaped sandwich toward him.

"Thanks. It looks great." When Annie didn't acknowledge his praise, he felt lower than a slug.

She folded her own sandwich in a paper towel, then jumped off the chair and dragged it back to the table.

Jake seated himself across from her. Each bite of peanut butter and jelly stuck to the roof of his mouth like rubber cement. He glanced at the clock. He should get back to the horses. Without the help of Little Bear, his work hours would have to double if he planned to have the horses ready by the end of August.

But his daughter appeared so lonely and dejected, sitting there eating her sandwich, that he didn't have the heart to leave her alone until Maddy returned.

"You know, after Maddy leaves, I'm going to need an awful lot of help from you."

Her chin lifted. "You are?"

"Yep. Little Bear isn't coming back this summer."

"He's not?"

Jake shook his head. "I was thinking…" He waited until he had her attention. "You're pretty smart. Maybe I could teach you how to measure out the horses' vitamins and their food. And you could help clean and polish some of the tack." He figured Annie would be in the way more than not, but he'd promise just about anything right now to erase the hurt from her eyes. "And I sure could use your help in the kitchen." He popped the last bite of bread in his mouth. "You make a mean sandwich."

Some of the sadness faded from her eyes, replaced by a hint of wariness. Although seeing Maddy leave would hurt, a part of him was glad that she'd come into his and Annie's lives, even if it was for such a short time. If not for Maddy, who knows how many days, months, years, would have gone by before Jake understood the importance of telling his daughter how much she meant to him and how much he loved her. "So, what do you say? Can I count on your help around here?"

She nodded, then dropped her gaze to the tabletop. "Daddy?"

"What?"

"Could we go visit Maddy sometime?"

He heard the hope, the uncertainty, the need, in his daughter's voice and cursed himself for not protecting her feelings better. For both their sakes, he wanted Maddy out of their lives before it was too late to fix the hurt.

"I don't think so, honey."

"Why?"

He shook his head. "We just can't." No way could he stand being on the fringes of Maddy's life. Not after what had gone on between them upstairs in his bedroom. The thought of standing back and watching her fall in love with another man, share his bed and his life, was enough to make Jake physically ill.

He skirted the table, knelt by his daughter's chair and tugged her into his arms. "It'll be okay, honey. We've got each other."

But who was he trying to convince more—his daughter or himself?

MADELINE STOPPED THE CAR at the intersection of Main and Harwood in Ridge City. She glanced at the café. The tables near the windows were already occupied, and the parking spaces out front were filling up fast.

The idea of sitting among the crowd of locals and subjecting herself to more gossip put a damper on her appetite. She shifted her gaze to the mercantile. She supposed she could look around inside and kill some time. She drove through the intersection and parked the rental in an empty space directly in front of the store.

After grabbing her beaded wedding purse, she went inside. "Coot? You in here?"

"That you, barbed-wire bride?" a voice echoed from the back somewhere.

Madeline laughed as she headed down the center aisle. "Yes, it's me."

A shiny, bald head popped up from behind a stack of boxes. Coot flashed his gums. "Howdy." He came toward her, the scratchy sound of his dragging shoe echoing loudly throughout the quiet store.

She doubted the old man had many customers during the day, and those who did come in probably didn't stay to chat. Funny, but a couple of weeks ago she wouldn't have had the time of day for a man like Coot. Now…well, being near the old man was strangely comforting. Even the strong musky odor of his hair tonic had a soothing effect on her. "How are you?"

He grabbed her hand and clasped it between his gnarled fingers. Eyes twinkling, he gave her the once-over. "Them Wranglers look mighty fine on ya, missy."

She started to laugh but in seconds her eyes welled up. "Jake thinks so, too."

A frown replaced Coot's smile as he tightened his hold on her hand. "Jake never was a slow one. Not like some of these young fellers 'round here, who ain't got the brains of a gnat."

She smiled and wiped discreetly at her eyes. Coot, bless his heart, didn't pry and ask what was wrong. He let go of her hand and returned to the pile of boxes. "Got me a shipment of new souvenirs today."

She winced at the sight of his knobby arthritic fingers struggling with the clear plastic sealing tape. "I'd be happy to lend a hand."

"Ya sure ya don't have anything better to do than help out an old fart like me?"

"Nope. And I'm in no hurry to get back to the ranch." That was an understatement. She needed to catch her breath. To prepare herself for a goodbye that was guaranteed to be emotionally messy.

Coot's expression turned thoughtful. "I'll take ya up on yer offer, then."

For a few minutes they worked side by side in companionable silence. Madeline knew it wouldn't last. She had a feeling it was killing Coot to hold his tongue.

"I guess yer stickin' around to take care of that young 'un of Jake's. Darn shame Catherine's sister done busted her hip."

"I'll be leaving later today." She swallowed the lump in her throat and pulled out another souvenir, a snow globe with teeny-tiny dollar bills floating in the water around a little pink-and-green casino.

Voicing her plan caused the ache in her heart to throb more painfully. She'd known all along she'd be leaving in two weeks. Still, she hadn't been prepared for the hurt she'd felt when Jake had stood in the kitchen doorway, reminding her to pack her things. Obviously, their lovemaking hadn't meant as much to him as it had to her.

Yet she had no one to blame but herself. In Jake's defense, he'd done everything he could to keep things platonic between them. She'd been the one to throw herself at him.

"Ya plannin' on huntin' down the fool who left ya high and dry?"

She grinned, imagining Coot, shotgun in hand, chasing her ex-fiancé through her father's law office.

"No, I'm not chasing after anyone. Things have a way of working out for the best sometimes, and I believe this is one of those times."

"Don't seem right, if ya ask me. Yer pappy ought to pepper his backside with buckshot and teach him a lesson fer messin' with his little girl."

Guilt surged through her. She'd left a message on her father's voice mail, telling him her and Jonathon's trip to the Bahamas had been canceled and that she'd decided to go off on her own and do some sight-seeing. She didn't leave Jake's number, but told her father she'd call as soon as she returned home. She had no idea where Jonathon had run off to. For all she knew, he'd returned to Seattle and was back at work. The thought made her smile. Let *him* explain things to her father.

Over two weeks had passed since her ex-fiancé had stood her up. Madeline tried to summon up some anger, but strangely enough, all she felt was relief. Relief that she'd narrowly escaped a bad situation and an unhappy marriage that would have undoubtedly ended in divorce. She shuddered and thanked her lucky stars no children had been involved.

Thinking of children, she pictured Annie in her mind. She was such a sweet girl. A lucky girl, too. Even though she'd lost her mother at a young age, Sara had loved her enough to give birth to her, when it would have been very understandable if she'd aborted the pregnancy after being raped.

Madeline hadn't been prepared for the feelings Annie stirred in her. She'd never considered children while pursuing her advertising career. When she and Jonathon had become engaged she'd brought up the subject once, and he'd agreed to children eventually. Spending time with Annie made *eventually* seem a little more urgent.

"Them ladies down at the perm factory say yer some kind of famous actress."

She rolled her eyes. "I'm not an actress. I work in sales for an advertising company." A few weeks ago, if anyone had asked what she did for a living she'd have said she was vice president of sales for a major West Coast advertising agency. Funny, but now when she thought of her prestigious position at Smith and Bower, the first thing that came to mind was *Whoop-di-do*.

Returning to Seattle and shifting her life back into high gear again held little appeal. Not to mention enduring all the gossip, the sad looks, the questions about her and Jonathon's breakup. To tell the truth, Seattle didn't *feel* like home anymore.

Spending time with Jake and Annie at the ranch made her see herself in a different light. She rather liked eating supper at home, instead of fighting a crowded restaurant with a group of coworkers. And how much she enjoyed *quiet* surprised her. No phones ringing, no pager going off. She was beginning to wonder if hers was the heart of a simple country girl.

The knowledge did little to comfort her. Although it had never really come up between her and Jake, she sensed he was uneasy with the fact that she was a successful, independent career woman. But there was more to it than that. She lived a lifestyle most single women, if not men, would envy. A lifestyle Jake's struggling ranch couldn't compete with.

A lifestyle she wasn't sure she desired anymore.

Once again she acknowledged that Jake wasn't like most men she'd known or worked with. He didn't strive to earn a lot of money for money's sake. He wanted his horse ranch to be successful so he could make a decent living for himself and Annie. But most of all, laboring hard day after day, training horses, made Jake happy. Most men worked at a job they hated, hoping their sacrifices and bigger salaries would buy them happiness.

Yet despite Jake's seeming contentment with training horses, in her heart she wished more for him. She thought of the money she'd saved over the past few years. A sizable amount. It would go a long way in improving the ranch and hiring additional help so he could expand his operation. If only he'd give the two of them a chance.

"Them old hair-shop biddies ain't gonna be too happy if'n ya up and leave."

Startled, she stared at Coot. "Why?"

"Folks 'round here ain't been to a weddin' in a long time."

*Wedding?* She shook her head and carried an armful of snow globes to a display shelf set up a few feet away. "There isn't going to be a wedding." She wasn't even asking Jake for a wedding. She just wanted a *chance.*

Coot grinned, his eyes disappearing in the folds of loose skin on his face. "Jake's a stubborn fool. Someone ought to show him what he needs."

She narrowed her eyes. "And you think that someone ought to be me?"

"I sure as hell ain't gonna crawl under the covers with him."

"Coot!"

"I don't know what's goin' on between the two of ya, but ya better skeddadle back to that ranch and set things right. Ya can't hide out here forever."

Impulsively, she leaned forward and hugged the geezer. "Thanks, Coot." Time was running out, but she still had a few hours to change Jake's mind.

## Chapter Eight

"I need you, Catherine." Jake had a stranglehold on the telephone receiver as he sat in the desk chair and stared out the office window, mentally cursing fate and bad luck. His housekeeper had called to tell him she wasn't coming back. At all.

"That's debatable, young man. What's this I hear about some lost bride living with you?"

Ah, the joys of small-town living. "She's leaving today."

"Your bride is leaving?"

He clenched his jaw. "She's not my bride."

"Ask her to take care of Annie for the rest of the summer."

"I can't." The same old gnawing guilt ate away at Jake's stomach when he thought about how badly he wanted Maddy to stay. But the past made it impossible for them to have a future. If Maddy ever found out how he'd betrayed Sara's trust, their relationship would be over.

And he didn't know if he could survive Maddy leaving him after he'd given all of his heart to her. It was better this way. Time would heal the pain.

"Gladys says Annie really likes the bride."

"Yeah, she does." He shoved a hand through his hair. That was a major part of the problem. Annie was looking for a new mom and his *bride* was her first choice. If Maddy stayed the rest of the summer… No. Maddy had a job—no, a career—to get back to, a life waiting for her in Seattle.

He didn't want to admit it, but he liked Maddy. A lot. A little voice inside his head shouted, *Liar!* Okay, fine. He was man enough to admit it—as long as it wasn't out loud. His feelings were deep, tangled and unsettling. And a hell of a lot more than *like*.

"Can't this bride stay a little longer until you find a new housekeeper?"

"Annie's getting too attached." He didn't want to go through another bad spell with his daughter like the one she'd suffered after Sara's death.

Sara had been a good woman at heart. She'd coped as best she could after getting pregnant and having her parents disown her. He'd never doubted that. But he'd doubted himself and his own efforts to make her happy and the marriage successful.

He'd hurt Sara. He didn't want to hurt Maddy. She meant too much to him. And if that wasn't enough to convince him to send her packing, then the thought of Annie losing yet another mother figure was more than enough.

"If I were you, Jake, I'd get an ad in the *Courier* as soon as possible. You know, Harriet Blecker has a niece staying with her for the summer. She's only sixteen, but perhaps she'd be willing to do light housekeeping and laundry to earn a little extra cash."

Harriet Blecker had a mouth bigger than a crater. By the end of the first day the whole town would know what color his underwear was and what brand of deodorant he used. And the thought of a hormonal teen sticking her chest out every time he walked by was enough to make him run for the casinos.

"Are you sure I can't change your mind, Catherine?"

"I'm getting too old to chase after young 'uns. Once my sister is back on her feet again, we plan to take one of those senior-citizen cruises."

Obviously he wasn't going to persuade his old housekeeper to return. "Thanks for taking good care of Annie these past couple of years. We'll miss you."

He thought he heard a sniffle on the other

end of the line. "I'll keep in touch. Tell Annie I love her."

"Sure thing." Jake hung up and sucked in a long, painful breath. What the hell was he going to do now?

"I guess you still need me." Madeline hovered in the doorway, hands behind her back, fingers crossed. Eavesdropping wasn't polite, but right now she couldn't care less about protocol. Learning that Jake's housekeeper didn't plan to return shifted things in her favor.

Jake stiffened, then inch by slow-moving inch, he raised his head until their gazes clashed. "How long have you been standing there?"

The civil tone in his voice might have fooled her if not for the sparks spitting from his eyes. Frustration, anger, maybe even embarrassment, oozed from every pore in his body. A smart woman would know when to leave well enough alone. But sometimes smart wasn't always best.

She swallowed the retort on the tip of her tongue and settled for a calm "Long enough."

They faced off like two wary wolves. He crossed his arms over his chest and leaned back in the chair. At that moment she realized what was different about him. Instead of his customary Western shirt with pearl snaps, he wore a tight black T-shirt. He reminded her of such a bad boy...rakish, dangerous, tempting.

He rolled his shoulders. "I thought we already covered all the reasons it wasn't a good idea for you to stay."

She lifted her chin. "We did."

"Then there's nothing left to discuss."

Determined not to let his no-nonsense tone scare her off, she crossed the room until only the desk stood between them. Slapping her palms on top of his calendar, she opened her mouth to spout off a long list of reasons she *should* stay, when the scent of faded aftershave and…Jake drifted under her nose, distracting her.

Even though his hair stood on end from his running his fingers through it and a five o'clock shadow covered his jaw, he was so darned handsome her whole body vibrated with desire.

She yearned for the soft-sweeping touch of his fingers across her skin, yearned to lay her head on his chest and hear the reassuring beat of his heart beneath her ear. Yearned to be one with him again.

She lifted her gaze and met his bold stare. "I believe we both know one good reason I should stay." There. Let him chew on that for a minute.

His blue eyes darkened. "I have Annie to think about. She's already attached to you. It would be that much harder on her when you leave at the end of the summer."

She wished she could ask if it would be harder

on him, too, but didn't dare risk hearing his answer. To her way of thinking, there was a very real chance that she wouldn't leave at the end of the summer. Something inside her said this man might be *the one*. She yearned for more time to be with him, to let her heart appreciate him more fully. And if it wasn't meant to be, then she'd know by the end of the summer.

Stealthily, she skirted the edge of the desk and moved closer to the chair, then went down on her knees in front of him. "You don't have a whole lot of options, Jake. You have to train the horses. And someone has to watch over Annie."

His gaze strayed from her eyes to her mouth. Nervously, she licked her lips, and his quiet grunt sounded like a firecracker going off in the room. His nearness made forming a coherent thought hard, but she pressed her point. "Annie likes me, Jake. Let her be happy this summer."

"What about your job?"

Right now, Madeline wasn't sure she wanted a career in advertising anymore. Wasn't sure about anything anymore. "I'll take a leave of absence."

His eyebrows dipped. "They'll let you do that?"

Jake had no idea how valued her work was at Smith and Bower. No idea how many hundreds of thousands of dollars she brought in for the company each year. She'd request a leave of absence and they'd approve it without question. "Phew, I have carry-over vacation from two years ago. It won't be a problem."

"What about your father?"

"I'll call him. He'll understand." At Jake's frown she added, "I'll make him understand."

"What about the rental car?"

He was stalling; she knew it. But at least he hadn't said no yet. "I'll keep it for the summer. Annie and I can use it to drive around in."

He frowned. "That's going to be expensive." He rubbed his forehead. "Maybe I can help out with the cost."

"Jake. It's okay. I can cover the car."

His face muscles tightened and Madeline suspected he was wondering how much money she made. But he'd never ask. The cowboy had too much pride.

"Salary?"

She smiled. "Room and board is fine."

Their eyes locked in a battle of wills. Then miraculously, his face softened, the lines alongside his mouth fading. He lifted his hand, and it hovered near her face a second before sliding across her cheek. "And us?"

The heat from his palm seared her skin, and she swayed closer. She liked that he'd used the word *us*. At least he thought of them as a couple. "What do you mean, Jake?"

His fingers slid into her hair and tugged her head closer. His breath caressed her chin. "Sex. What about us and sex, Maddy?"

Excitement rushed through her, followed by the sting of guilt for using her body to get her way. A second later, she slammed the door on her conscience. Now was not the time to be noble. The combustible chemistry between her and Jake was the best shot she had of convincing him to allow her to stay the summer. They'd use the summer to find their way as a couple. To find out if forever was in their future.

Even though she believed that what she felt for Jake was deep and true, being jilted by her former fiancé had left her a little shaky and uncertain. A tiny part of her heart insisted that she be darn sure that what she felt for Jake was an I-can't-live-without-you kind of love. After all, a child was involved. And the last thing Madeline wanted to do was hurt Annie.

He traced the arch of her eyebrow with the tip of his finger. "How the hell am I supposed to keep my hands off you for another minute, let alone several weeks?"

"What if you didn't have to worry about keeping your hands off me?"

His nostrils flared and his gaze raked over

her body, stripping away each layer of clothing, piece by piece.

Joining him in the visual game of striptease, she changed the rules and ran a pink fingernail down the center of his chest, over his washboard belly. His fingers clamped around her wrist. Her gaze collided with his, heat and sparks flying between them with such speed she feared their clothing would burst into flames.

Jake's mouth hovered above hers. "Are you saying what I think you're saying?" He crowded her with his body until not even air could get between them.

She nodded, not trusting her voice.

He slid his free hand under her hair, wrapping his long, calloused fingers around her neck. "At the end of the summer it's goodbye? No fuss, no regrets?" His lips feathered over hers, barely touching, barely tasting.

"Yes," she breathed into his mouth. He pressed her palm against the front of his jeans as his lips settled on hers. He kissed her in a way that left no doubt in her mind what he wanted to do with her right then. Right there.

A feminine thrill filled her at the groan that vibrated in his chest. It was as if he couldn't quite get close enough to her.

"Daddy!" Annie's voice called from upstairs.

Jake tore his mouth from hers and stood so

fast he almost knocked Madeline on her backside. He faced the window, his chest heaving, and adjusted his jeans. The sound of Annie's footsteps in the upstairs hallway reached their ears.

Madeline backed up a couple of steps, biting her lower lip to keep from laughing. But when he turned toward her, she caught her breath at the determined look on his face.

"August." He fisted his hands at his side. "No matter what, you'll leave at the end of August."

Madeline knew what he was doing. Putting up walls, barricading his heart. He wanted her as desperately as she wanted him, but underneath all his bluster, he was afraid of caring again. Well, she was afraid, too, but not so afraid that she wouldn't take this risk with him. "Agreed."

She had the rest of the summer to open the cowboy's eyes. If sex was what it took, then she'd gladly offer up her body. Naked, flesh to flesh, heartbeat to heartbeat.

He glanced around, suddenly nervous, reminding her of a boy asking a girl to the school dance for the first time. The rare show of vulnerability touched her heart, made her feel connected to him. Then he looked at her. Straight in the eye. His desire was there for her to see, but it was his *need* for her that made her heart flutter wildly in her chest. His blue eyes deepened, turned dark and promising, offering her a glimpse into his soul, where she saw a hunger for more than just the passion that blazed between them.

He moved to the doorway, then stopped and faced her. "I have one condition."

She arched her eyebrow. "A condition?"

"No sex."

What! How in the world did he think the two of them could keep their hands off each other for two months? The set of his jaw told her his *condition* was nonnegotiable. Still, maybe there was a way around this. "Okay. But I have a condition of my own."

His eyes narrowed, but he remained silent.

"I reserve the right to try and change your mind."

It was hard to tell, but she swore his face paled. The nerve along his jaw pulsed for several long seconds. "Fine. But don't make the mistake of thinking I'll go down easy."

"HELLO, MS. REDDING, this is Madeline. Is my father available?" She'd called her father's office three days ago and his office manager informed her that he was tied up in meetings most of the week. When Madeline refused to leave a phone number so he could return her call at his convenience, the woman had told her late today would be her best chance of catching him.

"Hello, dear. If you'll hold for one moment I'll ring him."

While she waited, she stared out the kitchen window, willing the jittery muscle spasms in her stomach to cease. She didn't think her father would take the news of her extended vacation well.

"Listen, Madeline, I only have a few minutes. I'm headed into another meeting shortly. Where are you? Jonathon said you'd changed your mind about going to the Bahamas with him and decided to visit friends, instead."

So Jonathon hadn't told her father about Vegas. Interesting. He was probably worried about his partnership in her father's firm. "Hello, to you, too, Father. How was the business trip to Canada?" She cringed when a rough burst of irritation came through the line.

"I don't have time to chat, Madeline. Is something going on between you and Jonathon? He isn't talking."

She opened her mouth to speak, but her father cut her off. "The wedding is still on for November, isn't it?"

She didn't want to lie to her father, but trying to explain things long distance wasn't going to work. She'd play along with Jonathon's story. "I wanted to visit some old friends."

"Friends? All your friends are in Seattle. Where are you, young lady? I have to tell you, Madeline, this behavior is so unlike you. I'm very concerned."

*But not concerned enough to cancel a business meeting and talk to your daughter.* "Father, I'm fine. Really. I called because I wanted you to know I won't be returning to Seattle until the end of August."

"August! Daughter, what's gotten into you? You'll end up throwing your career down the tubes."

"My career is fine. In fact, they were happy to see me take some vacation time."

"What about Jonathon? Does he know you're not returning until the end of the summer?"

"No, he doesn't. You can tell him if you'd like."

"Don't you think he'll be upset?"

*No.*

"Jonathon is an up-and-coming lawyer, who's going to leave his mark on this city. He's driven and committed. You won't find better husband material anywhere."

It suddenly occurred to her that her father had picked out a man for her who was just like him. She thought back to her youth and shuddered. She didn't want a marriage just like her childhood…cold and lonely.

"The meeting is starting. I have to cut this call short. Where can I reach you? I'll phone within the next few days or maybe the middle of next week—my calendar looks clear then."

"I'll call you, Father." She watched from the window as Jake removed his shirt and wiped the sweat from his neck and shoulders with it. "I'm busy doing a lot of sight-seeing. It's best if I contact you."

There was a long pause on the other end of the line. "Madeline, just tell me one thing. Is another man involved in this sudden decision to visit friends?"

"Father, I can't talk about it right now."

"I sure hope you know what you're doing, young lady."

*So do I, Father. So do I.* "Talk to you next week."

"Fine. But I'd feel better if I had a number to reach you at in case of an emergency."

Guilt broke her down. What if her father had a heart attack and someone had to get ahold of her? She had to prove to her father she hadn't lost all her marbles. So she gave him Jake's number and said goodbye before he could ask what state the area code was in. He'd probably have Ms. Redding find out within the next ten minutes.

Madeline hung up the phone, wondering if she'd done the right thing in contacting her father. She went back to the kitchen window and watched Jake saddle one of the horses, the sight of him allaying her doubts.

If she thought he'd cave in to the sexual attraction between them she was sadly mistaken. Each time she got within three feet of him he spun on his boot heels and all but ran in the opposite direction. Most of the time he hid out in the barn with his blasted horses. Good Lord, the man fought the attraction between them as if it were a life-or-death battle. Until now, she hadn't known he could be so bullheaded, making her wonder what other surprises he had hidden inside him.

*Ah. But tonight would be different. Tonight, he was going down.*

She'd planned this Saturday evening since Tuesday, when she'd gone to Coot's Mercantile and asked him to phone in an order for a lingerie set from one of the store catalogs. She smiled at the memory of Coot's bald head turning red when he'd rattled off her size, color preference and desire to have the items overnighted. Bless the man's heart, he'd never asked whom she planned to wear the scrappy bits of lace for. *As if he didn't already know.* Then she'd purchased two boxes of emergency candles and left, ignoring Coot's toothless grin.

The tantalizing smell of fried chicken warming in the oven wafted through the kitchen. A sense of pride and accomplishment filled her as she thought of how hard she'd worked to prepare Jake's seduction dinner.

Following Betty Crocker's recipe for fried chicken and potato salad wasn't easy. It took patience—something she didn't have a whole lot of these days. She'd read somewhere once that the way to a man's heart was through his stomach. At the time she'd thought it didn't make much sense. Now she prayed it held some truth.

Earlier in the afternoon she'd called Gladys and asked if Annie could spend the night again. After a short hesitation, Gladys had agreed. When Madeline had dropped Annie off at the neighbor's, she'd informed Jake supper would be at six instead of five.

Now as she surveyed the kitchen she couldn't help but think how romantic it appeared. She'd found a beautiful lace tablecloth stored on a shelf in the pantry. Hoping Jake wouldn't mind her using something of Sara's, she'd covered the oak table with it and put a vase of wildflowers in the middle. A glance at the clock told her she had only a few minutes before Jake came up to the house. She grabbed the box of matches and worked her way around the room, lighting each candle, then closed the curtains, leaving the dim room glowing with warmth and shimmering light.

After hurrying upstairs, she changed out of her clothes. Spritzed perfume behind her ears and on the inside of her elbows, then changed into the black satin-lace bra and panty set she'd kept hidden under her bed until now.

Just then she heard the back door slam. She checked herself over in the mirror one more time. Satisfied she looked like a femme fatale, she slid her feet into her old satin wedding shoes, donned her chef's apron and hurried downstairs.

*See if he can resist me now.*

Breathless with anticipation, she called out softly as she entered the kitchen, "You're right on time."

"I believe I might have arrived too late. Did I miss the wedding?"

Horrified, Madeline stared at the stranger. She opened her mouth to speak but had no idea what to say, so she snapped it shut. The back door opened and Jake called out from the porch. "Maddy, I invited Reverend Thomas for supper." He stepped into the kitchen and froze.

His gaze slowly took in the room, moving

from candle to candle, then to the table with the fancy cloth and flowers. Then to her. His eyes widened in shock as he took in her outfit. He cleared his throat. "I guess you two haven't been properly introduced. Reverend Thomas, this is Madeline Tate, Annie's new nanny."

Her face felt as though it was on fire and her hands shook as she tried to pull the chef's apron higher up her chest. Jake, the rat, ran a hand down his face to smother his grin. How dare he find her predicament amusing. Good grief, she was standing in front of a preacher, practically nude!

Her chest tightened with humiliation, but pride and anger at the cussed cowboy kept her from fleeing the kitchen. "Reverend Thomas, it's nice to meet you. Of course you're welcome to join us for supper. Jake, if you'll pour the reverend some lemonade and blow out these candles, I'll change into something, something... well, something."

She turned on her heels and exited the room, giving both men an eyeful of her black lace panties. She heard the choking sound Jake made and hoped he'd suffocate on his own spit.

The gray-haired reverend looked at Jake and grinned. "Nannies sure have changed since my day."

Jake wasn't sure what to say, but he felt he had to say something. "It's not what you—"

The reverend held up a hand. "I'm not asking questions, Jake. I stopped by because Gladys pulled me aside after services last Sunday to tell me she's worried about you and Annie."

Jake swore silently that one of these days he'd have to take his meddling neighbor in hand. "I know she's worried. But Maddy's stay is temporary. She's leaving at the end of the summer. I don't have any choice. Someone has to watch Annie so I can work to pay the bills."

The clergyman stared at him as if he were a dense schoolboy, and Jake resisted the urge to squirm under his gaze. "Gladys told me she offered to help with Annie this summer. She thinks of Annie as one of her own."

*Yeah, well, Gladys ought to find wives for her sons so she can have her own grandchildren and stop borrowing other people's kids.* "I appreciate the concern, but I've got everything under control."

Jake felt ridiculous standing in the candlelit kitchen talking to a man of God, so he blew the candles out one by one, then opened the curtains. He tried to ignore the warm sensation that filled his insides when he thought of how hard Maddy was trying to seduce him, but he couldn't. Never before had a woman pursued him with such enthusiasm.

"Jake. I'm not here to judge you morally. I, better than anyone in this community, know what you went through during your marriage to Sara."

Jake still felt a twinge of embarrassment as he recalled sitting in the reverend's home, confessing every little detail of his marriage and how he blamed himself for his wife's death. He'd been so scared when Annie had stopped talking after Sara died. Scared he wouldn't be able to help his daughter, scared he wasn't good enough to be her father.

He'd panicked and run to the reverend, asking—no, begging—to be forgiven for his sins. He hadn't planned ever to tell anyone about his marriage, but he'd found himself going back to the reverend's house several times after that first night, seeking advice, a sympathetic ear. "I'm not going to let things get out of hand with Maddy."

The clergyman stared at him thoughtfully. "Do you have feelings for her, Jake?"

"Of course I *feel* something for her." He clamped his mouth shut. He'd always been up front with the reverend, but he sure as hell didn't like talking about his sexual attraction to his daughter's nanny. "She's great with Annie." He shoved a hand through his hair and leaned back against the counter. "Annie likes her. Likes the attention Maddy gives her."

"And what about the attention she gives you? Do you like it, Jake?"

"You're getting a little personal here, Reverend."

"I might be a reverend but I'm also a man. And I was married once."

Surprised, Jake spoke before thinking. "What happened to your wife?"

"She divorced me."

Jake was speechless.

The reverend pulled out a chair and sat down, his shoulders slumping. "Mary had an affair after we'd been married two years. She said the whole reverend thing had turned her on when she'd first met me. But after a while I wasn't exciting anymore. So she moved on to someone else."

Jake couldn't think of anything to say but "I'm sorry."

"When you came to me after Sara died and confessed your troubles, I felt as if I were reliving my own marriage. Like you, I'd experienced what it felt like to desire a woman who didn't desire me back. You probably won't believe this, but helping you went a long way in helping myself let go of Mary and our marriage."

"Did you want the divorce?" Jake didn't know if it was any of his business, but he was curious.

"Yes and no. I still had feelings for Mary, even though she wasn't sexually attracted to me anymore. If she'd wanted to stay and try to work things out I would have welcomed the chance. But she didn't. In the end we just weren't a good match. Not like you and Annie's nanny."

"What makes you believe Maddy and I are a good match? You just met her."

"I saw the way you looked at her, Jake."

"Well, how the hell was I supposed to look at her? She was wearing lace underwear!"

The reverend smiled. "There was more than lust in your eyes. And I saw the way she looked at you."

"Yeah, I saw it, too. She looked ready to beat me with a broom."

The reverend chuckled. "She stared at you like you were her whole world, Jake. Maybe you should give this woman a chance."

Maybe if he kept his mouth shut the reverend would take the hint and drop the subject.

"Have you considered that Madeline might have been sent here for a reason?"

So much for taking a hint. "A reason? That's a little superstitious for a man of God, isn't it?"

"Not at all. God has a plan for everyone on

this earth. Madeline may be part of his plan for you."

Jake shook his head. God didn't reward sinners. "Maddy's only here for a short time. I'm grateful to her for taking care of Annie, but that's it." He rubbed his chest, wondering at the heaviness pressing against it from the inside.

"Don't let your experience with Sara keep you from living, Jake. You helped her when she needed you most. You tried to heal her, you sheltered her, offered her your love and protection."

*Then betrayed her trust.*

"Let the past go. Life is too short to live it without loving someone."

"I've got Annie."

"A man needs more than his children."

Jake stared at the reverend, and for the first time saw beneath the white collar and black suit. He was in his late forties, trim and fit for his age. Jake supposed a lot of women would still find him attractive. He wondered if the reverend ever thought about marrying again and having a family. "I appreciate your concern, but I've got everything under control."

The reverend stood and pushed the chair in. "If you want to talk, you know where to find me."

"You're not staying for supper?" The reverend

couldn't leave him alone with Maddy. Not after she'd… she'd…bought new underwear for him!

The reverend smiled. "I believe there's a young lady upstairs who went to a lot of trouble to make this evening enjoyable for you."

Jake's neck heated.

"Now that Annie's nanny is going to be a part of the community this summer, I expect to see all of you in church, starting tomorrow."

In seconds, the porch door slammed shut, leaving Jake alone in the kitchen with the smell of snuffed-out candles and fried chicken wafting around him. He glanced toward the doorway leading to the hall that led to the stairs that led to the second floor that led to…trouble. Pure, unadulterated, sexy-as-hell trouble.

He opened the oven door, grabbed a handful of hot chicken and headed out to the barn as if his pants were on fire.

MADELINE'S SHOULDERS ITCHED—A sure sign the fifty or more church members were staring holes in her back. They'd arrived only seconds before the service started, thereby avoiding introductions to the other parishioners. Obviously, Jake had planned it that way.

Why in the world had she allowed him to talk her into going to church this morning? She should have fought him harder. But every excuse she'd come up with he'd deftly defeated and in the end she couldn't resist the soft kiss he'd placed on her cheek and the whispered "Please" in her ear.

So she'd donned her best pair of jeans, the only clean pair, and her least offensive T-shirt, the one with Country Girls Rock stamped on the front. She cursed Jonathon for stealing off with her luggage and the several beautiful outfits that would have been more appropriate for church.

They sat in the third pew from the front, with Annie between her and Jake. The parishioners' curious stares made her feel like a fox trapped in a chicken coop with no way out. She kept her face forward and listened to the six-member choir, singing behind the reverend.

She was still in shock over last night's fiasco. Her dream of watching Jake succumb to her charms had turned into a nightmare. All the hard work she'd put into making the meal, her carefully chosen attire—everything had been in place for a sexy, intimate evening. Until the man standing ten feet away had blown her seduction plot to smithereens.

Never before in her life had Madeline been so embarrassed. Not even being left at the altar in Vegas was as embarrassing as being seen in her skivvies by a man of God.

Embarrassment aside, the most painful part

of the evening had been waiting for Jake to return to the house after the reverend had left. But
he hadn't. Instead, the coward had hidden out in
the barn again. Teary-eyed, she'd taken a long,
cool soak in the tub, munched on cold chicken
and wondered if she should raise a white flag.

But no matter how difficult things got between her and Jake, Madeline refused to let
Annie down by breaking her promise to stay
the summer.

"Before I begin the service today, let's take
a moment to say good-morning to our fellow
worshippers." The reverend smiled pointedly
at Madeline, but she slid her gaze to the wall
behind him. Good grief, he had a lot of nerve
smiling at her after he'd seen her underwear!

A horrible thought hit her full force. What if
today's sermon dealt with sins of the flesh? She
glanced around, searching for an alternative escape route just in case. Annie tugged her arm,
urging her to stand. Jake was shaking hands
with a man behind him and Madeline smiled
stupidly at no one in particular. Annie, bless her
heart, came to her rescue.

"Hi, Mrs. Sloan. This is Maddy." Annie lifted
Madeline's hand and pressed it to her heart.
"She's my new nanny and I love her."

Madeline's throat threatened to swell shut.
Again she marveled at how this child had found

a way into her heart in such a short time. The thought of leaving her behind at the end of August was too painful to consider. Swallowing hard, she greeted the middle-aged woman. "Pleasure to meet you, Mrs. Sloan. I'm Madeline Tate, from Seattle."

The woman's eyes twinkled. "It's nice to finally meet the barbed-wire bride. You're quite famous." She leaned closer and whispered, "I'll introduce you to several ladies who've expressed a desire to—" she waggled her eyebrows "—help you out."

*Help me out?* Her confusion must have shown on her face, because the woman added, "Help you catch Jake."

Most of the church members had quieted and sat back down, just as Annie blurted, "Why do you want to catch Daddy?"

Madeline clamped a hand over Annie's mouth and tugged her down onto the wooden pew. She pointedly ignored the knowing grin on the reverend's face. When she cast a sideways glance at Jake and saw that his neck looked as though someone had painted ketchup on it, she hid her smile behind a discreet cough. Served the man right for dragging her to the Lord's house when both of them had sinning on their minds.

Thank goodness the rest of the service went without further embarrassment. After the reverend led the congregation in a final prayer, he stood by the doors, greeting the parishioners as they exited the church.

She leaned close to Jake and motioned to behind the pulpit. "Maybe we should use the back door."

"Leaving without saying hello to Reverend Thomas wouldn't be polite." His expression remained impassive, but his blue eyes sparkled with mirth. He found her situation amusing, did he? *Well, we'll see just how amusing he thinks I am in a minute.*

A short time later they reached the reverend. Madeline held out her hand. "I enjoyed the sermon today, Reverend." Not that she could recall a single word of it.

"Thank you, Ms. Tate. It's good to see you again."

"I imagine it's just good to see me in clothes, period." She winked at the reverend, his widening eyes the only clue she'd shocked him.

Ignoring Jake's sudden coughing fit behind her and the openmouthed stares of the parishioners eavesdropping nearby, she tugged on Annie's hand and proceeded out the door and down the church steps.

Before she even reached the sidewalk, a gray-haired woman with too much starch in her clothes and a ridiculous hat with some sort of bird perched on top of it blocked Madeline's path. "So you're Jake's new—" she narrowed her eyes "—nanny?"

Madeline forced a smile. "No, I'm Annie's new nanny. I believe Jake's old enough to take care of himself."

"Tsk, tsk. One would think so, but..." The older woman gave Madeline the once-over, then stuck her nose in the air.

"Oh, Madeline, there you are." Mrs. Sloan approached. And just in time, to Madeline's way of thinking. She'd been about to slap that silly bird off the old biddy's hat.

"I see you've already met Harriet Blecker. This is Maureen Crumble and Phyllis Martin. And please, call me Nancy."

"It's nice to meet all of you." Madeline glanced over her shoulder, wondering where Jake had disappeared to.

"We heard you were staying the summer," the woman named Maureen said.

"Well, I have better things to do than gossip." Bird head sniffed, then scurried away.

Madeline must have allowed the relief she felt at the woman's departure to show on her face, because the other women laughed and Nancy patted her arm. "She's not so bad in small doses."

"As I started to say," Maureen continued, "we

wanted to be sure you knew about Ridge City's Fourth of July celebration next Thursday. We're always looking for an extra pair of hands to help with our decorations. Oh, and you'll need to bring a dish for the potluck supper."

Madeline wondered if there was an ulterior motive behind the invitation, but their expressions appeared sincere. "I'd love to come. It sounds like fun."

"Good." Phyllis took her arm and guided her away from the church steps, toward a gnarled oak shading the lawn. "The gossip mills have been churning since you arrived in town."

Madeline tugged her arm free. Three eager faces stared at her. She felt like a defenseless bunny cornered by a pack of coyotes. "I wish I could stay and chat with you ladies, but I need to get back to the ranch and put a roast in the oven for supper." She knew for a fact there wasn't a roast in the whole house.

She turned away from the group and bumped right into Jake's chest. He clasped her upper arms to steady her and smiled at the women. "I thought we'd eat Sunday dinner at the café today. I haven't had their meat loaf in a long time."

*Drat.* The last thing she wanted to do was eat meat loaf with everyone in town watching her. But Jake seemed to want to delay their departure for the ranch as long as possible. "Sounds great." After offering a "See you later" to the ladies, she followed him across the lawn to where Annie was chasing around with a bunch of girls.

They drove to the café, Annie chatting their ears off about her friends. If Jake thought the restaurant was a safe zone he was in for a surprise. Everyone grinned as the waitress showed them to a table in the middle of the room. One man even gave Jake a thumbs-up when they passed by.

Obviously, the locals were eager to participate in a little matchmaking. Well, all except Gladys. She sat in a booth with her husband and another older couple, her face puckered as if she'd just sucked a lemon.

"Annie, what should we do when we get home?" Madeline asked after the waitress took their drink orders.

"Can we fill up the pool and swim?"

"Sure." Madeline eyed Jake. "Maybe your dad would like to swim with us." The idea had possibilities. She could picture the three of them sitting in the kiddie pool, she and Jake sipping a beer and Annie drinking Kool-Aid.

"Sorry, ladies, but the owner of the Bar S is coming to check on his horses this afternoon."

*I just bet you're real sorry.* Madeline waited until the waitress left after bringing their Cherry

Cokes. "How come you didn't mention this before now?" She felt a prick of irritation that he seldom bothered to keep her informed about anything dealing with the ranch or his progress with the horses. He was trying so hard to keep his distance, not just physically but emotionally. Her mind argued he wasn't worth all this trouble, but her heart disagreed.

"Sam William called this morning when you were in the shower." Jake shifted in his chair and stared at her. "I didn't tell you because it doesn't concern you."

Stung, Madeline reached for her soda. Ever since the reverend's surprise visit last night, Jake appeared angry with her. Or maybe he just regretted bringing her to church today. Regretted flaunting her in front of the whole community. Maybe it hadn't occurred to him until now that once they were seen together she suddenly became more than just a rumor, more than just some barbed-wire bride hiding out at his ranch.

Maybe he realized that people would think of them as a couple now.

"Should I have something ready to eat when he arrives?"

"No. He won't stay long. He's on his way to Arizona—"

"I'll be damned," a voice interrupted. "I guess

the rumors are true. Is this the barbed-wire bride everyone's been talking about, Montgomery?"

Maybe it was her imagination, but Madeline swore Jake stiffened in his seat before standing and offering a hand to the man who'd stopped by their table. "Mac," Jake greeted him. He motioned to Madeline. "Madeline Tate, this is Mac Glenwood. His ranch is a half hour south of here."

Madeline held out her hand and choked back a squawk of surprise when the rancher kissed her fingertips lingeringly. Her gaze skirted to Jake. His expression was so dark she glanced up to see if a thundercloud had settled over his head. Annie, thank goodness, was oblivious to the tension crackling in the air around the small table.

"Nice to meet you, Mr. Glenwood."

"My pleasure, Madeline. Call me Mac." He grinned at Jake, then returned his attention to her. "Knowing Montgomery, I'm positive he hasn't shown you the local sights. I'd be happy to tour you around the area this afternoon."

"I wasn't aware we had any *sights* around here, Glenwood," Jake challenged.

Madeline opened her mouth to decline the invitation, then snapped it shut. Maybe a little competition would light a fire under Jake. "I'd love to see the area, Mac." She smiled sweetly at Jake's glowering face.

"You'll have to take Annie along," Jake grumbled.

Mac didn't appear happy about it, but he didn't object. "That's fine. I've got some business at the feedlot. I'll be back in an hour and we can leave from here."

"Thank you again for the invitation, Mac."

"My pleasure, Madeline." The rancher set his Stetson on his head, nodded to her and Annie, then left the diner, greeting those he knew on the way out.

Jake leaned across the table. "Through making a fool out of us?"

She coughed delicately. "I didn't think there was an *us*."

Jake flinched. "For your information, he eats up women like you and spits them out for fun."

*Here we go again.* "Women like me?"

"Yeah, women like you. Beautiful, smart, sexy."

She believed Jake thought she was attractive, but she was beginning to think that was all he thought she was.

After the waitress brought their food, Madeline teased, "Why, Jake. I never knew you had a jealous streak."

"I'm not jealous." His protest came out a bit

too loudly, and several heads turned in their direction.

Madeline smiled. "Whatever you say, dear."

## Chapter Nine

"'Snow White kissed each dwarf goodbye. Then the prince lifted her up onto his horse and they rode to his castle on the hill, where they lived happily ever after.'"

Madeline closed the book and smiled at Annie, who lay snuggled in bed with her favorite stuffed frog. She tenderly brushed a strand of hair off the little girl's cheek, then bussed the soft, soap-scented skin.

Although it wasn't yet dark outside at eight-thirty, she had pulled the blinds and drawn the curtains, which made the room dark enough to need the night-light.

"Maddy?" Annie's sleep-slurred voice wrapped around Madeline's heart and tugged.

"What, sweetie?"

Thick brown lashes fluttered. "Can I call you 'Mommy,' now?"

*Mommy.* The single word managed to turn Madeline's insides mushy and warm. She cast a glance over her shoulder, and sighed in relief at the empty doorway. If Jake overheard Annie's question he'd pack Madeline's bags himself and drive her to the nearest bus depot. Knowing the coast was clear, she let down her guard and allowed Annie's words to fill her with joy. It would be so easy to love this child as if she were her own. "Sweetie, I think your dad might say it's a little soon for that."

"Daddy says Mommy had brown hair like me." Annie yawned and burrowed deeper under the light blanket. "Sometimes I can't remember Mommy."

She'd been so wrapped up in Jake and wondering whether they might have a future together that she'd hardly considered the possibility of instant motherhood. At twenty-five, she wondered if she was too young for the responsibility. Then she remembered how well she and Annie got along these past weeks and pushed aside her fears. "How about if you come up with a nickname for me, instead."

Solemn brown eyes watched her. "Like Princess?"

Madeline smoothed the covers across Annie's shoulders. "Princess it is. Sweet dreams, honey." She slipped from the room, closing the door partway.

She had at least two hours to blow before

Jake came in for the night. That is, if he didn't chicken out and sleep with the horses in the barn. Tiny tremors flickered across her skin as she envisioned how she wanted the night to end—their arms and legs entwined on the huge sleigh bed in his room. The excitement lasted no more than a moment before a voice in the back of her mind cautioned not to push too hard too soon. The blasted cowboy was just stubborn enough to dig in his heels to prove some stupid, irrelevant, chauvinistic male *point.*

Well, she wasn't taking any chances of that happening. She stopped in the kitchen and grabbed two longnecks from the fridge, then headed outside to the corral where Jake was working Quicksilver. Again. As far as competition went, she wasn't quite sure how to compete with a horse for Jake's attention. Good grief! She never thought she'd be jealous of the stallion.

She descended the steps and crossed the ranch yard. Quietly, she flung a jean-clad leg over the top rail of the corral and straddled it. Jake had his back to her, speaking in low tones to the animal while scratching the stallion's ear. The four-legged brat stared at her over his master's shoulder with a look of *Ha, ha, he likes me better* in his big brown eyes.

Jake turned toward her. She hadn't expected a

welcoming smile, but a little less hostility would have been nice. If she wasn't so darned afraid of the horse, she'd meander over and wrap herself around Jake's body, then use her lips to erase the scowl on his face. She might lack common sense where men were concerned, but she had enough sense to know when to steer clear of fifteen hundred pounds of possessive horseflesh. She stayed put on the rail and lifted a beer in invitation.

He studied the bottle for what seemed like forever, then wrapped the horse reins around a post. His long-legged stride ate up the distance across the pen. The closer he came, the harder her heart pounded. He stopped next to her knee and accepted the beer.

"Thanks." He downed the amber liquid in four swallows. "Annie asleep?"

"Yes." She wanted to mention the new nickname Annie had given her but didn't think it wise if she planned to seduce him tonight.

He eyed her T-shirt. "So. What *sights* did Glenwood show you?"

Well, that was certainly fast. She thought he'd hold out a bit longer before he caved in and grilled her about her sight-seeing venture with his neighbor. "He showed me his ranch. Then we drove down to Stephenville for ice-cream cones. Annie liked him."

"Annie likes frogs." He crossed his arms over his chest and leaned against the fence rail. "He's divorced."

"Yes, he told me that."

Jake's brows rose. "Did he tell you why he's divorced?"

"No. And it isn't any of my business."

"He cheated on his wife."

"Really, Jake, I don't care about his marriage."

He spun toward her without warning and grabbed hold of her thigh, his fingers pressing into her flesh. "You'd better care if you're going to get involved with him while you stay here this summer." He loosened his hold, his fingers sliding down her muscle like a caress before he lifted his hand away.

"I hardly consider taking a drive with the man getting involved."

"Honey, he didn't ask to show you around today because he was just being neighborly. Hell, every man in that diner saw him stare at you like a rutting bull after a prize heifer."

"Gee, no one's ever called me a heifer before."

Jake frowned. "You know what I mean."

"No, Jake. I don't. Tell me."

Jake gazed at her for the longest time before glancing away. "He looks at you, Maddy, like I do in my dreams."

*Oh, my.* Madeline's heart fluttered inside her chest. "You can put your mind at ease, big guy. He didn't make any moves on me."

"Yet," Jake grumbled, stabbing the toe of his boot into the ground, stirring up dust.

His little-boy pout went straight to her heart and she was glad she'd lied. No sense riling Jake by confessing that Mac had tried to make a move on her. When Annie had been preoccupied with her ice-cream cone, Mac had squeezed her derriere and whispered that he'd like to show her other things besides his ranch. After giving him an elbow in the gut, she didn't think Mac would be calling on her again anytime soon.

Madeline feathered her fingers through the damp hair along the back of Jake's neck. Startled, he lifted his head. "I don't intend to get involved with anyone but you," she whispered.

His throat muscles rippled before he spoke. "Then why did you go with him?"

"Because I wanted to make you jealous."

He stared at her with his soul in his eyes. "Maddy, all I have to do is picture you and another man and I'm jealous as hell."

"Jake—"

He held up a hand. "I have no right to be jealous. But you're the first woman—the only woman—who's ever tied me up in knots like this. And I'm not too good at dealing with it."

Hoping to ease the tension some, she asked, "Are you finished for the night?"

Something dark and dangerous flashed in his eyes. "Yeah." He motioned with the empty beer bottle toward the horse. "That stubborn cuss is finally making some progress."

"How did your meeting go with the owner of the Bar S today?"

"Sam seems happy with the progress I've made. I'll start working the horses with cattle soon."

"You have cattle on your ranch."

"Nope. I borrow a few head from the Winstons." He took off his hat and wiped his forehead. "I train their new horses and they loan me their cows."

She nodded, thinking that Jake's damp, sweat-glistening face was far more fascinating than talk of cattle. "Can I help you in the barn?"

His eyebrow lifted in surprise.

"I'm not afraid of getting dirty." She hated when he did that. Stared at her as if a strong wind would blow her over or getting her nails dirty would reduce her to a bawling baby. Then his eyes darkened. Heat poured from his expression as he made no attempt to conceal his interest in her mouth. "How dirty are you willing to get?"

Hallelujah! The gods were smiling down on her tonight.

She swung her leg over the rail and landed with a plop on the ground outside the pen. Then she held out her hand for his empty beer bottle, took it and headed for the barn. As she disappeared inside, she peeked over her shoulder, and caught his gaze glued to her backside.

*And he thought the horse was stubborn!*

THE LITTLE TEASE.

Jake flung another pitchforkful of horse crap into the wheelbarrow outside the stall while watching Maddy's fanny poke up in the air as she bent over the feed barrel.

They'd been working side by side for an hour, cleaning stalls and bedding the horses down for the night. She finished filling the bucket, then sashayed down the center of the barn, toward the last stall on the left. After setting it inside, she wiped her hands on the front of her jeans, pivoted on her foot and sashayed back his way.

He had to be imagining it. They were both sweaty and hot, yet he swore he could smell her sweet feminine scent as she drew near. Something musky mixed with that expensive perfume she wore. He felt himself harden. A condition that had plagued him for weeks.

"I'll go check on Annie and bring something cold back to drink," she offered.

Like another beer would quench the kind of thirst he had right now? To keep from grabbing her as she brushed by, he gripped the rake handle so tightly he felt a wood splinter jab into his palm.

After she left the barn, he wheeled the last load of dung out to the compost pile, then killed time doing chores that didn't need doing. When a half hour passed, he figured she'd chickened out.

He shoved aside his disappointment. What had he expected? From the moment she'd landed in his backyard twenty-four days ago she'd fired off more signals than a referee from a Monday-night football game, and he'd ignored most of them. He'd been pretty damn proud of his effort to hold her at bay…until now…when he stood aching for her touch, her smile, the feel of her hands on his skin. He would have made love to her tonight. Because he was too tired. Tired of fighting this…this…whatever it was between them.

Oh, hell. He might as well admit that the *whatever* between them had become a lot more involved than he'd been prepared for. After watching Glenwood hit on Maddy in the café today, he admitted that he was in over his head.

He was falling for the barbed-wire bride and he didn't know what the heck to do about it. The only thing he did know for sure was that he'd go crazy if he had to fight this sexual tug-of-war between them for an entire summer.

He stripped off his shirt and went into the tack room to wash off. After cleaning his hands first at the small stainless-steel sink against the far wall, he turned on the hose and stood over the metal drain in the middle of the concrete floor to soak his head, letting the cool water run down his back and over his chest, dampening the waistband of his jeans.

A sound caught his attention, and he lifted his head, blinking away the rivulets of water streaming over his eyes. Poised in the doorway, a plastic tumbler of cold tea in hand, Maddy stared at his naked chest. He straightened, pointed the hose toward the ground and watched as she lifted the cup to her mouth. The thin column of her throat rippled delicately with each swallow, and he longed to move his mouth over the sensitive flesh.

She finished half the drink, then moved closer and offered the rest to him. He rotated the rim until the reddish-pink lipstick imprint touched his mouth. He drank deeply, then licked the remainder of the lipstick off before setting the cup in the sink behind him.

Their labored breathing set the mood better than any love song or candlelit dinner. The time had come to surrender his feelings. He was just a man. A man on the verge of falling in love for the first time in his life. A man with the woman of his dreams standing before him, offering him things he didn't deserve but was desperate enough to accept.

A small voice in his head demanded that he be noble and walk away. Forget nobility. He'd take what she offered regardless of the consequences. Regardless of who got hurt.

He wanted. She wanted. To hell with the rest of it.

He lifted the hose and she gasped with shock as the cold water soaked her clothes. A zing of pleasure shot through him when he saw that she wasn't wearing a bra underneath the T-shirt. Fascinated, he watched the wet cotton cling to her breasts, molding their shape and size.

He stepped closer and thumbed one of the stiff peaks. When he cupped her sensitive flesh, her moan of pleasure went straight to his heart. The urge to have all of her was too powerful for him to wait until they got back to the house. He needed her now. Here.

He hauled her body up against his, trapping the hose between them. He doubted even the cold water could put out the fire burning them.

Grasping the back of her head, he pressed his mouth to hers. Her lips were every man's fantasy. His fantasy, and he didn't think he'd ever get enough.

She sighed, and Jake just about lost it. He stepped back and let the hose fall to the ground. Grabbing the hem of her T-shirt, he tugged it over her head. She was gorgeous. He caressed her fullness and gazed into her warm green eyes. "I need you, Maddy."

She smiled. "I want you, too, Jake."

Together they pulled at their wet clothes and shoes until they both stood naked under the harsh room light. He stroked her cheek. "You deserve better than this, Maddy." He wasn't sure if he meant their surroundings or him.

"I deserve you, Jake."

He laved kisses across her shoulder as his hands roamed the soft swells of her body. Her head fell back and her hands raked through his hair, urging him closer, until he thought he'd smother in all her softness. He wasn't aware of time passing, but eventually he noticed that their feet looked pickled from standing in water so long.

He lifted her in his arms and moved away from the drain. "Maddy." He waited until she looked at him. "Whatever happens between us…" He set her on the ground. "I want you to know that tonight is more than just sex." He made himself stop before he sounded like a fool. Besides, a man had his pride to consider. And his pride might be the only thing left inside him after Maddy went away.

She bent her head and used her mouth to drive him crazy. When she kissed his nipple, he about shot off the floor. Gritting his teeth, he struggled to hold still as her kisses went lower and lower and lower.

A growl rumbled up his chest, vibrated in his throat and erupted into the small room when her hand wrapped around his length and stroked. His eyes slammed shut, the ecstasy more than he could bear. The intimacy of Maddy's gesture shattered him and he fought the tightness in his throat. On the brink of losing control, he pulled her near and buried his face in her hair.

He yearned to please her. To show her how much she meant to him. She lifted a leg and settled it over his hip. He moaned at the feel of her heat cradling him. "Slow down, Maddy. I don't have any protection out here."

She nibbled his neck and smiled wickedly. "I do." Stepping away, she rummaged through a pocket in her wet jeans, then triumphantly displayed the foil packet.

"Beauty and brains. I'm a lucky man." He

reached for the package, but she moved her hand back. "I'll do it."

Jake wasn't sure if he could handle that. Surprisingly, he held himself together while she rolled the condom on.

She flexed a hand against his chest, her eyes dark and sensuous, her breathing quick and erratic, her mouth swollen and open. She forced him back until his hips bumped the metal sink. Using the sink for balance, he lifted her onto him and sank into her.

He went still. He wanted to kiss her, taste her, breathe her. Kissing Maddy while he was inside her made him feel that he was a part of her, bodily and spiritually. As crazy as it seemed, he couldn't tell where his body stopped and hers began.

After several long, deep kisses he started moving. Slow and easy, afraid he'd lose control if he did what his body was screaming for…to pound into her. But Maddy's hands and mouth shattered his control and he gave up the fight.

He wanted it to go on forever, but his legs started to shake and he wasn't going to be able to hold out much longer.

"Let go, Maddy. Fly with me." He shifted his hips. Her breathing quickened, and her nails dug into his shoulders. Then he bent his head and suckled a breast. Her body tensed, and a soft keening escaped her throat as she flung her head back and shattered in his arms.

He followed a moment later, muffling his shout of satisfaction against the soft mounds of her breasts.

How on earth could he ever let this woman go?

## Chapter Ten

Madeline unplugged the Crock-Pot, lifted the lid and sniffed appreciatively at the spicy aroma of simmering beans. *Bless you, Betty Crocker.*

Earlier in the week, Nancy Sloan had called to remind her of the July Fourth celebration in the town square. She'd asked if Madeline would bring a pot of beans to the celebration and show up a little early to help decorate. Having never celebrated the holiday before—at least, not that she remembered—Madeline looked forward to the day's festivities.

Then the nightmares had started. Each nightmare had been a different town's Independence Day celebration. But the results had been the same. She and a ghostlike Sara had stood side by side next to their own pot of beans as judges had sampled them. Each nightmare had ended the same—Sara had been awarded the blue ribbon and Jake had taken Sara's see-through hand and left the picnic with her.

Madeline had admitted that competing with a ghost was childish. But deep in her heart she wanted only to make Jake proud and not embarrass him in front of his neighbors and friends.

So, she'd pulled out a stack of old cookbooks from the pantry and all week she'd pored over them at night after Annie had gone to bed and while Jake had trained the horses. For the past several nights she'd experimented with different recipes, and neither Annie nor Jake had complained about eating beans with every meal. Yesterday, she'd finally decided on a combination of two recipes. After a trip to town to replenish the ingredients, she'd put the bean concoction together and had allowed it to simmer all through the night.

She dipped a spoon into the pot and sampled the end product. At the rich tangy-sweet flavor, her mouth watered. "Mmm."

"I think I'm jealous."

She whirled at the sound of Jake's husky voice. Arms crossed over his chest, hat tilted low across his forehead, he lounged in the doorway, looking like a desperado. Her heart did a little flip and her face warmed under his narrowed-eyed perusal.

Two could play this game. She moved her gaze down his body, taking in every detail. The scrape across the back of his right hand. The tear in his shirt at the elbow. The grease stain on his knee. The layer of corral dust coating his boots. He was hot, tired and so darn sexy she was tempted to put the lid back on the beans and tug him by the belt loops to the bedroom, where she could massage all those big achy muscles.

She motioned to his disheveled appearance. "Did you fall off your horse?"

He grinned. "When do we have to leave?"

"Soon. Annie's upstairs putting her swimsuit on under her clothes. How long will it take to put up the decorations?"

He shoved his hands into the front pockets of his jeans. "I don't know. I've never attended any of the local celebrations."

To cover her shock, she turned away and stirred beans that didn't need stirring. "Oh. I assumed you and Sara and Annie..." Great. She should have kept her mouth shut. The last thing she wanted to do today was bring up Annie's dead mother.

She waited for Jake to make a quick escape. But she didn't hear the familiar clomp and stomp of his boot heels against the linoleum. Only silence filled the kitchen, stretching her nerves taut. She chanced a peek over her shoulder. Head bent, Jake studied the tips of his boots, a frown marring his handsome face.

He breathed deeply, then exhaled slowly and

lifted his head. "Sara was nervous around people. We avoided public places, shopping, eating out." He shrugged. "There's always something that needs to be done on a ranch, so it didn't matter to me one way or the other if we socialized much." He removed his hat and hung it on a peg by the door. "Maybe that was the wrong thing to do. Maybe I should have forced Sara to leave the ranch. Maybe I should have driven Annie to see the fireworks." The muscle along his jaw bunched. "Maybe I should have done a lot of things. But I didn't."

Madeline wasn't sure how to respond. Going with gut instinct, she set the lid on the pot, then went to him. A wary look entered his eyes when she laid her palm on his cheek. "You can't force someone to do something she doesn't want to." He opened his mouth to object, but she cut him off. "If you'd picked her up and set her in the truck and taken her places she'd only have grown to resent you for it."

"But I was her husband. I should have known what to do. What she needed."

Madeline wondered how much time Jake would need to stop beating himself up over his dead wife. She wrapped her arms around his dusty torso and tucked her face against his gritty neck. She inhaled the familiar scent of sweat, horses and outdoors, all of which she'd come to associate with security and comfort. And Jake.

He was a complicated man. She was just beginning to understand what made him tick. Desperately, she wanted to be the woman who could help him forgive himself and move on with his life.

She lifted her face to his and waited, hoping he'd accept the kiss she offered. He hesitated a moment before dipping his head and capturing her mouth in a warm caress. His arms came around her and dragged her closer. This kiss was different from any of the others they'd shared. There was nothing sexual about it. It was a kiss of comfort, of caring and sharing. Their lips gentled each other's for a long time; neither she nor he were in any hurry to end it.

Eventually, they had to breathe, and she lifted her mouth from his. "Don't blame yourself for the past, Jake. You were there for Sara. You were always there for her."

A stark look glazed Jake's eyes, and he flinched at her words. The muscle beneath her fingers tightened and his face became an expressionless mask that scared her more than the desolate expression in his eyes moments earlier.

"You were patient and kind and you stayed, Jake."

His whole body seemed to turn to granite.

Save for the slight rise and fall of his chest, he remained motionless.

Desperate to ease the agony tearing him to pieces, she gripped his arms tighter. "You could have left your wife. Walked away when the going got tough, but you didn't. You took your vows, your commitment to her and your marriage, seriously." When he still didn't speak, she nuzzled her face against his chest and hugged him hard. "You're an incredible man, Jake Montgomery. Any woman would feel proud to have you as her husband." *Especially me.*

Her heart ached with love for the big cowboy. She wondered if he had any idea how special he was. She had to find a way to show Jake he was exactly the kind of man she wanted to spend the rest of her life with. To have children with. To grow old with.

But now was not the time. Today, she wanted everyone to have fun. Attempting to lighten the mood, she lowered her hand to his backside and squeezed one firm bun. "Get a shower, cowboy. The wagons pull out in twenty minutes."

His smile didn't reach his eyes. "Yes, ma'am." He kissed her cheek and ran a hand over her hair. "Thank you, Maddy."

She soaked in the contentment his soft touches always made her feel. "For what?"

"For today."

Her throat threatened to swell shut. "You can save your thank-you for later tonight."

The shadows left his eyes and his old grin was back. "Yes, ma'am."

As Fourth of July picnics went, this one wasn't so bad, Jake thought as he watched the line for Maddy's beans grow longer by the minute. He figured that in about one hour the smell of skunk would be more welcome than the stink of a hundred cowboys with their bellies full of baked beans. A nasty buzz sounded near his ear. He whipped his hat off and swatted at the horsefly.

Trying to find relief from the sweltering afternoon sun in six inches of shade, he shifted to his right. The damn tree was over one hundred years old and had more dead wood on it than leaves. But he wasn't about to wander off in search of a cooler spot when he had the best view of the bean table from where he stood and could also keep an eye on Annie.

Several yards away, a play area had been set up for the kids. His daughter stood ankle-deep in a plastic play pool, splashing and giggling and having fun with several girls her own age. The realization that she'd missed this event year after year partly because of him sat in his stomach like a big, heavy boulder.

He swallowed back the rising knot in his throat. He'd dealt with Sara's death by throwing himself into ranch work. It was all he knew to do. And he'd pretty much ignored Annie, leaving her with the housekeeper day in and day out. Not only had he failed Sara, he'd abandoned Annie when she'd needed him most. And why? *Guilt.*

How could he face his daughter when he was to blame for her mother's death?

Right then, Annie glanced his way and waved. He smiled and waved back. He'd sacrifice anything and everything for his little girl. That Annie was a happy, loving little person despite Sara's death amazed him. He believed somewhere deep inside him that God had brought Annie into the world for a reason. He believed the world was a better place because his daughter was in it.

Watching her play with other children made Jake more determined than ever to see to it she had friends over to the house more often. And he'd look into those dance lessons she was always talking about. There would be plenty of time for that after Maddy left.

And Maddy would leave. He had no doubt that by the end of the summer she'd become bored with country life. Maybe even bored with him. She'd be ready to return to her corporate job and her corporate friends. Her corporate life.

A guffaw from near the buffet tables set up along one side of the square grabbed Jake's attention. He noticed several things at once. The line for Maddy's beans had grown to twenty in number. Harriet Blecker's sixteen-year-old niece, who manned the coleslaw table nearby, had no customers and appeared ready to claw Maddy's eyes out. Deputy Karl had positioned himself at the far end of the table and proceeded to direct traffic through the line. And Maddy looked…beautiful. Actually, *stunning* was a better word. Her ponytail was askew, her T-shirt had bean stains on it and the lipstick she'd applied in the truck on the way to town was gone. Yep, she was stunning.

Jake felt kind of funny observing the other cowboys ogle and flirt with Maddy. He wasn't used to men giving his woman the once-, twice-, all-the-way-down-and-up over. The prick of jealousy aside, pride nudged its way into his chest, making him feel like a puffed-up rooster. He wanted to cut through the crowd, grab Maddy by the back of the neck and haul her up against him then kiss the daylights out of her in front of God and everyone. Must be a guy thing, he figured. He was proud that the vivacious redheaded, bean-ladling woman belonged to him. For the summer, anyway.

"Oowee. Ain't she somethin'?"

Embarrassed to be caught daydreaming, Jake cleared his throat and nodded a greeting to Coot. The old man ambled toward him, balancing a plate with a piece of fried chicken drowning in a pool of beans between his knobby fingers.

"Tourists keeping you busy at the store this summer, Coot?"

"Making ends meet. If they hadn't put that blasted interstate through Cutter's Creek five years ago I'd have retired by now. As it is, only folks who get lost end up in Ridge City." He motioned to the lawn chair next to the tree. "Mind if I sit a spell?"

"Heck, no. Have a seat." Jake didn't feel like sitting but grabbed the other lawn chair Madeline had insisted on bringing along today. The least he could do was visit with the old man while he ate. He didn't know Coot that well, but he'd heard his wife had died over fifteen years ago and he'd never wanted to remarry. Jake didn't think he had any kids, either.

"The bride came by with yer young 'un a while back. Prettiest little thing and growin' like a weed."

"Annie's a good girl."

"Next time ya come to town, bring her by. I always have a few surprises for the little ones."

What would it hurt the next time he came to town to drop in and check on Coot? "I'll do that."

A sparkle lit up his wrinkled face. "Annie and the bride sure hit it off."

Jeez, would people ever stop referring to Maddy as *the bride?* "Yeah, the two girls are always cooking up trouble at the ranch."

Coot chuckled, then turned his attention to the plate of food in front of him and chowed down on the chicken leg.

Jake took the opportunity to study Maddy again. She lifted her hand to brush aside a loose strand of hair from her face. She was becoming more disheveled by the minute, and he couldn't help but think she must be tired from standing in the sun all afternoon. But her bright smile turned cantankerous old farts into drooling fools.

At first, he'd thought she was just being nice. But after two hours of watching her interact with others, Jake realized she was genuinely enjoying herself and the people around her. If he hadn't witnessed it from afar, he'd never have believed a city woman like Maddy could have fun at a small-town picnic.

"How'd them skivvies fit on her?" Coot grinned, his cheeks puffing out with food.

Jake thanked his stars he didn't have any food in his mouth or he'd have choked at the question. He wondered how far the old man's loose tongue had spread the news of Maddy's special purchase from his store catalog. He eyed the cowboys standing in the bean line. Were they hoping to catch a glimpse of her lacy bra or panties?

"I suppose it ain't none of my business." Coot sounded glum.

"That's right, old man, it isn't."

Undaunted, Coot flashed a toothless grin and went on. "I convinced her to get the black. She wanted the red, but I said they'd clash with her hair color."

Jake shifted on the chair, uncomfortable talking about Maddy's unmentionables with a man old enough to be her grandfather.

"Heard Roy and Roger makin' bets on ya 'n' the gal."

"Bets?" No use pretending he didn't know what *gal* Coot was referring to.

"Roy bet ten bucks ya'll haul the bride off to Vegas before summer's out. Roger says ya won't."

Jake frowned. He didn't much care for people speculating on his and Maddy's future. Besides, he had a feeling Vegas was the last place she'd want her wedding. He should keep his mouth shut, but curiosity and male pride reared its ugly head. "Why doesn't Roger think I'll marry Maddy?"

"Says she's too fickle. Figures she'll git bored 'n' hightail it outta here before summer's out."

Well, heck. That wasn't anything Jake hadn't considered himself.

"Now, if ya was to ask me, I think the bride fits in real nice 'round here."

Jake couldn't argue there. She acted more at ease behind the bean table than most of the locals who were born right down the road. Heck. He'd lived here over six years and he stood off by himself, while Maddy, who was a stranger to most folks, talked up a storm with everyone around her.

While Coot finished his meal, Jake tried to envisage Maddy dressed in business attire, hair in a tight bun, giving a sales pitch before a group of men in a conference room. But picturing her face serious and stern was hard. Since he'd met her, she'd shown more emotion than any woman he'd ever known. He'd seen her cry, laugh, pout, smile and more. She was full of life.

Coot thumped him on the back, startling him. "Yes, sirree, ya got it bad, son." The old bugger chortled.

Jake shifted in the chair, not sure he liked Coot seeing through him.

"Ya best give some thought to makin' an honest woman outta the bride."

The hairs on the back of his neck stood up. "Are people talking, Coot?"

"Kit Harper's sayin' yer givin' the bride the honeymoon she missed out on."

Jake wanted to kick something, preferably Harper's butt. In his mind any man who went around claiming to be named after Kit Carson was an idiot. Hauling off and punching the daylights out of all the dummies smearing Maddy's reputation with lies was damned tempting.

But they aren't lies, a voice inside his head taunted.

The hayseeds could joke all they wanted, but unless he said so, they'd never know for sure if he and Maddy were sleeping together. *Wrong.* There was no way in hell any man would believe Jake could live under the same roof with a woman as beautiful as Maddy and not touch her. Or at least try. He hated to believe her living in his house had compromised her reputation. But it had. Jake wished like hell he had the right to defend her honor. *You'd have the right if you married her.*

*Marry Maddy for real?* No. No matter how

much he might want to spend the rest of his life with her, his past got in the way of the future.

"So ya gonna marry the gal?"

Jake started at Coot's question and wondered if he'd spoken his thoughts.

But didn't all guys think about marriage at least a little after having mind-blowing sex with a woman? No man wanted to lose a good thing. Still, a good marriage needed more than just great sex to last. He knew firsthand a marriage could survive without it.

Trust played a big role in a happy marriage. Sara had trusted him. And he'd failed her in the worst possible way. He sure as hell didn't want to go down that road again. Especially with a woman like Maddy.

The day he'd found Maddy tangled up in his barbed-wire fence she'd started patching the hole inside him, filling up the empty space with her smiles, touches, words. He tried to look ahead to a time when she wouldn't be there, and didn't like what he saw.

"Best watch it. Some young feller's gonna snatch her right out from under yer nose."

Aside from her being physically attracted to him, Jake wasn't totally sure of Maddy's feelings for him. He believed she cared for him. Was tempted to think she cared deeply. He knew for a fact that she wasn't the kind of woman to sleep with a man unless her emotions were involved.

But in the back of his mind he had to take in account that she didn't have a lot of experience with men. He'd gathered from Annie's comments that Maddy had led a sheltered life. And even though she acted as if she was over her ex-fiancé, Jake had to consider that she might still be hung up on the guy.

How nice it would be if he'd wormed his way into her heart and she couldn't live without him. Not that he thought for one minute he deserved such devotion. And he had to keep things in perspective. Even if Maddy did have deep feelings for him, nothing could come of them. He wasn't good enough for her. "Has Maddy ever talked about her plans for the future, Coot?"

Jake wondered if Maddy ever thought about the future and he'd been in those thoughts. She never mentioned her career. Never said if she was looking forward to going back to her job. Never talked about her friends. He didn't even know if she kept in touch with her father. He tried to feel offended that she hadn't shared her plans with him, but how could he, when he hadn't even taken the time to ask her those questions himself?

The old man shook his head. "Nope. She seems mighty confused, if ya ask me."

Confused? Jake didn't think so. Frustrated, maybe. He sensed it bothered Maddy that he wouldn't talk more about his marriage to Sara. If he didn't care so much for Maddy, he might share more of his past. But the idea of spilling his guts to her scared him spitless.

Jake knew that after Maddy heard what he had to say, she'd never look at him again with the same sweet, innocent expression on her face. He didn't want to see disgust or fear in Maddy's eyes. Not after what they'd shared together already.

*How do you know if you don't give her a chance?*

He glanced toward the food tables and caught her watching him. His chest tightened. Every time she looked at him with those expressive green eyes all soft and glistening he believed he could conquer worlds, move mountains. Sometimes he even believed he could bury the past.

Later tonight when he was buried deep inside her, he'd confess his feelings for her. He'd tell her how she eased the hurt inside him. She deserved more than that from him, but that was all he could give her.

And when the end of August came, he'd find the words to make her understand that what they'd shared this summer had meant more to him than anything else in the world. Then he'd set her free.

A bead of sweat slid down his temple. God help him if he couldn't find the courage to let her go.

"CAN WE SEE the fireworks?" Annie asked, tugging on Madeline's belt loop.

Madeline put down the wet rag she'd used to clean off the picnic table and scrutinized the little girl, laughing gently. Ketchup stains dribbled down the front of her flower-print T-shirt. Dirt smudges decorated both cheeks and a small scrape covered her left knee. Chocolate ringed her mouth, her pigtails were askew and she was missing one sock. She was adorable. Annie had had a wonderful time today and Madeline was fiercely thankful she'd convinced Jake to attend the town's celebration.

The day had been a long one, and the locals were sacked out in lawn chairs and blankets spread out under shade trees. Children were asleep in parents' laps and there were long lulls between conversations. Even the colorful red, white and blue streamers drooped along the edges of the buffet tables. Madeline thought about how exhausted she was, how much she wanted to go back to the ranch and take a long, cool soak in the tub. But her fatigue was no match for the sweet innocent eyes staring up at her. "I'd love to go, sweetie, but it's up to your dad."

She looked over Annie's head to where Jake stood conversing with a group of men under a tree. The day's heat and humidity hadn't affected him. He appeared fresh and vibrant and sexy, standing with both hands stuffed into his back pockets. Today he'd worn a golf shirt that displayed his biceps to perfection. She hadn't been the only one to notice. Harriet Blecker's niece had all but drooled every time Jake had come up to the buffet table to ask how things were going.

She might have been jealous of the young teenager if not for the fact that each time Madeline's gaze found Jake's, he already had his eyes on her. Even now, the memory of his heated stares sent tiny shivers racing across the surface of her skin. Jake might be the most handsome and virile man at the picnic, but what the other females didn't realize was how wonderful he was on the inside. Even if Jake had a big wart on the tip of his nose he'd still be irresistible.

Now, if only she could find a way to convince him to open up to her. She sensed he was holding something back about his marriage to Sara. She wished she knew how to make him trust her. How to convince him that nothing he told her could change the way she felt about him.

Annie jumped up and down. "Can I go ask now?"

Madeline checked her watch. It was already 8:00 p.m. Coot had mentioned the fireworks were in Stephenville and started at dusk. "Sure. I'll get our things together."

She shook out the picnic blanket, lifting the edge high enough to conceal her smile as she watched Annie march into the circle of men. The child tugged on Jake's elbow, demanding his attention. As he knelt in front of her, she used wild arm gestures to convey her request. Madeline assumed he didn't want to go by the sudden dip in his eyebrow, but to his credit, he waited to speak until his daughter finished pleading.

Madeline folded the blanket and set it on top of the cooler. Jake raised his head and their gazes collided, her stomach jumping at the intensity of his stare. She could guess exactly what kind of fireworks he wanted to set off tonight. He continued to stare, waiting for some kind of sign from her. They'd been separated most of the day and she yearned for some quiet time with just Jake.

She shifted her gaze to Annie, and the hopeful expression on the little girl's face cinched her decision. Her and Jake's quiet time would have to wait. Annie deserved to see the fireworks. And truthfully, Madeline was excited at the idea of sitting on a blanket with Jake and Annie and watching the sky explode with color and light and sound. She smiled and gave a thumbs-up, then laughed at Annie's squeal.

Taking Annie's hand, Jake excused himself from the group and headed toward her. "Annie really wants to see the fireworks, but they're all the way over in Stephenville. You sure you're up for it?"

Annie's expression changed from eagerness to worry as she watched the adults. Madeline wanted to commend Annie for the superb acting job she was witnessing. "I don't mind."

Annie's eyes shone with anticipation. Madeline thought that if what they saw tonight was half as bright as the sparkle in the child's eyes, they'd be in for a real treat.

"I don't mind driving you girls over. C'mon, let's pack the truck and get going. As late as it is, we'll have to park on the other side of the hill to see anything."

And they did. It turned out the fireworks were shot off at the edge of Stephenville's city limits. Hundreds of cars and trucks lined the shoulders of Highway 10 going in both directions. They were among the last to arrive, and Jake managed to find a spot just over a small hill. He parked facing away from the town. "We'll sit in the truck bed."

After he spread the blanket across the tailgate, he lifted Annie up, then she and Jake sat on either side of her. Madeline breathed deeply, wishing, for one selfish moment, that just her and Jake were parked in the middle of this field, with nothing but darkness and the sound of chirping insects surrounding them.

Then the first thunderous boom came, taking both her and Annie by surprise. They giggled like schoolgirls as they watched the sky light up. Jake lay back, arms crossed behind his head, and chuckled at their excitement. For over twenty-five minutes the sky flashed with glimmering blues, sparkling silvers, rich reds and greens.

Madeline liked the resonant booms as much as the bright colors. Her favorite firework was the one that sounded like a machine gun going off and ended with an explosion of twinkling white lights that looked like falling stars.

She hated to take her eyes off the heavens, but even the fireworks couldn't block out the sensation of Jake's gaze burning into her. She sucked in a quiet breath when the tips of his fingers caressed the skin under the hem of her T-shirt.

Annie's shoulders drooped, and she curled

herself into a ball, laying her head in Madeline's lap. The poor little thing had finally run out of steam. Just then the sky exploded into a million sparkling stars. She pointed and gasped, "That's it!"

Jake's fingers tensed against her back. "That's what?" he whispered, his voice thick with intimacy.

She stared in awe at the heavens. "That's what it's like when you…when you…" She sighed, realizing the conversation was a little too intimate for their surroundings.

He sat up, leaned over his daughter and murmured against Madeline's mouth, "That's how *I* feel, Maddy. You make my whole world explode." He kissed her softly, just a touch of tongue to tease and entice. She followed his mouth when he pulled back, wanting more.

His lips claimed hers in a powerful kiss. She wasn't sure if the next explosion was in her heart or the sky. He plunged his tongue inside her mouth, telling her without words what he wished he could do right then. She wished for it, too.

Madeline wasn't aware of time passing, but the sound of gunning engines invaded her consciousness. Jake drew back slowly, leaving behind the taste of him in her mouth, the feel of him on her lips.

His heavy breath puffed across her face. "We need to talk when we get home."

Her heart lurched in her chest. The darkness that had provided such intimacy was now her enemy. She hated that she couldn't see his eyes, couldn't read his thoughts in those deep blue orbs.

Had he changed his mind about her staying until the end of the summer? She clutched his muscled thigh. "Tell me now, Jake."

He pried her fingers from his leg and brought them to his mouth. One by one he kissed each tip, then the center of her palm. "Soon. Let's get Annie home to bed first."

"Is it bad?" Oh, Lord, had she no pride? Obviously not, where this man was concerned.

His quiet chuckle eased some of the tension in her, but she still had to know. "You're not going to ask me to leave, are you?" When he didn't answer right away, she panicked. "I won't go. I promised Annie I'd stay the summer. I can't—"

"Shh, babe. Take it easy." He kissed her mouth, her cheek and her forehead. "I'm not asking you to go."

She clamped her hands over his forearms. "But it's about us, right?"

He rested his forehead against hers. "Yeah, it's about us. How you make me feel."

"How do I make you feel, cowboy?"

He chuckled. "You don't give up, do you?"

She pressed her face to his neck and breathed in deeply. Was Jake thinking marriage? Hope surged through her. It didn't matter that he still hadn't said the word *love*. At least he acknowledged there was something between them. That was enough for now. "Okay, I'll listen."

Jake grinned. "Without distracting me?"

She shook her head. "No promises."

He hugged her close. "Fair enough."

The hour drive back to the ranch was the longest in Madeline's life. Why did she sense that Jake thought their future, if they were to have one, depended on her reaction to what he had to say? What could he possibly have to confess that would make her change her mind about wanting to be with him forever?

She stared at Jake's profile as he drove. One might use the word *rugged* when describing his looks. His tanned skin came from working in the sun, not from a tanning salon. His muscles were real, not the result of protein powders and health clubs. But underneath all that ruggedness was a warm, loyal, giving heart.

Tonight, she wanted very much to do the giving. To show him with kisses, touches, whispered words how much today had meant to her. How much he meant to her.

"What the hell?" Jake muttered as he swung the truck in a circle near the corral.

Madeline slapped her palms against the dashboard and gaped out the windshield. Jake put the truck into Park and turned off the engine but kept the headlights shining on the surprise by the house.

She couldn't believe her eyes. There in the glow of the headlights, wearing a tailored suit and tie, leaning against the trunk of a silver Lexus, was her worst nightmare.

"Who is he?"

"My ex-fiancé."

## Chapter Eleven

Jake stared out the truck windshield at the man by the brand-spanking-new Lexus. A spasm gripped his body, twisting his gut into a pretzel. He sucked in a breath, the oxygen burning in his lungs like hell. He clutched the wheel until white-hot pains shot through his knuckles, as he searched for something to say, anything that would release him from the sudden panic that had overtaken his body.

Madeline frowned. "What in the world is Jonathon doing here this late at night?"

*This late at night? What in the hell is he doing here, period?* Right about now Jake didn't think anything could make the tight band of fear cinching his chest ease, but hearing the note of displeasure in Maddy's voice helped some.

He swallowed hard, wondering if she wanted a response. Wondering if he was even capable of giving one. The infamous ex-fiancé shifted against the rear bumper and waited, arms crossed over his chest, as if he had all the time in the world to waste until Madeline got out of the truck. *Cocky son of a gun.*

Jake glanced across the seat, wishing Maddy's face weren't hidden in the shadows. Someone had to say something. It might as well be him. "You going out there to talk to him, or do you want me to turn the truck around and get the hell out of Dodge?" He knew what answer he wanted to hear.

"Yes."

His heart did a little flip. "Yes, stay, or yes, get the hell out of Dodge?"

"Yes, stay. I guess I'll have talk to him."

He reached for her hand, and was startled to find her fingers icy cold. "You don't have to talk to him. I'll make him leave."

She squeezed his hand, then pulled away and grappled for the door handle. His lungs seized up again. Before he could stop himself, his hand shot across Annie, who slept peacefully between them, and clutched Maddy's thigh. He wanted to warn her to be careful, tell her not to listen to a word the creep had to say, but his throat closed shut.

She pried his hand loose from her leg and patted it as if she were consoling a child. Is that how he was behaving? Shame filled him and he cursed himself for acting like an idiot.

"Put Annie to bed, Jake. I promise this won't take long."

He waited for some sign of reassurance that when this "won't take long" was over, everything between them would still be the same. But without a word she opened the door and slid from the front seat.

Jake watched her as she walked toward the guy. He thought of staying in the truck until she finished talking to the jerk. After all, this was his ranch; he could sit in his truck all night if he wanted. Leaving Maddy alone with her ex-fiancé was one of the hardest things he'd ever do, but she was a grown woman. She could handle the guy. More important, if they were going to have a future together, he had to show Maddy he trusted her. Might as well start now. He reached for Annie, intent on taking her into the house, but froze when the lawyer pulled Maddy, *his Maddy,* into his arms and tried to kiss her.

His stomach churned with jealousy and rage. Maddy belonged to him. He had the door open and was halfway around the hood, when she turned her face away. The jerk's lips smacked nothing but air.

*Good for you, darlin'.*

He didn't want to leave her alone with the guy, but he wasn't sure he could control his temper if he stuck around. Hauling off and sucker punching the idiot was too damn tempting. Not trusting his emotions, he took extra care lifting his daughter from the seat and settling her in his arms. Annie went right on sleeping, snuggling her head under his chin. Absently, he rubbed her back, finding comfort in her warm little body curled against him.

Grinding his teeth, he left on the headlights, shut the cab door, then headed toward the Lexus. The city slicker threw his shoulders back and lifted his chin as if trying to appear taller. Jake still towered over the other guy by a good four inches. He couldn't tell for sure, but the lawyer didn't appear to have a whole lot of muscle under his thousand-dollar suit.

Jake thrust out his hand. The guy hesitated, then offered his own, and Jake bit back a grin when he felt the baby-smooth skin and thin fingers slide across his palm. He squeezed extra hard, and eased up only after the lawyer winced. "Jake Montgomery."

"Jonathon Carter."

Well, that was about all he had to say to the guy. He shifted toward Maddy. He wanted to insist she come inside with him but didn't. "You going to be all right out here?"

"I'll be fine. I won't be long."

He nodded, afraid that if he touched her he wouldn't let her go. He shot Carter a warning look. "I'll be right inside the door. Yell if you need me." All his strength was required for him to climb the porch steps, fit the key into the lock and enter the house. He flipped on the porch light. No telling what that idiot outside would do if he was left alone in the dark with Maddy.

He carried Annie upstairs, frustrated this Carter jerk put a damper on what was one of the best days Jake could remember in a long, long time. He laid his daughter on the bed, removed her clothes and smiled in spite of his bad mood at the chocolate-ice-cream stains on her shirt. Then he took her nightie from under the pillow and tugged it over two snarly pigtails. Next he hauled her to the bathroom and set her on the toilet. She swayed, before falling forward and resting her head against his shoulder. He'd just about given up that she'd pee, when he heard a faint tinkling. Relieved that she wouldn't be making any late-night visits to the bathroom, he carried her back to bed, tucked the sheet around her shoulders and kissed her grimy little forehead. After closing the door partway, he stood in the hall. Just stood, not knowing which way to go or what to do.

Feeling edgy, he went downstairs and looked out the foyer window. Madeline was waving her hands wildly around her head. Jake grinned. She was letting the lawyer have it with both barrels. When Carter stepped back, Jake knew Maddy wasn't in any physical danger from the guy.

He didn't want to get caught peeking out the window like some Peeping Tom so he went into the kitchen and walked out the back door. He sat on the stoop and waited, wondering what kind of crap Carter was filling Maddy's head with. He didn't have to wonder long. The wind shifted, carrying their raised voices around the side of the house and right to the back door. Good. He leaned against the porch step, crossed his arms behind his head, stretched his legs out and settled in real good.

"How in the world did you find me?" Madeline asked.

"Caller ID. Your father had Ms. Redding track down the number."

*Her father? When had Maddy called her father, and why hadn't she told him?*

"Forget how I found you, Madeline. The important thing is that I still love you. It didn't take long after leaving you in Vegas to realize that I made a terrible mistake."

*He called ditching her at the altar leaving?*

"You didn't leave me, Jonathon. You abandoned me. At our wedding."

*Go get him, honey.*

"Do you know how humiliated I was when

the minister escorted me out a side door and asked for the balance of the chapel fee?"

"Baby, I—"

"And if that wasn't bad enough, you checked out of the hotel and took *my* luggage with you. I drove clear across the state of Nevada in my wedding dress!"

"I wasn't thinking. I panicked. Hell, I didn't know which piece of luggage was mine and which was yours. Remember, you came over to my place and packed for me?"

The sound of crunching gravel reached Jake's ears and he pictured Carter pacing in front of Maddy, trying to come up with his next line of bull crap.

"If you had doubts, Jonathon, you should have told me."

"I didn't have doubts. Something unexpected occurred."

"Are you talking about the phone call you got right before we were supposed to leave for the chapel?"

"Yes."

"But you told me to go on ahead so they wouldn't give away our reservation."

"I know what I said, Madeline."

Jake tensed at the sharp note in Carter's voice. The guy was walking a thin line. One wrong move and he'd send the lawyer packing with or without Madeline's approval.

"Jonathon. You drove a long way to see me. At least tell me the truth."

"Look, baby. It's complicated."

*Baby?*

"Give me the condensed version."

"Why can't you just accept that I behaved like an idiot?"

*Idiot. Moron. Imbecile. Jerk-off. Butt-head.*

"Because I can't."

There was a long moment of silence and Jake wondered if Carter considered taking a hike over offering Maddy an explanation.

"Before our relationship became serious I was involved with another woman."

"What do you mean 'involved'?"

"A casual affair. A fling. I told this woman from the start that I wasn't interested in a serious relationship. Then I met you and stopped seeing her."

*Yeah, right.*

"She became jealous and threatened to make trouble for us. I thought if we went to Vegas and got married, she'd get it through her head that I didn't want anything to do with her anymore."

"So, why did she phone that day in Vegas?"

"To tell me I'd gotten her pregnant."

Maddy's gasp went straight to Jake's heart.

Damn, he wished he could take her in his arms right then and ease her pain.

"My God, Jonathon. Why didn't you say something? Why did you lead me to believe we were still getting married?"

"Because! This other woman means nothing to me. I refused to let her destroy our plans for the future."

"What future? Jonathon, another woman is having your baby."

"*Was* having my baby."

Jake held his breath. What the hell was Carter implying?

"Madeline, I flew back to Seattle and confronted the woman. Turns out she lied. She wasn't pregnant. She was hoping I'd give you up for her."

"What if she had been pregnant, Jonathon? What would you have done?"

"I'd have taken care of the problem, Madeline. I wasn't going to allow that woman to destroy my future. Our future."

"What do you mean, 'taken care of it'?"

"I would have given her money for an abortion."

Jake couldn't see Maddy's face, but he was sure Carter's words had shocked her.

"I was going to tell you everything, Madeline.

Then you didn't return to Seattle, and I didn't know where to find you."

Jake waited for Maddy to say something, but she remained silent.

"Madeline, I love you. You're the only woman for me."

*Don't believe him, honey. He's lying.*

"How do I know you're sincere?"

*C'mon, Maddy. Don't be fooled by this guy.*

"We make a great couple. I understand better than anyone how important your job is to you, and I'd never hold you back from making the most of your career."

"Is my father aware of this other woman? This mistake of yours?"

"No. No one knows, Madeline. I give you my promise, not a word of this will ever reach anybody's ears."

Silence. Loud enough to burst Jake's eardrums. Then hundreds of tiny voices in his head started shouting at him to storm around the house and plow his fist into Carter's face before Maddy got sucked in by more lies.

"I don't know what to say."

Jake groaned. *Say goodbye, Maddy.*

"What's the deal with this cowboy? Is this the *friend* you told your father you were visiting?"

"Yes."

"Is there something going on between you two?"

"Maybe."

*Maybe?* Jake's blood pressure soared.

"I can see where you might find a guy like him interesting in bed, but baby, what do you two have to talk about? The stock market? His portfolio? The latest art exhibit? Opera? Symphony? Get real, baby. You have nothing in common. You deserve someone in your own league, Madeline."

"That's not fair, Jonathon."

"Does your father know that you're shacking up with a cowboy?"

"Don't be crude. I'm not shacking up with him. I'm working as his daughter's nanny."

"Nanny?" Carter's laughter rumbled through the night air. "Good God, what would your father think? His daughter employed as a nanny."

"That's enough, Jonathon."

"Listen, I'm no saint. If you're willing to forgive and forget, then I can do the same with Billy the Kid in there."

Jake's face burned at the insult.

"Let's start over, Madeline. I found an apartment down by the water. Remember the flat we looked at in the Historic District before we set the wedding date? Well, I got it. It's ours now."

*A flat?* Jake turned and stared at the back of

the house. As far as houses went, his was nothing special. Put it up against an entire floor of a historic building and it didn't stand a chance.

"Jonathon—"

"Your father's worried about you."

*Smooth. Real smooth, bastard.* Changing the subject when he knew damn well Maddy was going to set him straight.

"Worried? He shouldn't be. I spoke to him and explained I needed time to think about the future."

"He's worried you've gone off the deep end. Wouldn't you be if your daughter suddenly ran off to be a nanny when she'd been making over two hundred thousand dollars a year as an advertising executive?"

Jake shot off the porch step and set a hand against his thumping chest. Maddy made over two hundred thousand a year? Good God. She was rich! He hadn't made that much in five years training horses.

"It isn't as if I've run off to the ends of the earth."

"You might as well have. This place is out in the middle of nowhere and it sure as hell isn't the Ritz-Carlton. C'mon, baby, you're used to fine dining, executive parties, Nordstrom's department store."

Jake hadn't pegged Maddy as the type to

while away a day shopping. She'd looked so fine in a pair of jeans and a T-shirt that it never occurred to him she might prefer satins and silks to denim.

"Oh, please. I know there's more to your showing up here at Jake's ranch than just wanting a second chance. Lay it on the line, Jonathon. What's the real reason you're here?"

The wind stopped blowing. The crickets stopped chirping. Even the owl in the tree by the barn ceased hooting. Jake waited, his body tense, as if Carter's answer had the power to determine his and Maddy's future.

"Your father offered me a partnership."

"Did he say you had to marry me to get the partnership?"

"It was implied. But that's not why I want to marry. I love you, baby."

*What a bunch of bull.*

"My father never mentioned any of this the last time I talked to him."

"He expected you'd come to your senses before now and return to Seattle on your own. Besides, I think he misses you."

"Hard to believe my father misses me that much. We've lived in the same city all our lives and sometimes we go a month without seeing each other."

"He isn't getting any younger, Madeline."

"He's not ill, is he?"

Jake held his breath, praying for Maddy's sake that the old man was as healthy as a thirty-year-old triathlete. Okay. He prayed for his sake, too.

"Not that I know of."

"I realize my father's concerned. But he doesn't always know what's best for me."

"And you believe *this* is best for you? Living in a run-down house in the desert, taking care of a kid who's not even yours and being a housekeeper for some country hick?"

The hairs on the back of Jake's neck stood on end and vibrated. He could picture the smug expression on Carter's face and his fists itched to pummel the guy's gut.

"I'm needed here."

Jake's heart stalled. *Oh, darlin'. You have no idea.*

"Madeline, I give you my word. If we marry, I swear I'll be totally committed to you and our marriage."

Jake rubbed his face, shocked by the sting biting the back of his eyes. He thought of a lifetime commitment to Maddy and couldn't imagine a better way to spend the rest of his years than being her man.

"I'm not the same girl you dated in Seattle, Jonathon. I've changed." Her soft chuckle filled the air. "I seriously doubt you'd approve of the new me."

"We meant something to each other once. Don't we deserve a second chance before you throw away our future?"

She didn't answer. *What are you thinking, Maddy?*

"Go pack your things. Let me take you home, so your father can see for himself that you're fine."

"Jonathon, this is all too sudden."

"Don't give up on us, baby."

*Damn, but the guy sounded like a whining kid.*

"At least say you'll think about it. We were together almost a year. That's something you shouldn't walk away from without giving it serious consideration."

*Don't listen to him, Maddy. He didn't consider anything when he left you high and dry in Vegas.*

"I don't know, Jonathon."

"You're being unreasonable, Madeline. You're not the type of person who would be happy living like this for very long."

"I can decide for myself what will make me happy."

"I'm not leaving until you promise me you'll consider what I've said."

If Maddy couldn't get Carter to leave, Jake would step in and tell the guy he'd worn out his welcome. And have a hell of a good time doing it.

"All right. Fine. I'll take into account everything you said. But I'm warning you right now—I made a commitment to watch over Annie until Jake finishes training the horses. I won't be returning to Seattle until the end of August."

"But—"

"No, Jonathon. I committed to this and I'm going to see it through."

"What should I tell your father?"

"I'll call him tomorrow and explain."

Jake couldn't listen anymore. On the verge of being physically ill, he vaulted to the top of the porch and rushed into the house. He headed straight to his office, where he was sure he'd stashed an old bottle of Jack Daniel's somewhere in one of the desk drawers.

Looked as though he'd be having his talk with the bottle tonight, not Maddy. No need to make a fool of himself and confess his feelings for her, when she planned to run back to that fool Carter at the end of the summer.

*Whoa there, buddy. Why the hell are you so miffed that she's willing to consider getting back together with her ex-fiancé? Shoot, you'd planned to make her leave at the end of the summer, anyway.*

Because!

Because he'd lied to himself when he thought he could just get by with telling Maddy he loved her. Because he'd tried to convince himself that letting Maddy go at the end of the summer was best for everyone. Maddy. Him. Annie.

But it wasn't. For one crazy moment, he'd actually thought happiness might be within his reach.

For one crazy moment, Jake had actually thought of asking Maddy to stay.

Forever.

As SOON AS the red taillights of Jonathon's Lexus disappeared over a swell in the dirt-packed road, Madeline marched over to Jake's truck and shut off the headlights. She stood cloaked in darkness, surrounded by a symphony of cricket chirps, feeling only relief at her ex-fiancé's departure.

She'd lied to Jonathon. She had no intention of contemplating a future with him. Any man who would even consider ridding his life of his own child because it interfered with his career plans was someone she wanted nothing to do with.

He must have assumed she was as dense as a

pine forest if he believed she would marry him now. He deserved a kick in the pants. Preferably the front of his pants. Jonathon was and always would be a schmuck.

Part of her resented his untimely intrusion, yet part of her felt grateful. Seeing her ex-fiancé again, listening to his voice, feeling his fingers on her skin when he'd clutched her hand, put to rest any lingering feelings she may have unknowingly harbored for him.

Jonathon Carter wasn't half the man Jake Montgomery was. What she felt for the cowboy was deeper, richer, more enduring than anything she could have hoped to feel for her ex-fiancé. Madeline lifted her face, stared at the stars glittering in the sky and breathed in a lungful of damp, earthy country.

This was where she belonged. In her heart, this was home now. Tonight, she'd do her best to convince Jake that she could be happy here with him.

She headed for the house, smiling at the memory of Jake's tight jaw and flashing eyes before he'd taken Annie into the house earlier. He'd reminded her of a rottweiler straining at the leash.

*Good.* She could use all the help she could get when it came to persuading the stubborn man she was everything he needed. Even if that help came in the form of jealousy.

She stepped through the front door, a little disappointed to find the foyer empty. She could have sworn she'd seen his figure in the window earlier. A sudden picture of him upstairs, lying in wait on the bed wearing only his boots, came to her mind. She cupped a hand over her mouth to stifle the giggle that bubbled in her throat. Maybe she'd share the fantasy with him later tonight.

She flipped off the foyer light, went upstairs, peeked in on Annie, then padded to Jake's bedroom. Here, she stood outside the closed door, one hand pressing against the fluttering excitement in her belly, the other raised in the air. She tapped. "Jake?"

No answer. She turned the knob and poked her head around the door. The hall light illuminated the dark room enough for her to see the bed hadn't been disturbed. If he wasn't in the house there was only one place he could be—the barn. He was probably grumbling to the horses that his plans for the evening had been rudely interrupted by her ex-fiancé.

She could sympathize with Jake, but the night was still young. And she couldn't forget that he'd wanted to tell her something. Something she hoped had to do with their future.

She headed out the door and across the yard. She knew just how to tease Jake back into an ardent mood. She'd kiss him. All out. And she would do that little wiggle with her tongue, which always made him groan.

The barn was dim, only one light turned on. She'd expected him to be cleaning stalls or building a new stall. Something that involved a lot of pounding and cussing. "Jake?" she called softly. No answer. Had he taken one of the horses and ridden off in the dark? She didn't know much about horses, but riding them in the dark couldn't be safe.

Her gaze slid by every stall, and noted that all the horses were accounted for. Not until her eyes landed on the last stall in the back did she see the stream of light spilling out from under the door of the tack room.

The memory of making love with Jake in that room came back with stunning clarity. Her skin prickled. Her heart raced. Her head hummed. Visions of his body pressing into hers, his breath in her ear, his hand between her thighs, coaxing, seducing, making her beg.

She walked quietly through the barn, careful not to disturb the horses. She wished she looked more presentable, wished she'd taken the time to clean up before coming to him, then she remembered the hose in the tack room and smiled. Maybe they could help wash each other.

She stopped in front of the closed door and took a deep breath. Without announcing her presence, she entered the room. Jake sat on a hay bale, his back to her, shoulders slumped, hands dangling between his thighs.

"Jake?"

His head snapped up, but he didn't turn and look at her. A good ten seconds passed before he spoke. "Go to bed, Maddy."

*Hmm.* Not exactly the loving reception she'd hoped for. Lord, the man was stubborn. She obviously had her work cut out for her if she planned on salvaging the night. One way or another she'd break down his defenses. Right now, she wanted to forget about Jonathon, forget about her father, her job, everything. Everything but Jake.

She crossed the room and set her hands on his shoulders. He stiffened but didn't pull away. Gently, she massaged the knots in his back. After several minutes, his muscles relaxed, and she leaned forward, rubbing her breasts against his shirt, touching her lips to his temple. She sucked in a quiet breath at the sight of the bottle of liquor dangling from his fingertips. The half-empty bottle of booze.

"Are you drunk, Jake?"

"I'm trying, Maddy. Damn, but I'm trying."

She tamped down the urge to yell in frustration. Instead, she moved in front of him and knelt at his feet. "What do you mean you're trying, cowboy? I thought we had plans to…to—"

"Screw?"

She swallowed a gasp at his crude remark. If he were any other man he'd have blown off Jonathon's unexpected visit. But Jake wasn't just any man. He was a cowboy. A breed of men who lived their lives by a set of values and a code of honor as old as the West. She had a feeling it would take some doing to prove to Jake she was really over Jonathon.

He swayed as he tipped the bottle to his lips.

Her eyes narrowed. "You *are* drunk."

He wiped his hand across his chin, where a drop of amber liquid clung. "I wish."

She snatched the bottle from his grasp.

"Hey, give that back."

She dumped the remaining whiskey down the drain of the tack-room sink, then tossed the bottle into the garbage bucket.

He popped off the hay bale like a jack-in-the-box and moved toward her. Rather, swayed toward her. "You got a lot of nerve, woman. Coming in here and disturbing a man when he's feeling sorry for himself."

She retreated a step, but the sink got in her way.

He glowered over her, his eyes hot with anger.

If he thought he could intimidate her, he had another think coming. She poked a finger in his chest. "Don't you dare take that tone with me, Jake Montgomery. We had a date to make love tonight, and you're standing me up. I want to know why."

His eyes slammed shut, then a moment later he shook his head and crushed her to him.

Madeline could feel the desperation pouring off his body as he rocked her in his arms. There was something final about the way he held her. Fear made her lungs burn. She wiggled against his hold, but his arms were like steel bands around her rib cage. "You're scaring me, Jake."

He bent his head, nuzzling her neck with his nose, nibbling the underside of her chin, dipping the tip of his tongue into her ear. Her knees collapsed, and she clutched his upper arms to steady herself. Her head lolled back as his hands cupped her face and he sprinkled tender kisses across her forehead, the bridge of her nose, her cheeks, chin and eyelids.

When his mouth finally settled over hers the kiss wasn't at all what she expected. She wanted deep, wet and hot. She got soft, slow and chaste.

Panic like she'd never known stung her eyes as she thrust her tongue inside his mouth, begging for more. Begging him to take her. But he denied her.

He tore his mouth from hers and stumbled back. The foot of space between their bodies felt more like an abyss. His blank gaze settled on her face. "We can't, Maddy." His chest shuddered as he struggled to control his breathing.

"Can't what? Make love?" She reached out with one hand, but he took another step back, the movement sending a piercing pain through her heart.

"It won't work."

Her lungs tightened until it hurt to breathe. "If this is about Jonathon's visit...let me reassure you—"

"It's not about Carter. It's about me, Maddy." He shoved a hand through his hair and turned his back to her.

"I don't understand."

The silence went on until she thought the air in the room might splinter if either of them spoke. Refusing to have a conversation with his back, she marched around him. "If you're dumping me, at least have the guts to do it to my face."

His shoulders stiffened. Good. If they were going to sling arrows, she deserved a couple of direct hits, too. Slowly, as if each movement caused great pain, he lifted his head. His blue gaze, clouded with agony, clung to hers, and she held her breath, battling the fierce sting in her own eyes. *Oh, no, Jake. Please, no.*

"You're an incredible woman, Maddy. A woman any man would feel honored to call his own."

"Any man but you?"

He winced.

Another arrow. Another direct hit. How come it didn't bring her pleasure?

"You deserve better than me."

"Why do I have a suspicion this has nothing to do with you believing I'm too good for you?"

He pressed his lips into a tight line and stared over her shoulder. "You deserve more than a horse trainer, trying to make a name for himself on a struggling ranch."

"You're lying. This isn't about the differences in our background."

"Leave it alone, Maddy."

"I never thought you were a coward."

The bleak look in his eyes broke her heart.

"Maybe you're right. Maybe I do deserve better."

His eyes snapped at the blunt statement. Thank God the wounds weren't real, or he'd be bleeding like a stuck pig right now. *Please say you love me, Jake.*

He drew himself up to his imposing six-three height. "Leaving…leaving tomorrow would be best."

A cold chill rattled Madeline's bones. She didn't know if she could take much more, but she refused to give up without a fight. "Best for who? You, me or Annie?"

He rubbed his forehead and stared at the concrete floor. "You're not going to make this easy, are you?"

"Should I?" Startled by the rasp in her voice, she swallowed hard, trying to dislodge the thick lump in her throat.

"Okay. We'll do this your way, Maddy. I want you to leave because of me. I don't want a future with you. I apologize if I've led you on."

She couldn't breathe. Her lungs burned and everything in the room tilted. Not even standing in the wedding chapel, waiting in her gown for her no-show groom, hurt this much. *Because you never loved Jonathon.*

She hadn't loved her former fiancé in the all-consuming, everything-I-am, can't-live-without-you kind of way she loved the stubborn cowboy standing five feet away. It wasn't easy, but she forced the words past her frozen lips. "What about Annie?"

He shrugged. "I'll tell her something."

"How about the truth? That you got what you wanted from me and now you don't want me hanging around."

His gaze slid away from hers. "Don't, Maddy. Please."

Hurting more than she ever thought she could, she moved closer to the big lug. His eyes refused to meet hers, so she pressed her fingers to his cheek and applied enough pressure until he turned his face toward her.

"I didn't realize it right away, but I fell in love with you the first time I saw you, stomping toward me with a fierce scowl on your face and maybe even a hint of amusement in your eyes at finding a woman in a wedding gown caught on your barbed-wire fence."

She stroked the beard stubble along his jaw and willed the tears away. "Even though you were angry and frustrated, your hands were gentle on my body, gentle with my dress. I knew right then that underneath all that macho-cowboy bluster was a man capable of real feelings."

He shut his eyes, but he didn't pull away from her hand.

"I'd just been dumped by my fiancé, yet all I could think about was the way my heart tripped over itself every time our eyes met."

"Stop." He stepped out of reach and backed farther into the corner.

Madeline hugged herself as raw grief filled her, making her limbs tremble and her teeth chatter. "I don't know what to do, Jake. How to make you believe that the love I feel for you is real, deep, the forever kind." She waved a hand around her head. "I can't imagine my life anywhere but here. With you and Annie."

His face remained expressionless. Was he made of stone? If not for the dark pain in his gaze, she would have thought her words hadn't affected him at all.

"If this is about your marriage to Sara, then we need to talk about it. I don't believe she would want you to punish yourself the rest of your life. Maybe you weren't everything she needed in a husband. But if you're half the man I know you are—"

"You know nothing about the man I am."

"I know you're kind, caring, maybe a little too headstrong—"

"Maddy, I killed my wife."

## Chapter Twelve

Madeline's breath caught in her throat and she struggled to get air into her lungs. He killed his wife? *No!* The Jake she knew wasn't capable of murder. "Look at me."

Slowly, he shifted his gaze to her face, and what she saw made her want to burst into tears. Desolation. Anguish. Pain so intense she found it hard to believe he hadn't crumbled to the floor. "You don't have the eyes of a killer."

A sad, faraway expression came over his face. "I didn't stab Sara or shoot her. But what I did killed her just the same."

"Tell me what happened, Jake. You can't throw something like that at me and expect me to…to… I don't know! Just walk away? I deserve an explanation."

He shook his head. "It doesn't matter what happened, Maddy. Nothing I say will change the fact that I'm not good enough for you. You deserve better than me."

"Shouldn't I be the one to decide if I deserve you or not?" Her legs threatened to give out on her, so she crossed the room and sat on the hay bale. She waited, listening to his labored breathing, feeling his pain press in on her.

"You won't leave until I confess it all, will you?"

Her head came up. "No. I won't."

A rush of air escaped his lungs. "Fine. We'll do this your way." He stood with his back to her in the doorway and stared out into the barn's interior. "I didn't press Sara for sex while she was carrying Annie. I could tell she was still dealing with the rape. Every time I touched her arm, or grabbed her hand, she'd jump a foot off the floor."

Madeline wanted to go to him. Hug him. Instead, she raised her feet and balanced them on the edge of the bale, then wrapped her arms around her knees and settled for hugging herself.

"After Annie was born, I waited six months. Then I tried talking to her about sex. I wanted her to understand I'd be careful. I'd go slow and stop if she wanted me to." He cleared his throat. "She asked for more time."

He shoved a hand through his hair and turned around, his eyes bright with emotion. "I waited two years, Maddy. Two years after Annie was born and I never cheated on Sara that whole time."

Madeline's heart clenched.

"Then one day I was filling the truck with gas and this pretty, young girl pulled into the station. It hit me that I hadn't had sex in almost three years. I got mad. Mad at myself. Mad at Sara. Mad that I couldn't control my body's reaction to a pretty girl."

Madeline was afraid to say anything for fear he'd stop talking. She sensed that he'd been holding this inside far too long, that it had eaten a hole right through his heart.

"I waited until Annie was sleeping that night. I asked Sara if I could just hold her in bed."

Madeline ignored the tear that slid down her face and pooled in the corner of her mouth.

"At first she let me put my arms around her. But when I tried to kiss her, she pushed me away."

*Oh, Jake.*

"I wouldn't let her go. I kept kissing her. Telling her it would be okay. Telling her I couldn't wait any longer." He scrubbed viciously at the wetness on his face. "I swear to God, Maddy, I didn't hear her tell me to stop. I didn't even know she was crying." He sucked in a ragged breath and punched the door frame with his fist. "I didn't know!"

Madeline cringed. Jake's misery went so deep he hadn't even felt the blow against his hand.

"Sara panicked and grabbed the bedside lamp. She hit me on the head." He rubbed the skin near his hairline. "She accused me of being no better than the guy who had raped her."

Madeline lost the battle with her emotions and cried soundlessly.

"I had to get out of there. I couldn't trust myself around her. And the look in Sara's eyes... I've never seen such fear in a woman's eyes before. I packed a bag and took off. I didn't know where I was going or how long I'd stay away. I just knew I couldn't be in that house with Sara, not after what I'd almost done to her."

"It's understandable—"

He held up a hand. "I was gone two weeks, Maddy. During that time an ice storm hit the area. One of the horses got loose and ended up getting stuck in the stream behind the barn. Sara worked for hours trying to get the horse free. It was my first stud and she was aware that horse meant the world to me. She fell into the icy stream, soaking her clothes. But she stayed there until she got the horse out."

Jake leaned against the wall and stared at the floor. "When I returned with my tail between my legs, she was sicker than a dog. She wouldn't see a doctor. Then she fainted dead away at the sink a few days later and I rushed her to the E.R. She had severe pneumonia and her lungs were more than half full of fluid."

He hung his head. "I begged her for forgiveness. Begged her to fight to live. Told her Annie needed her. Promised I'd never touch her again if she'd just get well." He flung his head back, knocking it roughly against the wall. "She died two days later."

Madeline couldn't speak. She tried to swallow the lump lodged in her throat, but it wouldn't budge.

"Can't you see, Maddy? Sara trusted me to take care of her. I violated that trust in the worst way. Then I abandoned her."

Madeline was off the hay bale in an instant. "You're being too hard on yourself, Jake."

His laugh sounded sinister. "I'm not being hard enough. Because of me, my daughter doesn't have a mother."

Madeline wanted desperately to touch him but feared if she did he'd storm off and she'd lose any chance at making him see sense. "Sara was an adult, Jake. Maybe things did get out of hand that night between the two of you. But your running off didn't kill Sara. We all get sick at one time or another. Sara chose not to see a doctor when she became ill."

"But I wasn't there to drive her to the doctor."

"Did you leave her without a vehicle to drive?"

"No. There was an old truck in the barn that was drivable."

"And she could have called Gladys for help. Don't you see? Your abandoning her didn't make her lose the will to live. Sara wanted to die. Sometimes people are so frail inside that no matter how much you help them or love them, they just can't go on."

"I wish I could believe that, Maddy. God, how I wish I could."

"I'm nothing like Sara. I'm not frail, Jake. I don't need your protection. I don't need you to take care of me. I just need you to love me. Don't throw away what we have because you think you deserve to be punished for the rest of your life."

"It's not that easy."

She felt anger slowly replace sympathy for Jake. Why couldn't she make the stubborn cowboy admit how wrong he was? "Do you still want me to go?"

He gazed at her face as if trying to memorize her features. "Yes." His voice rasped. "I want you to go."

She dug deep down inside herself and found the courage to keep from falling at his feet and begging him to change his mind. "Promise me one thing."

His eyebrows dipped.

She gently touched his face. "Promise me that one day you'll find a way to forgive yourself. For your sake, Jake. And for Annie's, too."

He tore his gaze from her face. "What do you want me to tell Annie?"

"Tell her that her father needs to learn that love can heal even the deepest wounds."

Feeling close to tears again, Madeline left the barn and returned to the house. Seattle was a long way away. She might as well get on the road tonight.

"YOU'RE LATE." JAKE jammed the Stetson on his head and clamped his lips together to keep from spewing a mouthful of obscenities.

"You said eight o'clock, Mr. Montgomery." Harriet Blecker's niece, Tiffany, glanced at her watch. "Oops." Her glossy watermelon-colored lips curved in a smile as she dipped her head to one side, causing her long blond hair to slide over one eye.

At first, her blunt attempts at seduction had amused Jake. He'd chalked up the girl's behavior to teenage hormones. But after a week of dodging accidental touches and rubs, seeing her arms and legs turn blue because her clothes were so tight, of Annie complaining that she didn't play with her the way Madeline had, he'd about had it.

Tiffany was fifty minutes late, and he didn't have the time or the patience for her adolescent sex games. He told himself the little rodeo-groupie-in-training was the reason for the dark cloud hanging over his head this morning, but he knew it was a lie. His grumpy mood had nothing to do with Annie's new sitter and everything to do with missing Maddy.

She'd been gone two weeks, but it felt like a hundred years.

"I'll be fixing the fence this morning." At 5:00 a.m., a hand from the Winston ranch had called to give him a heads-up on a break in the fence line running along Jake's property. The cowboy had chuckled and said the section was the exact spot Jake had found his barbed-wire bride.

Well, Maddy wasn't *his* bride anymore.

He dreaded going back to the place he'd first met Maddy. The pain of her leaving was still too fresh, too acute. If not for Cyclone roaming that pasture, he'd have let the downed fence lie until he was good and ready to fix it. Like, fifteen years from now. But he couldn't afford a lawsuit if the mangy bull got it in his thick skull to take off and terrorize the good citizens of Ridge City or some unsuspecting tourist passing through. He snatched the truck keys from the hook by the back door. "Annie's watching TV. Keep her in the house until I get back."

He didn't wait for Tiffany's usual "You be careful now, Mr. Montgomery," before storming out the back door. He must have a ton of dead brain cells to have hired the girl to care for his daughter the rest of the summer.

But what was he supposed to do when he had a corral full of horses to train, and Maddy had run out on him and Annie? *Whoa there, buddy. She didn't run out on you. You ran her off.*

He hopped into the truck, gunned the engine and sped down the road, tires spitting up gravel. He knew he couldn't have forever with Maddy, but why hadn't she fought him harder? He'd wanted her to refuse to leave. The fact that she'd left without much of a fight told him where he stood with her.

His eyes burned at the memory of seeing her stow her few belongings in the rental car that night. She hadn't bothered to search him out to say goodbye. So he'd stood in the barn doorway, feeling as though the world had stopped revolving, as she drove out of his and Annie's lives. He remembered grabbing on to his anger and holding it close. Not until Annie came down for breakfast the next morning did he almost fall apart.

The pain didn't lessen with each passing hour, passing day, as he'd thought it would. He'd been worried as hell ever since she'd driven away. For three days he'd wondered if she'd made it back to Seattle safely. He'd called Directory Assistance and discovered there were over one hundred and fifty Tates in the Greater Seattle Area. Then he'd remembered the name of the ad agency she worked for. The uppity receptionist had answered the phone, but wouldn't give out any information on their employees.

What would he have said to Maddy if he'd been able to talk with her? *I'm sorry? I need you to watch Annie? I want you back, but not forever?*

He'd thought of calling her father's law firm but chickened out twice after dialing the number. In truth, he'd been afraid to find out that she'd gone back to her idiot ex-fiancé, Jonathon.

Jake reached the end of the road, turned right onto the highway and headed north. The break in the fence was a ten-minute drive away.

He eyed the land around him, waiting to feel comfort in the vast nothingness that had drawn him here years earlier. He'd found refuge for himself and Sara in the miles and miles of open space. But Sara was gone now. And suddenly all this nothingness felt more like a prison than a haven.

Sara's death had gutted him emotionally. Years of pretending that eventually everything would be okay had come crashing down on top of him like a rockslide. He'd wandered around in a daze for a week. After the first seven days, the numbness had worn off and the guilt had threatened to suffocate him. Then Annie had quit talking, and blaming himself, he'd fallen into deeper despair.

He'd been so sure he'd feel the same deep despair, guilt and pain when Maddy left. Damned if anything ever went as expected.

First, Annie didn't clam up the way he'd feared. Instead, she'd fussed at him for running her nanny off, until he'd felt lower than pond scum. Second, the guilt he'd expected never came. Instead, frustration ate at his insides until he'd finished off a bottle of antacid tablets in five days.

Third, he'd felt anger. At himself, for lacking the guts to stand up for what he wanted. Then at Maddy, for giving up on him so easily when he got a little bullheaded. And at Sara, for not wanting to live.

He shook aside his jumbled thoughts and eased the truck over to the shoulder of the road near the fence break. After grabbing the wire cutters and a pair of gloves, he headed toward the gaping hole.

*How in the hell had* this *happened?* He examined the fence, noticing three strings of rusted barbed wire had all decayed and broken, bringing down a whole section. He returned to the truck for new wire, and after a half hour of twisting and tugging, he'd fixed the fence.

As he stepped back to survey his work, he caught a movement out of the corner of his eye. Fifty yards away, Cyclone stood watching.

"Come on, you old bastard. Let's see if you can get through this."

Snot hanging from his nose, the bull pawed the ground, snorted, then trotted toward the fence. Every couple of yards the animal picked up speed.

Well, hell. He hadn't really meant it.

Confident the wire would hold, but not stupid, Jake took several steps back. The bull gained speed, his hooves pounding the dry ground, kicking up clouds of dust.

Because Jake was so sure the bull would lock his legs and skid to a halt, a second passed before he reacted. The beast was twenty feet away before he realized the animal had no intention of stopping. He grabbed his tools and hit the ground running.

He just cleared the front end of the truck,

when the bull turned at the last second, preventing himself from being gored by the barbs on the wire. The animal spun in a tight circle, kicking up dirt and grass, flinging his tail high in the air and bellowing something fierce.

Dumbfounded, Jake watched the crazy creature. After thirty seconds the bull settled down and stared at him, large nostrils flaring, white foam drooling from his mouth.

The damn bull was psycho. He should get rid of the animal, but he'd promised the old man he'd bought the ranch from that he wouldn't put him down. That he'd let him die of natural causes. He figured the bull's volatile behavior was a way of expressing sorrow at the previous owner's disappearance.

"Git! Go on, now!" He waved a work glove in the air. Cyclone stared at him for a few seconds, then ambled away, back toward the old oak five hundred yards out. Jake walked a quarter mile in each direction, checking the fence, tightening the places that sagged a little too much.

He was on his way back to the truck, when he noticed Cyclone headed his way again, this time at an easy trot. Jake's boots cemented to the ground, and he couldn't have moved if his life depended on it. Dangling from the bull's mouth, dirty, dingy and torn, was the skirt from Maddy's wedding gown.

*Well, I'll be.*

Cyclone stopped three feet from the fence. Cautiously, Jake moved closer. The animal remained motionless; didn't even blink. An eerie feeling slithered down Jake's back. The bull almost seemed to be telling him something. He braced his feet and reached over the fence until he clutched a fistful of the satin material, careful to lock his knees and keep his thigh muscles bunched in readiness should Cyclone toss his head and try to pull him over the fence. Jake gave one firm tug on the material, and to his amazement the bull opened his mouth and let go.

*If that don't beat all.*

Jake stepped back, his gaze shifting from the filthy material, covered in bull spit, to the old cantankerous beast with a docile look in his eye. His chest tightened unexpectedly at the feel of the satin material in his hands.

"You think I'm crazy for letting her go, don't you?"

He remembered the morning he'd found Maddy strung up on the fence line. She'd been something else. All fiery hair and snapping green eyes. He'd barely managed to keep his eyeballs from popping when he saw all that glory hanging out of her dress in front of God and every cowboy within a hundred miles.

His chest rumbled with a silent chuckle. She'd wanted so badly to save her wedding gown. Man, had she been ticked when he'd tugged her right out of the skirt and Cyclone had trotted off with it.

A spasm gripped his chest and the material blurred before his eyes. *Damn.* He did not need Maddy. He might *want* her, but he didn't *need* her.

He rubbed a hand over his face, cursing the wetness clinging to his fingertips, and took a deep shuddering breath—not an easy thing to do when his chest felt as if it had been split open with an ax. Desperation filled him. The thought of waking up the rest of his days without Maddy to go through life with sent a bolt of pain through his body, so intense it threatened to knock his legs right out from under him.

Deep in his heart, Jake knew Maddy was the one person who could make him whole again. With her love, he could find the courage to let go of the past. With her guidance, he believed he could be the kind of father Annie deserved, the kind of husband Maddy needed, the kind of man he'd always hoped to be.

He remembered Maddy's words. Was it possible that he hadn't failed Sara? That she had failed herself? For most of their marriage, he'd been there for his wife, but never once had Sara reached out to him.

*Maddy reached out to you. And you sent her away.*

He stared down the road. Life was a crapshoot. Who'd have thought going back to his hometown to bury his parents would turn into getting married, buying a ranch and becoming a father to a child who wasn't his? Who'd have believed he'd wake up one morning and find a bride caught on his barbed-wire fence?

And who'd have figured he'd go and fall in love with that bride? A woman so different from him, yet without her he didn't feel complete.

There were some things in life he couldn't control—Sara's happiness for one. Happiness came from within. Right now, Jake had to admit he wasn't happy. Not without Maddy in his life. And he was sure *she* needed *him,* but not in the way Sara had. All Maddy needed or wanted from him was his love. It couldn't get any simpler than that.

He glanced down at the cloth, then back at the bull. "Cyclone, if this is your way of telling me what a fool I've been, then thank you." He tossed the material back over the fence. The bull nabbed it with a horn and trotted away.

Jake headed back to the ranch. He and Annie had some talking to do…and then some packing.

## Chapter Thirteen

"Jonathon says you're being unreasonable. That you won't give him a chance."

Madeline's shoulders stiffened at the sound of her father's voice. She stood in her old bedroom of her father's home, surrounded by boxes, mounds of clothes, stacks of books, her Andy Warhol painting and other personal items she'd planned to store there until after her and Jonathon's wedding in November. Had it only been three weeks ago that she'd allowed Jake to run her off the ranch? The end of July was already near, but it seemed as if time had crawled to a stop after she'd returned to Seattle.

"I am not being unreasonable." A sharp pain clutched her heart at the worn look in her father's age-weary eyes as he leaned against the wall just inside the door. His rumpled suit and mussed hair gave her pause. She'd never seen her father rumpled before. She wondered if there were problems at the law firm.

"You won't return his calls, Madeline. That's not being reasonable. The man is walking around in a daze at the office."

"Jonathon is a poor loser. He doesn't like other people calling the shots."

A grin tugged at the corner of her father's stern mouth. "Isn't that the pot calling the kettle black?"

She blushed. She shouldn't have run off at the mouth about Jake sending her packing when she'd arrived home a week ago. No wonder her father thought she was a hypocrite.

"Mind if I come in?"

"Have a seat." She gestured to the bed. "If you can find one, that is." She shoved a pile of sweaters out of the way.

For several minutes she sorted her clothes, waiting for her father to say what was on his mind.

He sighed heavily. "You're just like your mother."

Madeline's hands froze as she reached for another box to put books in. Her father never talked about her mother. When she'd been younger, she'd asked questions: What was her mother's favorite color? Her favorite food? Her favorite movie? Her father had always smiled indulgently, patted her head and told her to go play. Eager now to hear what was on his mind, yet afraid her enthusiasm might scare him off, she settled for a noncommittal shrug. "How so?"

He pointed to the boxes full of books near the window. "She loved books. Any kind. Before you were born, she'd drag me into every antiques shop up and down the coast. She'd buy old diaries, how-to books, out-of-date medical manuals."

The thought of her mother—any woman, for that matter—tugging her stubborn father into dusty, dark antiques shops made her smile. "I love books, but I draw the line at reading diaries. I have enough problems of my own. I don't want to read about someone else's. Besides, I'd rather believe most people live happy lives."

Her father stared down at his shoes as if he found the design in the leather stitching fascinating. She studied him with veiled eyes, noting he had more gray hair along the sides and on top than he'd had a few months ago. The crow's-feet around his eyes were a little deeper, as were the lines alongside his mouth. Still, her father was a handsome, distinguished-looking man. His only problem was that he worked too hard.

"How come you never remarried, Father?"

His head snapped up and he stared at her in stunned surprise. "You dated a few women when I was younger. Wasn't one of them a lawyer, also? You two would have been a good match."

He rubbed his forehead and smiled sadly. "I've been thinking about this since you came back from Nevada."

"Thinking about marrying?"

"Thinking I owe you an apology."

"An apology? For what?" Her father had never apologized for anything in his life.

"For not being a good father all these years."

Her heart hammered in her chest as she watched her father grow older, more frail, right before her eyes. She set the box she was holding on the floor, then sat beside him on the bed.

"I blamed you for her death those first couple of years. It was wrong, and I'm sure your mother would be awfully upset if she knew how little attention I gave you growing up." His eyes shimmered with pain. "You look just like her."

"Oh, Dad." After a statement like that, calling him "Father" suddenly seemed too stuffy. The little girl inside her broke free, and she flung her arms around his neck, hugging him hard.

"It's probably difficult to believe, but I was a much different man when I married your mother. Rose was the love of my life. She brought joy and happiness to my world." He cleared his throat, gazing sightlessly across the room. "She was everything to me, Madeline.

My heart and soul. When she died…something inside me died with her. I changed after that. Threw myself into the practice, hoping the pain would go away. It worked during the day. But then I'd come home and see you, and the hurt would start all over. So I stayed late at the office, traveled more often." His eyes met hers and she sucked in a quiet breath at the tears welling in them.

"It's okay, Dad." She squeezed his hand.

He shook his head. "No, it's not okay, sweetheart. What is it you younger people say? I *sucked* at being a father?"

Madeline laughed and hugged him again. They sat in companionable silence for a minute, before she asked, "Were you happy that she got pregnant with me?" She held her breath, waiting for an answer. Her birth had caused her mother's death. Until now she hadn't realized how important his answer was to her.

For the first time in a long time her father grinned. A wide, open smile that lit up his eyes and made him appear ten years younger. "She was happy. So happy when she found out she was expecting you. She wanted several children, and she would have been a wonderful mother."

He stared down at his hands, his smile slipping. "How could I not love you? You're the greatest gift your mother could have given me to remind me of the love we shared for each other."

Madeline wiped her eyes. They should have had this talk years ago. They might have been so much closer had they shared their feelings.

Her father grasped her hands and held them. "I did you a great disservice, Madeline. The love I felt for your mother was so all-consuming that when she died...well, I didn't know how to handle my grief. Ignoring you most of the time, instead of being reminded of your mother every time I saw you was easier."

He brushed a hand down her hair. "Later, when you reached your adult years, the only way I could think to make it up to you was to protect you from ever having to go through what I did with your mother. I thought that if I could keep you from falling in love with a man, I could spare you much pain and hurt."

"Is that why you encouraged me to date Jonathon?"

He nodded. "I could tell when the two of you were together that you didn't love him. But he was a bright young man with a promising career ahead of him. It seemed a good match."

"And now?"

"And now, young lady, the way you've been moping around the house reminds me of the way I felt the first time your mother turned me down for a date."

Madeline laughed. "She turned you down?"

"Right in front of the entire rugby team." He chuckled, and his eyes sparkled. "Getting your mother to give me a chance took a lot of convincing. But it was love at first sight."

Madeline sighed. "Yeah, I know the feeling."

"I was wrong to try to force you to marry Jonathon. Your running off made me realize how lucky and blessed I was to have experienced true love at least once in my life. My time with your mother was short. But some people don't even get that."

Her father opened his arms and Madeline leaned in for another hug. "You're positive you're in love with this cowboy?"

She sniffed. "Yes, I love the blasted stubborn man." She lifted her head from his shoulder. "I don't think I can live without him, Dad."

He smiled. "If you love this man half as much as I loved your mother, then you have my blessing to go back there and try to change his mind about you."

Joy burst inside her at his words.

"Your mother made some things for you before you were born. I kept them in a cedar chest. It's in the attic. She would have liked for you to have had those things when you were younger."

His expression was again sad. "I couldn't stand having them around, honey. Too many reminders. So I packed them all away."

"I'm glad you saved them, Dad."

His face brightened. "I believe there's a wedding gown in that chest."

"Good. I'm going to need that gown where I'm going." The tears started again.

"You've never talked about retirement. Would you consider that in the near future?"

He stared out the window across the room. "What would I do with myself if I didn't have the office to go to every day?"

She squeezed his arm. "You could start doing things men your age do all over the world."

He smiled. "What sort of things do men my age do?"

"Well, they go fishing. They take their grandchildren to Walt Disney World. They chase after widowed women."

"Widows!" He shuddered.

"Dad, I know you loved Mom. But she'd never want you to spend your entire life alone. Somewhere out there is a woman who needs you as much as you need her."

His eyes softened. "Your mother was a romantic, too. God, but I miss her." They hugged again, and this time her father didn't stiffen quite as much as he had earlier. The hugs would get easier with time.

"Dad? I think you'd like Jake. Would you—I mean, do you think you could—"

"When do we leave, honey?"

"PULL OFF OVER HERE, DAD." Madeline pointed to the side of the road.

Richard Tate guided his daughter's brand-new Suburban to the shoulder of the deserted Nevada highway, put it in Park, but left the engine on in order to keep the air-conditioning running. It was midmorning, but already the temperature was over ninety degrees.

"This is where you're going to live, Madeline?"

She smiled at the disbelief in her father's voice as he stared out the windshield at the vast nothingness spread out before them.

"Isn't it beautiful? Oh, there's Cyclone!" The rangy bull stood on the other side of the barbed-wire fence, watching them.

"What *is* that thing?"

"Jake's bull. The one that tried to gore me when I couldn't untangle my dress from the fence."

Her father looked at her, and she burst out laughing at the incredulous expression on his face. "Do I want to hear about this?"

"Probably not. Needless to say, Jake rescued me in time, and it was all downhill from there for my heart."

"Well, daughter. What happens now?"

"Now I call in the reinforcements." Madeline fished her cell phone out of her purse and dialed Ridge City's only dispatcher. "Hattie, this is Madeline."

"Well, golly, girl. We've been waiting all morning for your call. Where are you?"

"I just pulled off the road by Jake's property."

"Same place as before?"

"Same place, same bull." Even the same day of the week—Friday.

"Okay. I'll put a call out to Deputy Karl. Then I'll get ahold of everyone else."

"Hattie, thanks for all your help."

"Honey, this town ain't been the same since you left. We're glad you're coming back."

"I'm glad to be back."

She hung up the phone. "All set."

"Madeline. Are you sure about this Jake Montgomery and his daughter?"

"Very sure."

"It's not too late to change your mind. I can turn the car around and drive you back to Seattle."

"Jake's the one, Dad."

"So tell me something else about this bigger-than-life hero you love."

She rolled her eyes. "I already told you he trains horses to work cattle. Right now it's just him, but one day he wants to expand his operation and actually breed cutting horses, then sell them to other ranchers."

"What kind of investment portfolio does this young man have?"

"I'm not sure that he has one, Dad." When her father opened his mouth to object, Madeline cut him off. "You won't find a man who works harder than Jake. He's a lot like you."

"Me? What do I have in common with a cowboy?"

"You're both full of stubborn pride and don't accept help easily."

Her father's eyes twinkled. "I see."

"Dad. I learned a lot about myself during my stay at his ranch. I learned that it doesn't take fancy clothes, diamond rings or five-star restaurants to make me happy. Jake's smile from a hundred yards away, his laughter, hearing Annie shout in excitement when she finds a frog—those are the things that make me happy."

"Frogs? This Annie sounds unusual."

"She's so smart and so exuberant about everything."

"I'm eager to meet her."

"Oh, look! My first wedding guest." Madeline pointed out the windshield to a truck pulling over near them.

As Coot approached the car, Madeline's father lowered the window.

"Well, if it ain't the return of the barbed-wire bride," the old man said.

"Hello, Coot. I'd like you to meet my father, Richard Tate. Dad, this is Coot. He owns the Mercantile in Ridge City."

Coot tipped his hat. "Right nice to meet ya, young man."

Her father's neck turned red at being called a young man. "Pleasure to meet you...Coot."

"More folks is headed this way." Coot stared down the highway. "Ain't had this much fun in ages 'round here." He winked, then went and held the passenger door open for Madeline.

Too late to chicken out now...not that she would. Still, the thought of being left at the altar—make that cow pasture—a second time tied her stomach in knots. She gathered the folds of her mother's voluminous wedding gown and stepped out of the car. The dress fit perfectly, but she felt more like a princess than a bride. Her mother's romantic streak definitely showed in the three layers of petticoats and six-foot train. One strong wind and she'd billow up like a hot-air balloon and float away.

In less than ten minutes a steady stream of trucks and cars headed in their direction, honking up a storm. *Oh, dear.* She'd told Hattie to invite only the Winstons and Coot, but the dispatcher must have called the entire town. The shoulder of the road was soon filled with people, some she remembered from the Fourth of July picnic, others she'd never even seen. When she spotted two motor homes with Florida plates pulling off the road, she had a feeling her wedding was about to become the main attraction in a three-ring circus.

Everyone greeted her with smiles and hugs, and she felt ridiculous when her eyes welled with tears at their warm welcome. Hattie stepped forward and grabbed her arm. "Have you changed your mind about Jake and decided to marry this handsome man, instead?" The dispatcher pointedly eyed Madeline's father.

For the second time in less than thirty minutes her father's face turned beet red. "Hattie, this is my father, Richard Tate. Dad meet Hattie. She's my wedding planner."

Richard Tate took Hattie's hand in both of his and gently held it. "It's a pleasure to meet you, Hattie. Madeline has told me wonderful things about Ridge City and its citizens. And you."

Hattie's eyes widened. The dispatcher was in her mid-forties and the size of a woodland sprite. Madeline wondered if she had fairy genes in her family. She waited for her father to let go of Hattie's hand, but he didn't. Her father was enthralled with the tiny woman. She'd never seen such amusement and interest in his eyes before when he'd looked at the opposite sex.

Hmm. Maybe her father would be visiting the ranch more than he planned. "Hattie?" Too caught up gazing into her father's eyes, Madeline asked again. "Hattie?"

"I'm busy, Madeline."

Her father's mouth curved into a smile and his eyes twinkled.

"Busy?" Madeline choked out.

"Yes, dear. Busy holding your father's hand."

Her father tilted his head back and laughed loud enough to draw attention from those standing nearby. "I dare say you're a breath of fresh air, Hattie."

"Be still my heart."

They all laughed, then Hattie turned serious and pulled her hand from her father's grasp. Amused, Madeline watched a look of disappointment cross her father's face.

"Has someone found Jake, Hattie?"

"Karl will have him here in no time. Why don't you pick your spot, so you're ready when he arrives."

Loud applause and cheers filled the air when

Madeline gingerly stepped over and around weeds and stickers as she made her way to the barbed-wire fence. She eyed the bull. "I don't know, Hattie. Cyclone is awfully close to the fence."

Hattie waved off her concern. "If he charges, slap his ugly mug with this." She held out a small card. Madeline took it and pressed her fingertips to her mouth to keep from blubbering when she read the printed wedding announcement.

July 25, 2004

City-slicker Madeline Rose Tate and cow-boy Jake Patrick Montgomery announce their plans to wed at high noon near the barbed-wire fence along the side of the road, somewhere outside Ridge City, Nevada. Look for the bull. Spectators welcome.

"Oh, Hattie, it's beautiful."

"Well, it didn't seem right, having a wedding without an announcement of some kind." She smiled. "I kinda thought the barbed wire around the edge was cute."

Madeline laughed and hugged the woman.

"Do you think you could snag the back of the gown on one of the barbs?"

"Are you sure? It's such a beautiful dress."

"I want everything to be just as it was the first time Jake and I met."

Doing as little damage as possible, Hattie wrapped the satin material around two barbs, then stepped back. "That should do it. You're hooked now." She spread the bottom of the gown around the satin pumps, and when Madeline looked down at herself, she truly felt like a princess bride. All she had to do was pray her Prince Charming would come for her.

"Now what?" Jake muttered.

A patrol car, its lights flashing, headed down the ranch road toward the house. He set Annie's duffel bag in the truck's backseat. "Sit tight, Annie. Let me see what this is about."

He glanced at his watch as the car drew near. He didn't have a minute to waste. This morning he rose before dawn, fed and watered the horses, cleaned out the stalls and filled the feed bins. He wrote out instructions for the animals, left his cell phone number at the bottom, then called and begged the Winstons to look after the horses. He didn't like leaving the animals in someone else's care, but without Maddy in his life, the horses didn't mean a damn thing anymore. After that he'd thrown some clothes for himself and Annie into a suitcase, grabbed his daughter's stuffed frog and packed the truck.

"But we gotta go now, Daddy. We gotta get Maddy so we can make her my real mommy."

Jake smiled at his daughter. Ever since he'd asked if she'd like Maddy to be her new mom she'd been more excited than a kid with her first glimpse of Walt Disney World. "We'll leave in a minute, Annie."

The patrol car pulled alongside the truck. Deputy Karl cut the lights, then lowered the window. "Jake."

"Karl. You picked a heck of time to drop by for a visit. Annie and I are headed to Seattle."

Karl grinned. "You don't say?"

Jake returned the grin. No use pretending the whole town didn't know he'd been sulking like a lovesick fool since Maddy had left. "What seems to be the problem?"

"We got trouble with that bull of yours."

"Cyclone? Did he break loose?"

"Hattie got a call from some tourist passing through. Couldn't make out what the problem was, but thought we'd better head out there and see for ourselves."

"I'm right behind you." Jake got into the truck and followed the deputy back to the highway. The last thing he needed right now was a recalcitrant bull on the loose, preying on unsuspecting tourists.

"What's wrong, Daddy?"

"We've got to check on Cyclone. He may have gotten out."

"What about Maddy?"

He thought of all the time he'd already wasted feeling sorry for himself when he should have called Maddy and begged her to forgive him. Begged her for a second chance. Begged her to let him come get her. "We'll leave after we check on Cyclone, Annie girl."

"Is 'Annie girl' my new nickname?"

Jake ruffled his daughter's hair. "Yeah, you like it?"

Annie giggled and flung her arms around his neck, then gave him a loud smacking kiss on the cheek.

Jake inhaled her baby-scented shampoo and thanked his lucky stars he'd come to his senses where Maddy was concerned. Ever since he'd told Annie they were going to Seattle to convince Maddy to marry them, she'd been a different girl. Warmer, more trusting toward him.

"Hey, you sit back down and put your belt on."

The patrol car raced along for five minutes before slowing. Jake stared down the road, astonished at the number of vehicles parked along both sides of the highway. The place looked like a carnival. What the hell was going on?

Karl pulled onto the gravel shoulder and stopped several yards from a large gathering of people. *Damn. Cyclone must have broken through the fence and hurt someone.*

Jake stopped the truck behind the patrol car, lowered the windows, then cut the engine. "Stay in the truck until I see what's going on."

"But, Daddy—"

"No buts, Annie. I'll be right back."

Karl walked toward him, grinning like a buffoon. "End of the road, buddy."

Maybe it wasn't Cyclone. The deputy wouldn't be smiling if someone had gotten hurt. Jake stared at a sea of familiar and unfamiliar faces. Annie snuck out of the truck and stood next to him, her tiny hand grabbing on to the front pocket of his jeans. "What happened, Daddy?"

He squeezed her little hand. "I thought I told you to stay in the truck."

Just then the group of people parted like the Red Sea. Annie tugged his jeans and pointed. "Daddy. It's Maddy! She's a princess again!"

Jake's heart did a double flip. The sea of people disappeared and the only thing in his line of sight was Maddy, decked out in another wedding dress. Stuck to the fence. His fence.

Her lips curved in a sultry smile. "Well, cowboy. Are you going to stand there all day, or get me off this fence?"

He fought a grin. "Depends." He took one step forward, thinking he knew what a stallion must feel like when he scents a mare. Because there wasn't anything he wanted more at that moment than to have Maddy in his arms.

Her eyes widened. "On what?"

He took another step and another, then stopped in front of her. "On whether or not you plan to stick around this time."

A feminine smile curved her mouth. "I'm going to be so sticky, cowboy, you'll never get me off you."

Raucous laughter rose around them, but Jake ignored it, focusing only on the lovely woman in front of him. He stroked one finger down her smooth, soft cheek. Her provocative scent surrounded him, drew him closer as he bent his head and whispered, "Ah, Maddy. You took my heart when you left."

"I'm bringing it back, cowboy." She peered over his shoulder and waved to Annie, who jumped up and down next to Gladys Winston.

Jake followed her gaze and grinned at the crowd. He straightened and announced, "Seems like my barbed-wire bride is back to stay."

Shouts and cheers filled the air. He turned

to Maddy. Eyes searching hers, he cupped her face with his rough, calloused hands. "I was so damn afraid of loving you, Maddy. You deserve better than this broken-down cowboy. But if you'll have me, I'll spend the rest of my life making you happy. And you have my solemn vow that until I draw my last breath I will always be there for you."

He lowered his mouth until he could feel her sweet breath caress his lips. "It took me a while, Maddy. But I finally realized that with your love I can put the past to rest. There's only the future. Only tomorrow. With you by my side."

Maddy opened her mouth to speak, but he touched her lips with his fingertips. He wanted to tell her everything before he lost his nerve. "I'm a simple man, Maddy. I can't promise I won't fail you at one time or another. But I can give you my word that I'll never walk away from you, from us."

"Oh, Jake. I love you so much." She raised her mouth to his, and he swallowed her sigh, then kissed her as if it might be for the very last time, vowing that every kiss he ever gave her would be as if it were their last. He would have kept on kissing her if not for the hand that clamped on to his shoulder.

"I don't believe we've been properly introduced."

Jake glanced over his shoulder at the stern-faced man standing a few feet away.

"Jake, I'd like you to meet my father, Richard Tate."

Jake shook hands with the older man. "Sir, you have my promise that I'll do my best by your daughter."

"I believe you, young man. Now, I'd prefer you keep your hands off her until you're officially married."

Jake noticed the twinkle in the man's eyes but remained stone-faced. "Yes, sir." He turned to those gathered around them. "Is there a preacher in the crowd?"

Bible in hand, Reverend Thomas made his way through the crowd and slapped Jake on the back. He leaned forward and murmured, "I can feel Sara smiling down on you today, Jake."

Jake's throat tightened as he stared at Maddy. A sudden sense of peace filled him, and at that instant he did believe Sara was happy for him. For Annie. Even for Maddy.

The few words spoken by Reverend Thomas went right over Jake's head as he lost himself in Maddy's sparkling green eyes. "Jake Patrick Montgomery and Madeline Rose Tate, I now pronounce you husband and wife."

Cameras clicked and cheers of congratulations rose in the air, but Jake didn't hear a thing, and he suspected neither did his bride. He was too busy kissing her, making a lifetime's worth of promises with his mouth.

"Jake?"

"Ah, Jake?"

"Jake, watch out!"

At the urgent shout an inch from his ear, Jake growled against Maddy's mouth and tore his lips from hers. "What!"

Fifty fingers pointed toward the pasture, where Cyclone pawed the ground and snorted. Jake grinned at Maddy. "Showtime."

Maddy's eyes rounded when the bull started charging. The crowd screamed and frantically waved hats and purses over the fence, trying to distract the nasty beast.

Jake grabbed Maddy around the waist and gave one mighty yank. The gown's train ripped away as he swung her up into his arms. Cyclone skidded into the barbed wire, but the fence held. He stuck his slobbery mouth through the wires, attempting to tug the torn material through.

"Oh no you don't. Not this time." Madeline wiggled in Jake's arms until he lowered her close enough that she could grab the other end of the material. A tug-of-war began between the bride and bull, with bets being placed and shouts of encouragement filling the air.

"Help me, Jake!" Maddy cried when the bull gained an advantage.

He chuckled at the way his bride's mouth thinned in determination, then he grabbed a handful of material and together they freed it from Cyclone's mouth. Jake and Maddy laughed as the disgruntled bull stomped away without his prize.

Annie tugged on Jake's arm. "My dream came true, Daddy."

Jake set Maddy on the ground so she could hug Annie. "What dream, Annie girl?"

"I got a real princess for a mommy." Annie shyly stared up at Maddy's father, then slipped her hand into his. "I've never had a grandpa."

Jake read the look of wonderment in his new father-in-law's eyes. Annie's new grandfather leaned over and picked her up. "I've never had a granddaughter."

"You haven't?"

"No, ma'am."

Annie's eyes brightened.

"I'm not sure what to do with a granddaughter. Can you help me?"

Annie frowned in deep concentration, then her eyes widened and she blinked like an owl. "You can take her to Disney World!"

All three adults burst out laughing and Jake

hugged Maddy close to his side. The four of them were going to do just fine as a family.

For the next half hour, he and Maddy smiled for the cameras and greeted their friends and neighbors. He wondered who the hell the old farts driving the motor homes were, but smiled just the same and thanked them for stopping by to offer their good wishes.

Someone mentioned a wedding dinner at the café in town. Jake knew he wouldn't have his barbed-wire bride to himself for several hours, but that was okay. He didn't mind sharing her with others, as long as he could hold her in his arms at the end of each day and wake up to her smiling face on the pillow next to his each morning.

\* \* \* \* \*

**YES!** Please send me the *Cowboy at Heart* collection in Larger Print. This collection begins with 3 FREE books and 2 FREE gifts in the first shipment, and more free gifts will follow! My books will arrive in 8 monthly shipments until I have the entire 51-book *Cowboy at Heart* collection. I will receive 2 or 3 FREE books in each shipment and I will pay just $4.99 U.S./ $5.89 CDN. for each of the other four books in each shipment, plus $2.99 for shipping and handling.* If I decide to keep the entire collection, I'll have paid for only 32 books because 19 books are FREE! I understand that by accepting the 3 free books and gifts places me under no obligation to buy anything. I can always return a shipment and cancel at any time. My free books and gifts are mine to keep no matter what I decide.

256 HCN 0779    456 HCN 0779

| Name | (PLEASE PRINT) | |
|------|---------------|---|
| Address | | Apt. # |
| City | State/Prov. | Zip/Postal Code |

Signature (if under 18, a parent or guardian must sign)

### Mail to the **Harlequin®** Reader Service:
**IN U.S.A.:** P.O. Box 1867, Buffalo, NY 14240-1867
**IN CANADA:** P.O. Box 609, Fort Erie, Ontario L2A 5X3

\* Terms and prices subject to change without notice. Prices do not include applicable taxes. Sales tax applicable in N.Y. Canadian residents will be charged applicable taxes. This offer is limited to one order per household. All orders subject to approval. Credit or debit balances in a customer's account(s) may be offset by any other outstanding balance owed by or to the customer. Please allow 4 to 6 weeks for delivery. Offer available while quantities last. Offer not available to Quebec residents.

# REQUEST YOUR FREE BOOKS!
## 2 FREE NOVELS PLUS 2 FREE GIFTS!

### HARLEQUIN®

*American ★ Romance*®

## LOVE, HOME & HAPPINESS

**YES!** Please send me 2 FREE Harlequin® American Romance® novels and my 2 FREE gifts (gifts are worth about $10). After receiving them, if I don't wish to receive any more books, I can return the shipping statement marked "cancel." If I don't cancel, I will receive 4 brand-new novels every month and be billed just $4.49 per book in the U.S. or $5.24 per book in Canada. That's a savings of at least 14% off the cover price! It's quite a bargain! Shipping and handling is just 50¢ per book in the U.S. and 75¢ per book in Canada.* I understand that accepting the 2 free books and gifts places me under no obligation to buy anything. I can always return a shipment and cancel at any time. Even if I never buy another book, the two free books and gifts are mine to keep forever.

154/354 HDN FV47

| | |
|---|---|
| Name | (PLEASE PRINT) |

| | |
|---|---|
| Address | Apt. # |

| | | |
|---|---|---|
| City | State/Prov. | Zip/Postal Code |

Signature (if under 18, a parent or guardian must sign)

Mail to the **Harlequin® Reader Service:**
**IN U.S.A.:** P.O. Box 1867, Buffalo, NY 14240-1867
**IN CANADA:** P.O. Box 609, Fort Erie, Ontario L2A 5X3

**Want to try two free books from another line?**
**Call 1-800-873-8635 or visit www.ReaderService.com.**

\* Terms and prices subject to change without notice. Prices do not include applicable taxes. Sales tax applicable in N.Y. Canadian residents will be charged applicable taxes. Offer not valid in Quebec. This offer is limited to one order per household. Not valid for current subscribers to Harlequin American Romance books. All orders subject to credit approval. Credit or debit balances in a customer's account(s) may be offset by any other outstanding balance owed by or to the customer. Please allow 4 to 6 weeks for delivery. Offer available while quantities last.

**Your Privacy**—The Harlequin® Reader Service is committed to protecting your privacy. Our Privacy Policy is available online at www.ReaderService.com or upon request from the Harlequin Reader Service.

We make a portion of our mailing list available to reputable third parties that offer products we believe may interest you. If you prefer that we not exchange your name with third parties, or if you wish to clarify or modify your communication preferences, please visit us at www.ReaderService.com/consumerchoice or write to us at Harlequin Reader Service Preference Service, P.O. Box 9062, Buffalo, NY 14269. Include your complete name and address.

HARDIR13

# REQUEST YOUR FREE BOOKS!

## 2 FREE NOVELS PLUS 2 FREE GIFTS!

### ⊞ HARLEQUIN

# SPECIAL EDITION

## Life, Love & Family

**YES!** Please send me 2 FREE Harlequin® Special Edition novels and my 2 FREE gifts (gifts are worth about $10). After receiving them, if I don't wish to receive any more books, I can return the shipping statement marked "cancel." If I don't cancel, I will receive 6 brand-new novels every month and be billed just $4.49 per book in the U.S. or $5.24 per book in Canada. That's a savings of at least 14% off the cover price! It's quite a bargain! Shipping and handling is just 50¢ per book in the U.S. and 75¢ per book in Canada.* I understand that accepting the 2 free books and gifts places me under no obligation to buy anything. I can always return a shipment and cancel at any time. Even if I never buy another book, the two free books and gifts are mine to keep forever.

235/335 HDN FV4K

| | |
|---|---|
| Name | (PLEASE PRINT) |
| Address | Apt. # |
| City | State/Prov. Zip/Postal Code |

Signature (if under 18, a parent or guardian must sign)

### Mail to the Harlequin® Reader Service:
**IN U.S.A.:** P.O. Box 1867, Buffalo, NY 14240-1867
**IN CANADA:** P.O. Box 609, Fort Erie, Ontario L2A 5X3

**Want to try two free books from another line?**
**Call 1-800-873-8635 or visit www.ReaderService.com.**

* Terms and prices subject to change without notice. Prices do not include applicable taxes. Sales tax applicable in N.Y. Canadian residents will be charged applicable taxes. Offer not valid in Quebec. This offer is limited to one order per household. Not valid for current subscribers to Harlequin Special Edition books. All orders subject to credit approval. Credit or debit balances in a customer's account(s) may be offset by any other outstanding balance owed by or to the customer. Please allow 4 to 6 weeks for delivery. Offer available while quantities last.

**Your Privacy**—The Harlequin® Reader Service is committed to protecting your privacy. Our Privacy Policy is available online at www.ReaderService.com or upon request from the Harlequin Reader Service.

We make a portion of our mailing list available to reputable third parties that offer products we believe may interest you. If you prefer that we not exchange your name with third parties, or if you wish to clarify or modify your communication preferences, please visit us at www.ReaderService.com/consumerchoice or write to us at Harlequin Reader Service Preference Service, P.O. Box 9062, Buffalo, NY 14269. Include your complete name and address.

HSEDIR13

# REQUEST YOUR FREE BOOKS!
## 2 FREE NOVELS PLUS 2 FREE GIFTS!

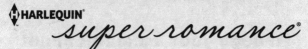

### *Exciting, emotional, unexpected!*

---

**YES!** Please send me 2 FREE Harlequin® Superromance® novels and my 2 FREE gifts (gifts are worth about $10). After receiving them, if I don't wish to receive any more books, I can return the shipping statement marked "cancel." If I don't cancel, I will receive 6 brand-new novels every month and be billed just $4.69 per book in the U.S. or $5.24 per book in Canada. That's a savings of at least 15% off the cover price! It's quite a bargain! Shipping and handling is just 50¢ per book in the U.S. and 75¢ per book in Canada.* I understand that accepting the 2 free books and gifts places me under no obligation to buy anything. I can always return a shipment and cancel at any time. Even if I never buy another book, the two free books and gifts are mine to keep forever.

135/336 HDN FV5K

| | | |
|---|---|---|
| Name | (PLEASE PRINT) | |
| Address | | Apt. # |
| City | State/Prov. | Zip/Postal Code |
| Signature (if under 18, a parent or guardian must sign) | | |

### Mail to the **Harlequin® Reader Service:**
**IN U.S.A.:** P.O. Box 1867, Buffalo, NY 14240-1867
**IN CANADA:** P.O. Box 609, Fort Erie, Ontario L2A 5X3

**Are you a current subscriber to Harlequin Superromance books
and want to receive the larger-print edition?
Call 1-800-873-8635 or visit www.ReaderService.com.**

* Terms and prices subject to change without notice. Prices do not include applicable taxes. Sales tax applicable in N.Y. Canadian residents will be charged applicable taxes. Offer not valid in Quebec. This offer is limited to one order per household. Not valid for current subscribers to Harlequin Superromance books. All orders subject to credit approval. Credit or debit balances in a customer's account(s) may be offset by any other outstanding balance owed by or to the customer. Please allow 4 to 6 weeks for delivery. Offer available while quantities last.

HSRDIR13